PENGU

THE WILD S

After twenty years in the Indian Civil Service, Philip Mason retired to England in 1947. In England he ran a small-holding for a short time after which he spent nearly twenty years researching manifestations of race prejudice and race relations in different parts of the world. He was also Director of the Institute of Race Relations.

Philip Mason has published seven books under the name of Philip Woodruff. These include *Call the Next Witness*, *The Founders* and *The Guardians*, which was later republished as *The Men Who Ruled India, an Account of the Indian Civil Service*. Since 1963 he has lived in the country and written among other things an account of the Indian Army called *A Matter of Honour*.

PHILIP MASON

THE WILD SWEET WITCH

In the most iron crag his foot can tread
A dream may strew her bed
And suddenly his limbs entwine
And draw him down through rock as sea-nymphs
might through brine.
But unlike those feigned temptress-ladies who
In guerdon of a night the lover slew,
When the embrace has failed, the rapture fled,
Not he, not he, the wild sweet witch is dead!
And though he cherisheth
The babe most strangely born from out her death—
Some tender trick of her it hath, maybe—
It is not she!
FRANCIS THOMPSON

PENGUIN BOOKS

Penguin Books India Ltd. 72-B, Himalaya House, 23 Kasturba Gandhi Marg, New
Delhi-110 001, India.
Penguin Books Ltd. Harmondsworth, Middlesex, England
Viking Penguin Inc. 40 West 23rd Street, New York, N.Y. 10010, U.S.A.
Penguin Books Australia Ltd. Ringwood, Victoria, Australia
Penguin Books Canada Ltd. 2801 John Street, Markham, Ontario, Canada L3R 1B4
Penguin Books (N.Z.) Ltd. 182-190 Wairau Road, Auckland 10, New Zealand

First published by Jonathan Cape as *The Wild Sweet Witch* by Philip Woodruff 1947
Published in Penguin Books 1989
Reprinted 1989
Copyright © Philip Mason 1947, 1988

Made and printed In India by Ananda Offset Private Ltd, Calcutta.

For Mary

FOREWORD

GARHWAL is a real district, whose hills and people, so far as they come into this story, I have described as well as I can. Since the district is quite different from any other in India, it would be silly to try to hide it under a changed name and most of the places are drawn just as I remember them; but the story itself is fiction. None of the characters are drawn direct from any single living person, although Mr. Bennett unites in himself some of the characteristics of three Deputy Commissioners in the nineteenth century whose names are still remembered.

Readers of recent fiction about India may think that my pictures of Mr. Bennett and his successors are too kind, but one can only write from one's own experience. Perhaps I have been lucky in the people I have known and the visitors who write books after a six months' stay have been unlucky.

The incidents which make up the story come more directly from experience than the characters, but they are usually based on tales heard from villagers which have been worn by time from their original shape, like pebbles in a stream, and they have been further modified to suit the main purpose. For instance, all I know about the forced labour is that there was an agitation against it after the war of 1914-18, and it was abolished. I have no idea what the Deputy Commissioner of that day thought about it nor what course the agitation took. There was certainly no Jodh Singh. Again, there really was a panther who killed human beings once or twice a week for some years; the villagers did think he was a man by day, who turned into a panther at night; and the Deputy Commissioner of the day did take a man into protective custody to prove he was not the panther. But my knowledge is based on hearsay; the true story of this panther is, I believe, being written by Major Jim Corbett, the author of *Man-eaters of Kumaon*, who eventually shot him.

The word I have translated 'warlock' really means a person who may turn into either a panther or a bear and some of the stories I have heard seem to indicate that the same person may turn into either and does not even know which form he is going to take when he starts his spell or incantation.

I have never cared for what Peter Fleming calls the 'nullah' school of writing, and expect other people to dislike Indian words they do not understand as much as I do the 'm'bongos' and 'b'wanas' in books about Africa. I think there are only three Indian words in this story: *kukri*, the heavy Nepalese chopping knife, which has been made familiar by the doings of Gurkha and Garhwali troops in two wars; *tahsildar*, a magistrate and revenue officer, who in the hills is a police officer as well; and *patwari*, a junior revenue official. He too in the hills is also a policeman.

Names, however, cannot be avoided, and the easiest way of explaining the pronunciation is to say that vowels are as in Italian, except the short *a* which has the sound of *u* in the English word butter. Thus Kalyanu is pronounced Kull-yah-noo, the first syllable rhyming with hull. 'Garhwal' is very difficult to pronounce well, but for all practical purposes the first syllable rhymes with 'her', and the second with 'marl'. By the same rough standard, 'Jodh' may be taken to rhyme with 'goad'.

I have a clear conscience about crops, states of the moon, and seasons; but the feast of lights mentioned in Part Three would really have come a few weeks earlier in relation to other events, and I suspect that the rope festival really took place in the spring, in order to fertilize the millet and maize crop. But it fitted this story to relate it to the winter crop of barley and I doubt whether anyone can say this is wrong, because there is no one living who has seen it.

CONTENTS

INTRODUCTION

Of his fictional works, *The Wild Sweet Witch* remains Mason's favourite. Set in the far reaches of the Garhwal hills of northern India, this novel recalls the three happy years that the author spent as a Deputy Commissioner in Garhwal district. His autobiography *A Shaft of Sunlight: Memories of a Varied Life* (1978) confirms, what one has suspected all along in the novel, his love for India. For the Garhwalis he had a special place in his heart and in the chapter "Kingdom in the Mountains" he praises them for their simplicity, fidelity, courage and their power of endurance. In this chapter he also tells us why, at the age of thirty and after having served in capitals like Lucknow and Delhi, he found the Deputy Commissioner's job in Garhwal the most satisfying:

> Walking among mountains was what Mary [Mason's wife] and I liked better than anything else—but there was much more to it than that. To be inaccessible is to be independent; instructions from the Government arrive late and are often so quaintly out of the question that they can be disregarded. Ministers do not come to see you. And in Garhwal, just because it was remote, power had so long been centred in the District Officer's hands that he had a prestige that in the rest of India was a thing of the past.

Mason liked power, but not for any imperial purpose. He wanted to help the people—to provide the rough and ready justice on the spot which the Garhwalis sought above all else. Once he had a woman with a putrefying leg placed under arrest so that she could be forcibly sent to a hospital. He admits he had no right to do so, but the people told him he was a king in Garhwal and it was no use being a king if he could not sometimes break the law.

No one who has read Forster's *A Passage to India* can afford to ignore this book. Forster portrays the British officials of Chandrapore with an irony amounting to loathing, and Mason in his novel sets out to correct the imbalance. In his "Foreword" he concedes that the portrait of the Deputy Commissioner, Mr Bennett, and those of his successors may appear too kind to the reader, but then he can only write from his own experiences. 'Perhaps I have been lucky in the people I have known and the visitors who write books after a six months' stay have been unlucky,' says Mason.

This mild rebuke of Forster, from one who himself was for over twenty years a member of the illustrious Indian Civil Service (ICS) that Forster attacked, is not without its point. But on the bigger issues concerning friendship between the British and the Indians, and the Indians managing their own affairs, the two writers agree. In fact, Mason is more forthright than Forster on the question of Indian independence. His Deputy Commissioner, Christopher Tregard, pulls the rug from beneath the feet of his countrymen who want to stay on in India because a segment of the

Indian people so desire it. Here is what he tells his wife Susan:

> It seems to me wrong for us, the English, as a people, to take refuge behind the peasant and say we must stay because he wants us. Every people must express itself through its vocal classes...and the vocal classes in India want us to go. It's true they're out of touch with the peasant, but that is just because we're here. It is a thing which can't right itself so long as we are.

Tregard's predecessor, Hugh Upton, also realises that it is time to go, and he asks what could be better than to go with dignity and good grace.

All the three Deputy Commissioners in *The Wild Sweet Witch* are drawn from people whom Mason knew and in each of them there is something of Mason himself. Mr Bennett expresses some of Mason's own love of the mountains, and his orderly, Kalyanu, is no doubt based on Mason's own orderly, Kalyan, who filled him in on many of the tales on bears and man-eating panthers. Hugh Upton, physically the very opposite of Mason, shows Mason's administrative sagacity and the fine line he had to steer between loyalty to his Government and his own sense of what was right and what was wrong. Christopher Tregard, who has some traits of Michael Nethersole (District Magistrate of Bareilly in 1930 while the author was there as a sub-divisional officer), comes closest to Mason in his love of Garhwal, in his exercise of a personal rule, and in facing candidly that the time to leave India had come. He is an example of the best of the ICS, of whom there were as many in India as Forster's arrogant Turtons and Heaslops, but of whose existence Forster never so much as hinted. Tregard's wife, Susan, is partly modelled on the author's wife, Mary, who loved Garhwal as much as her husband did and to whom this book is fittingly dedicated.

A character of compelling interest in Jodh Singh. After graduating from Lucknow University he returns to his home district in Garhwal to find himself leading a campaign against forced labour. His initial success (more the outcome of Hugh Upton's intervention with the authorities concerned than of his own initiatives) wins him popularity and convinces him of his mission to lead his people out of a mental and political morass. Though honest, and full of life and enthusiasm, his ideas are half-baked and impractical. He is quick tempered and highly emotional, and in matters of everyday intrigues he is no match for political adventurers like Congressite Ram Prashad Singh or wily Brahmins such as Ram Dat and Uma Nand. He first falls victim to a whispering campaign about himself as a creature who changes into a man-eating panther by night, and is ironically saved by the very man he is out to denounce—Hugh Upton. Some years later he is falsely accused of complicity in a murder, loses his mind completely, goes on a killing spree and is eventually shot by the police. Despite the violence towards the end, Jodh Singh is a character of noble and tragic dimensions.

Anglo-Indian fiction about the Raj by and large ignored Indian nationalists. When they did appear they were generally depicted as cowards motivated by self-interest. Mason's novel is singular in that it shows a nationalist, however misdirected, as brave and totally unselfish. Mason also reveals with considerable insight that the real enemy of Indian aspirations was not the British but Indian customs, ignorance, superstition and the divisions in Indian society itself. This is perhaps as true today as it was forty years ago when the novel was first published. Cornered and betrayed by his own people, Jodh Singh finally puts his trust in Christopher Tregard. It is no small irony that Tregard has to give the police the order to shoot Jodh Singh.

The Wild Sweet Witch is skilfully plotted. Though divided into three parts, and spread over several years, 1875, 1923, and 1938, the novel is closely knit by the theme and a judicious use of imagery and symbolism. Jodh Singh's elation at the abolition of forced labour in Part II has a close parallel with the rejoicing of his grandfather at killing his first bear in Part I. Jodh Singh's failure as leader of the procession in Part II has its counterpart in Kalyanu being badly mauled when he tackles his second bear, also in Part I. Both grandfather and grandson are carried away by the enthusiasm attending their initial successes and both, as a result, blunder in their second attempts. Mr Bennett saves the life of Kalyanu in Part I and this corresponds with Hugh Upton's efforts to protect Jodh Singh when he is suspected of having become a man-eating panther in Part II. Such is the spell cast by suspicion and fear that even Jodh Singh half believes the stories about himself, and in Part III he develops many of the traits of the animal he was earlier said to be. The panther imagery is worked out with minute care, and Jodh Singh's final rage and collapse completes the analogy. But what most unifies the novel is its setting—the varied yet unchanging face of the Himalayas. The book abounds in descriptive passages of great beauty; it evokes the sights, smells and the sounds of the Himalayas as no other novel that I have read.

First published by Jonathan Cape in 1947, *The Wild Sweet Witch* received a strong press. *The Manchester Guardian* called it an 'admirable book', the *Times Literary Supplement* a novel of 'much merit', and *The New Statesman and Nation* referred to it as 'a definite contribution to the Literature of India.' Penguin's reissue of this book is welcome, for it puts it beside their editions of the Indian novels of Forster, Joseph Ackerley and George Orwell. And this is where it belongs.

University of Regina   Saros Cowasjee
Regina, Canada, 1989

PART ONE

THE UPROOTING, 1875

I

EVERYONE in the hills knows that when the snow has melted and the flowers are in their first glory, the scent in the high pastures is so strong that it makes a man drunk and he is likely to do strange things and wake with a headache. Kalyanu knew the feeling well, for it was his custom every year to climb many thousands of feet to the summer alps and to stay there with the sheep and goats for the lambing. But now he was in the fields below the forest where the homestead stood; and yet it was the same constriction of the throat and lightness in the head, the same impulse of wild unreason, that rose and choked him as he stood looking at his field of ruined millet.

As soon as he had come down from the pastures, he had been round the fields to see how his brothers had managed while he was away. It was a hard life they led, here between the mountains and the river, and they had not much reserve if a crop failed them. The autumn millet fed them for most of the year, and they added to it any barley they were lucky enough to get if there was good snow or rain in the winter. But the millet was their life, and here were the best fields ruined by a bear. Rage filled him; it swelled in his chest and head, a drunkenness of rage as suffocating as that other drunkenness of height.

As the worst of it passed and he became conscious of more than blind fury, he spoke aloud:

'The bear must be killed,' he said.

He looked at the sun. It would soon be behind the mountains to the west; daylight is short in the high steep valleys. The bear would come again when the sun had gone and he must quickly get his brothers together for the fight. No one could be certain that the bear would come to the same field, but there was a chance. He looked at the damage, and the drunkenness rose in

15

him again when he saw how the beast had rolled in the crop after eating its fill. But he fought it down and looked for tracks in the moist soil which was never wholly dried by the brief warmth of midday. It was one bear, only one. It would be an old strong male. It would come again, that night or the next or the one after; they must wait every night till it came and then they would kill it. He went quickly down the hill to fetch his brothers, planning as he went.

His problem was not an easy one. Weapons were his first thought. There was not much iron in the upper hills of the Himalayas in the year 1875, because every ounce had to be carried up from the plains on the buyer's back and the journey took twelve days. As the buyer had to take his own food for the journey too, the less iron he carried the better. What there was, soft untempered stuff, would not take an edge and was most of it beaten into short blunt sickles or trowels. Wood and stone were the two materials of which there was plenty and they were used for almost every purpose. The only arms Kalyanu possessed were one degenerate kukri used for beheading goats, one axe, and several heavy wooden poles. The kukri was really quite unsuitable for a fight with a bear. It was small and involved coming to very close quarters before it could be used. The axe was better and would be invaluable in the last stage, but it was short and clumsy. Kalyanu had decided before he found the first of his brothers that they must stun the bear with poles and then use the axe to finish him off.

The four brothers were all working in the fields near the homestead and it did not take long to find them nor to collect their heavy poles and the axe and kukri. They started at once on the climb back to the damaged field. The path was one they had made themselves in their goings and comings to their fields, and to the forest above the fields where the women went to cut grass and collect sticks, and where they drove the cattle to graze. The way led first through the home fields, little shelves of ploughed land a few yards in width, with a slanting scramble after each shelf up a bank, about the height of a man, faced sometimes with stone, sometimes with the natural turf. The twisted triple ears of the green millet near the farm, like the plaited tails of tiny shire horses, were beginning to turn yellow for the harvest; farther up the patches of red millet were already a deep madder, ear and leaf and stalk alike. The air was moist with the fruitfulness of autumn and the scent of vegetation was heavy.

The path left the fields and struck up slanting across a long hillside too steep for cultivation, deep in grass which the women would cut before it was buried by the snow. But it was easy walking because the feet of themselves and their goats and their ancestors for generations had worn a firm ledge, seldom as much as six inches wide, but not difficult for anyone who did not think of the depth below. For the almost precipitous grassy side gave way farther down to a sheer rocky scarp, which fell away in cliff on cliff to the river, boiling in ice-fed spate in its narrow channel. The steady roar of tormented water and rolling boulders made a background to every other sound that Kalyanu and his brothers heard, although the river was thousands of feet below them.

The way led below a sheer rock face with a spring at the foot and then turned to zigzag directly upwards to the less extreme slopes which lay at the top of the cliff. Here the labour of their fathers and grandfathers and themselves had driven back the pines and gradually cleared a patch of snaky terraced fields, sloping outwards between rocky walls, fields a few feet wide that nothing could have ploughed but the little mountain bullocks as high as a man's waist, and that no one but a hillman would have thought worth the heart-breaking labour. But on this side of the river there were only two patches of ground where the slope was not so steep as to forbid even this hard-won cultivation, one near the homestead and the second up here, where the bear had rolled in the millet.

The sun was already behind the mountains as the brothers climbed the hill, but there would be reflected light from the sky for some time. The fight had to be very carefully planned, because one man with a pole is no match for a bear and if the bear was able to attack one of the brothers alone, that one would probably be killed. Kalyanu was thinking hard as he climbed. If all the brothers were close together from the start, hiding behind one rock, the bear would probably get away. A bear can move fast for a short distance and it would not stay to fight five men if it saw them all close together in a group. But if the brothers surrounded the field and were too far apart, one of them might be left to face the bear alone. It must eventually make away up hill, towards the forest, for there was a sheer drop on the lower side. A subtle plan was needed, based on the lie of the ground.

The three fields that were damaged were at the top of the patch of ploughed land and from Kalyanu's point of view at present they were well placed, for there was only one natural line for a retreat to the forest above, and that was fairly narrow. On one side was a bluff with a rock cliff fifty feet high, up which not even a goat could go, and on the other the debris of some fall of rock in forgotten times, huge fragments as big as a cottage, over which a bear could scramble, but which he would not willingly choose as his path. His natural line would be between the bluff and the fall of rock. He could, of course, go down and traverse below either of these obstacles, but he would not do this unless he realized that he had something formidable to face. And this was unlikely, for firearms were almost unknown and as a rule the men of the hills feared a bear more than the bear feared them. Once the bear was committed to the way between the cliff and the fall of rock, he would not easily be deflected. The plan must, therefore, be to make him start on that path, and then to take him in the narrow place, all arriving there at the same moment.

Kalyanu did not formulate this reasoning even to himself. He

certainly could not have put it in words, but by a swift sub-
conscious appreciation of the nature of the ground and the mentality of his enemy, he saw that it was the best course to take.
And since his brothers gave him unquestioning obedience, he
did not need to explain his reasoning to them. He hid two of
them among the rocks to the east of the narrow place and two
in the bushes in the thick shadow below the cliff on the west.
He himself would be farther down, below where he thought
the bear would be, and it would be his first task to make it move
towards the narrow place. He explained to his brothers what
they had to do. They were to lie still, even when they heard him
shout. He would not show himself when he first shouted, but
would try to make the bear think it had more than one man to
deal with, so that it would start for the narrow place, but it
must not be frightened, it must be slow and unhurried. Only
when Kalyanu showed himself and shouted a definite word of
command—'Strike'—were they to leap out from their hiding
places and rush upon the enemy. And then they must make sure
to arrive all at the same moment. They must not lose their heads
in the excitement and rush in without thought. He made each
of them repeat what he had to do.

The waxing moon rose early, but it was some time before it
cleared the eastern hills and shone on the fields and rocks of
Kalyanu's upper farm. The forest above the ploughed ledges
was of blue pine; the trees nearest to the fields glistened with
little points of light, but the mass of the forest made a black
menacing shadow. Inky black were the shadows below the rocks
and among the thick bushes at the foot of the cliff. The silvery
light on the narrow fields seemed clear as day by contrast, but it
was deceptive. You could not distinguish detail, and it was the
shadow rather than the object that could be seen. Black and
silver, forest and cliff and rock, the stage was set.

Kalyanu waited with fast-beating heart, a sick feeling in the
stomach. He strained his eyes to see their enemy. Surely that

19

shadow had not been there before? It was just the shape of a bear. It was very still. No, it was moving; a tiny movement. It looked different; it had moved as he blinked his eyes. It was the bear. Wait and see which way it goes. Wait. Wait. No, it has been still too long. No, it is nothing, a rock. Things look so different in the moonlight. Quiet, more waiting, and then again the heart pounds, the breath comes quick, the palms of the hands are wet on the polished wood of the staff, at a stone rolling down from above; the bear must have dislodged it. Wait again; wait and see; no, it was nothing.

Disaster might have overtaken the brothers if they had missed the bear that night and had tried a second night with senses dulled by lack of sleep and the boredom of waiting. But they were lucky. The bear came early, while they were still keen and alert, keyed and poised by Kalyanu's talk, their eyes bright, their bowels still conscious of the nearness of danger. The black bulk rolled forward in the moonlight, black as a moving shadow. Kalyanu waited till it was well into the field and then he yelled. He did not show himself, but shouted and moved from one bush to another and shouted again; he beat the bushes, threw stones at other bushes, and rolled boulders down the hill. The bear stood still suspiciously; then slowly it began to move uphill towards the narrow place. Still Kalyanu did not show himself; he waited, watching, forgetting to breathe, judging his moment; then he shouted: 'Strike!' and ran with all his strength and fire for the narrow place. The four brothers sprang from their tense muscles and dashed forward, hurling insults at the bear.

It was perfectly timed. The four younger brothers reached the centre of the narrow place a fraction of a second before the bear; Kalyanu was close behind, in a position of great danger if it should turn. But it did not turn; it swung clumsily but with incredible quickness to its left towards the cliff, meaning to pass between the two brothers coming from that side and to maul both as it passed. But the men it had to deal with were not trying to get away as it had expected; their stout poles swung high above their shoulders and came down with all their force, almost in the same second as those of the two on the right. Three blows fell on the head and neck and the fourth, that of the brother on the bear's extreme right, on the backbone. And at the same moment Kalyanu flung aside his pole and made his axe bite deep into the back above the root of the tail. Such a volley of blows, all at once like a clap of thunder, stopped the bear for the blink of an eyelid, but he shook his head and rose on his hind legs to strike right and left with the curved claws of his forepaws. But again that shattering volley of four blows fell on head and shoulders and a second time Kalyanu struck with his axe and this time the axe reached the backbone. The bear fell; at once all five were on him, yelling wildly, striking again and again till their poles were splintered and broken. The bear lay stunned and battered; with all his strength Kalyanu swung the axe and split its skull. He drew the kukri and cut its throat.

'He's dead,' they said.

'He's dead!'

They could not believe it. They were silent, looking at each other and panting. Then they all began to talk at once.

'Did you see how I hit him the moment he turned our way?'

'Well, he's dead now, and he won't roll in our crops again.'

'That was a fine blow Kalyanu caught him with the axe!' And so on. At last Kalyanu stilled the chatter and said:

'Let us drag this sod of a bear out of our field into the forest and leave him to the vultures. Then we will go home and eat. We will kill the home-fed sheep. And we will eat raw game. And when we have eaten we will dance. We will dance *Bakhtawar Wins*.'

They did certain things to the corpse and then they dragged it out of the field and they went back down the little twisty path to the homestead. The moon silvered the grass on the steep side below the bluff, as the wind sighed over it in a long ripple, like

21

a caress on the skin of a panther. The wind sighed again and the blue pines breathed deep in reply. The roar of the torrent below rose to them faintly and the wind sighed in the pines, the five men chattered of their triumph, but behind all trivial sound, behind the roar of the torrent, was the deep positive silence of the mountains, the silence, and the silver of the moonlight.·

The chatter broke out in a fresh spurt of excitement when·they came to the little cluster of houses where they lived, a stone-paved terrace with circular paved pits for treading out the corn, and round the terrace little stone cabins on three sides of a square, some for men and some for beasts. The women heaped up the fire and they dragged out the home-fed sheep. It has been in the dark and fed on grain for six months. The grain made it fat; it was kept in the dark so that the sun should not melt its fat. Its feet had grown so that they curved up before it like fantastic medieval slippers. Autaru, the second brother, led it up to Kalyanu. There was no Brahman in the little community of Bantok, but Kalyanu was priest of the godling they propitiated from time to time, a power who had ruled over this hillside before the Hindus came up from the plains. The godling lived in a tiny stone house at the foot of a cedar tree. They led the sheep before him and marked its forehead with a daub of colour and a few grains of barley. Then Autaru seized the sheep by the horns and leaned back, stretching the neck while another brother held the hind-quarters. Kalyanu struck once with the kukri and Autaru staggered one pace back with the head in his hands. A spurt of blood fell on him and he laughed, and they all laughed at him. They cut the sheep to pieces without skinning it, and singed the raw meat in the flames. Then they ate it with handfuls of salt. The liver they did not even singe in the fire but rolled little pieces of it in salt and red pepper and ate it. This is 'raw game'; for in Garhwal all meat is called 'game'.

They piled up the fires higher and stuck torches of pinewood round the paved courtyard. Then they began to dance the dance of *Bakhtawar Wins*. There was a family of aboriginals, the dark-faced Doms, who lived farther down towards the river and worked as the serfs of Kalyanu and his brothers. One of the children had gone to fetch them as soon as the triumphant party returned. They had brought the drums, one a great vessel of copper shaped like an egg with the top cut off, the severed end bound over with stout buffalo skin, the other smaller, with a narrow waist, a percussion surface at either end, bound with thinner goatskin. The drums were beaten with a curved and polished stick held in the right hand; the second man played also with his fingers and the butt of his left palm on the reverse end of his small tenor drum. There was no other instrument but the drums, and so no tune, only the cadence of the voice singing a ballad and the odd exciting syncopated rhythm of the drums, quickening and quickening to intolerable broken speed, dropping again to a slower throb, throbbing and pulsing in slow broken rhythm, quickening again, pulsing faster and faster at a climax in the story.

There was silence and silver moonlight on the cliffs and the hanging bulk of the hills, but in the paved yard before the houses the flicker and waver of torches and the broken pulse of the drums and a man's voice singing. The figures moving in a circle were short and square, the woollen blankets that they wore looped round their bodies and over their shoulders like a plaid, accenting the angle of the shoulder. They stamped and bowed in the dance, their arms rose and gesticulated, as they circled between the torches. The little circle of fire and human joy was as small as one star among the myriads of heaven.

The ballad to which they danced was the story of a king from over the passes in Tibet who crossed the high range and came down with his slant-eyed men into the valleys of Garhwal. They came with their felt boots, their barbarous furs, round copper shields studded with turquoise and silver, with spears and swords and bows, and they were very many. But Bakhtawar called together the people of the valleys and led them against the invaders. When they told him that the odds were against him, for the men of Garhwal were few and poorly armed, he told them that this was a land beloved of the gods, where the sacred Ganges rose, and where the gods had played and journeyed when the world was young; the gods will help us, he said. And sure enough, when they came close to the armies from across the mountains, the gods sent on the Tibetans a madness, that drunkenness that comes in the high pastures when the flowers are in bloom. They ate stones and grass and snow and turned their weapons upon each other; and the people of Garhwal fell upon them and killed many of them and drove the rest back over the passes. So to this day they dance the dance of *Bakhtawar Wins* to celebrate victory.

The dancers are first the people of Garhwal, marching up the narrow valleys to unequal battle; and then in turn they are the Tibetans on whom the madness has fallen. They become possessed by the gods and the drums quicken and quicken again, till it seems beyond belief that nerve and muscle can keep up the speed, and each dancer twirls away in a wild *pas seul*, twirling and spinning till he falls breathless and dizzy. Then on hands and knees he fills his mouth with grass or stones, and foaming and champing joins the dance again, till at last the rhythm drops and all sink exhausted to the ground. Then again the steady throbbing approach of Bakhtawar's army, and again the drums quicken to the climax of action and victory and defeat.

The drums died, the torches burnt low, the serfs went back to their hovels below and the people of the homestead turned to sleep. Kalyanu was happy. Like Bakhtawar, he had triumphed over impossible strength. He had earned his rest. The little homestead clung to the cliff's edge and there was only the silver moonshine, the roar of the torrent below, the sigh of the wind in the pines and the deep silence of the mountains.

II

THE mood in which Kalyanu and his brothers danced and feasted after killing the bear lasted for some days. They had indeed done something worthy of note. As a rule the people of the high valleys looked on the damage done by wild beasts as an act of the gods, something against which it was little use to fight. They took some precautions, just as they went through certain ceremonies to avert calamity, but with no very fervent belief that anything would come of it. They put up scarecrows and primitive booby-traps and, if things got too bad, would build themselves a little hut raised high above the ground on poles and in this would watch all night with the object not of killing but of scaring the marauder; but that was as far as they usually went. Gun-licences were rare and were usually given to pensioners from the army or to the descendants of the barons who had ruled the land for the Rajas in the days before the Gurkhas swept over the hills and conquered the country. And if Kalyanu had asked for a gun-licence, which he was not so presumptuous as to do, he would certainly have been told that he was not the most important person in his village, no account being taken of the fact that the rest of the village was on the other side of the river and the nearest bridge was thirty miles down stream. The bow was forgotten, though it had been the weapon of the heroes of Hindu story and ballad. And for some strange reason the pitfall was not used. The truth was that the hill folk were not a hunting people and knew little of the ways of beasts.

So it was a great thing to have killed a bear with clubs and an axe. Kalyanu woke next day with something of the exaltation of a young man successful in his first love affair. He regarded the world with the same feeling of confidence in himself and mastery over external incident; he could shape events as he wished them and make others dance to his piping. And just as the happy youth feels himself irresistible to all women, so Kalyanu believed that he had nothing more to fear from wild beasts. Bears were easy.

This confidence and self-satisfaction were still with him a week later when he decided to climb to the upper patch of ploughland and see how the crops were ripening. In the fields round the homestead, his brothers and the women were all at work, getting in the yellow millet. Men and women alike moved stooping through the crops, reaching out the left hand to gather together a bunch of stalks, cutting with a stroke of the blunt sickle in the right hand; there was none of the orderly division of labour that went with the work on an English farm at the same period, no sweeping line of scythes with the women picking up. Each worker drove his own path into the crop and collected the fallen corn when there was a load he or she could conveniently manage; each carried it on his own back to the homestead. Kalyanu regarded their activities with satisfaction and thought of the work still to be done. The snow had already fallen on the high pastures in a light powdering that would melt by day. Up there the ground would freeze hard every night and the clefts and corries where no sun came would gradually fill with snow; but it would be two months yet with any luck before it would lie on the upper fields. There would be time to finish the harvest in the lower fields, then to get in the millet from the higher; then to plough into some of the upper fields the rotted bracken that had been stored during the summer and sow the barley before the snow covered it. Next would come the ploughing and sowing of the lower fields. It was a great convenience that everything on the upper farm was so much slower; one could cut later and sow earlier up there; the labour force at Kalyanu's disposal would not have been enough to deal with the same acreage if the land had been all at one level and the crops had all ripened at the same time.

He turned from the busy scene in the fields round the homestead and set his face to the path leading to the upper farm. He
climbed easily and quickly; indeed it was hardly climbing to
him, for his muscles were so attuned to rough paths on the hill
face that they would have been more quickly tired on the level.
But he had never walked on the level.

Kalyanu had no ears for the roar of the river below, no eyes
for the scene he knew so well. His thoughts were on practical
matters, the harvesting of crops and the work he should set his
brothers to do. To an observer on the hillside beyond the river
he would have seemed a minute dark point moving steadily
across the grass slope below the bluff. Even the ploughed land
below him made only a tiny patch of colour against the immensity of the hillside. Its snaky terraces, the crimson of the red
millet, the yellow of the green millet, the brilliant orange of the
drying heads of maize, were touches with the point of the brush,
hardly to be picked up by the eye in the vastness of rock face,
grass slope and forest. Grass clothed the hill where it was not
sheer rock; forest poured into every corrie, glen or hollow where
a tree could stand. Below the homestead were long-leaved pines,
the light sparkling on their dancing upturned needle-points, their
airy glitter interspersed with the darker masses of cedar or contorted oak scrub; higher, the blue pine turned its closer darker
fingers to the sky with the same exultation. Even where the
trees could grow, the line of the ground was nearer the vertical
than the horizontal; it was a landscape crazily tiptilted out of the
plane familiar to the world of men and the tiny evidence of man's
presence could hardly be distinguished against those impending
precipitous masses.

When Kalyanu reached the first field he plucked an ear of
millet and rubbed it between his fingers to see how it was forming. He was pleased at the progress it had made. It should be
possible to start cutting this patch from the bottom upwards as
soon as the work below was ended. He climbed up from terrace

to terrace, appraising the crop in each narrow shelf. Half-way up he stopped and stood, gazing at the ruins of one field where a bear had again eaten its fill and rolled.

The anger he felt this time was quite different from that of a week ago. This was no surging of uncontrollable fury, because he no longer felt helpless. He knew how to deal with a bear. He would show the swine. He went quickly over the remaining fields, to see the extent of the damage, and he looked at the footprints. Not so large a beast as last time. Probably a female. His confidence needed no strengthening but his contempt was increased. He followed the tracks up through the crops to the narrow place at the top, where the first bear had been killed. This was where the female too had come in from the forest. Then he turned to go back and fetch his brothers.

It was a pity that Kalyanu did not examine the tracks more carefully or apply his mind more thoroughly to the problem. Had he done this, he would have seen that the tracks did not return to the forest by the narrow place, as they had come in. He had hunted heel, following the tracks back in the direction from which they had come; but though they came in by the narrow place, they went right through the crops, going on, not back. After eating and rolling, the bear had wandered downwards and westwards, passing out of the cultivated patch below the cliff that formed one flank of the narrow place. If he had noticed this, Kalyanu might have remembered the thicket of wild raspberries that lay beyond the plough on that western side. If he had troubled to think how a bear lived, it would have occurred to him that it must find much other food besides his crops and an occasional goat or bullock. He might then have reflected that this beast must have enjoyed the wild raspberries and that where a bear has gone once, it may go again; and had he thought thus, the story of his life, his son's, and his grandson's, might have been changed. But the Himalayan peasant is unobservant of the ways of beasts and birds except as they affect him directly. He does not even know of the strange habits of the cuckoo, whose word of fear rings through his hills in May and June just as it does in England. Kalyanu assumed that this bear would come in by the narrow place and could be made to go out by the same way, just as the first bear had done a week ago. He did not hesitate but went at once to fetch his brothers.

The five men stopped work in the fields, leaving it to the women to go on till dark, and climbed up the hillside once more to the ambush. But they did not come as they had a week before, full of wonder at their own daring, breathless, with a queer empty feeling in the bowels. They were only a little keyed up by the thought of what they had to do. They could joke among themselves quite naturally, for they knew now that bears were easy.

Kalyanu arranged them just as he had done before and they took up their stations. The moon had not yet risen, so that waiting should have been more nervous work than last time. But the tension that had made the heart pound at every moving stone and crackling leaf had gone when victory was achieved and, far from being on edge, as the night wore on, the younger brothers were inclined to doze. Kalyanu being separate from the others did not know this, but Autaru, the second brother, had to speak several times to his companion, the youngest, to keep him awake. They had all worked a long day in the fields.

No bear came that night and it was a weary and dispirited party who came back to the homestead in the dawn. They worked badly in the fields that day and when Kalyanu told them they were to watch for the bear again, Autaru was the only one who did not grumble. But there was no question of disobedience and they hid once more in the appointed places, Kalyanu agreeing, however, at Autaru's suggestion, that one of each pair of brothers should sleep.

The moon had risen and her silvery light made long inky shadows below rocks and terrace walls, when, an hour after this watch began, Kalyanu rose carefully to his feet, taking care to make no sound. He glanced over his shoulder to the east and saw the pines on the next ridge cut out in rigid black silhouette against the growing radiance; then turned again to look at the fields before him. As he looked, he stiffened in sudden attention. There it was. Yes, there was no doubt. There was the bear, right in the middle of the crops. That shadow had not been there before; it was moving slowly, very slowly, but undoubtedly moving, as the beast nosed here and there, making up its mind where to begin.

For about ten heart-beats Kalyanu was flustered. The bear was below him. How had it got there without his knowledge? Had it crept past him in the dark? It seemed now to be moving upwards; was it already retreating? But the moment of indecision passed. However the bear had got there, whatever irrelevancies it had introduced, the original plan must stand. It was moving upwards. He would wait till it was level with him and then he would hurl rocks and shout, and it would make upwards for the narrow place.

The bear moved very slowly and Kalyanu's patience began to wear thin. He was very short of sleep; and all the time this sod of a bear was spoiling his crops. He did not stick to his decision to wait till it was level with him. The bear was still on a terrace lower than his own when he let out his first yell and began to throw stones at the bushes and send them crashing down the hillside.

The bear raised her head at this sudden commotion and began to move away, slow and unhurried, for she was disturbed, not frightened. But she did not go towards the narrow place as Kalyanu had expected. She went back the way she had come, towards the wild raspberries, downwards and westwards. Kalyanu sprang to his feet.

'Strike!' he shouted at the top of his voice, and ran after the bear in a frenzy lest she should escape and the hours of waiting be wasted. He sprang down from the top of a terrace-wall into the field across which the bear was moving with rolling un-hurried gait. He swung his pole and brought it down with all his strength on the hairy black hindquarters. The bear turned with incredible speed; Kalyanu struck again with his shortened staff as she came at him on all fours, but quite ineffectively; the bear's quick lunge with mouth and paw went home. Her right paw broke his left leg below the knee; her teeth crunched deep in his right thigh.

As Kalyanu fell back at the foot of the terrace wall, Autaru arrived at the top with a yell and struck downwards with his staff at the beast below. It was a blow into which he could put no strength, for she was too far below him, and in a blind red fighting lust he sprang down beside her. His blow had been just enough to distract the bear from Kalyanu and to infuriate her. She rose on her hindquarters and struck with both forepaws a fraction of a second quicker than he could. Her left stripped the flesh from the side of his face and glanced off his shoulder; but before he could feel the agony her right fell with its full force on his head, crushing the skull and breaking his neck.

The youngest brother had been sharing the watch with Autaru in the bushes below the cliff and had been asleep when Kalyanu first shouted. He was only a few yards behind when he saw his brother drop lifeless, but he was fully awake by now and he acted with sense and courage. He did not leap down at once to the bear's level, to drop almost into her arms as Autaru had done, but moved off a few paces, dropped to her level and approached her warily, poised on his toes, ready for flight or fight. The bear had hardly noticed him, for she was still wholly unafraid, and was actually sniffing at Autaru and considering his possibilities as a meal, when he struck. Her lunge towards him with curved left forepaw was made almost as one might brush away a fly; she returned to her interest in Autaru. But her hooked blow had done all that was necessary; the youngest brother had sprung back and had dropped his staff as a guard, but the bear's strength and quickness were such that the staff was torn from his hands and broke his shin-bone where it struck him. He pulled himself away from the enemy with his hands, trailing his useless leg.

The third and fourth brothers arrived as the youngest fell. They had run as fast as they could and were wildly excited. They too would have flung themselves at the bear, no doubt with the same result, if Kalyanu had not spoken. But lying there sick with pain, he still knew what was happening and from the shadow below the terrace wall had seen the fate of his two brothers. He heard the others shout as they came up and called up all his strength to cry:

'No! Do not fight! You must look after us. Do not fight!' Then he fainted.

The two remaining brothers pulled up at Kalyanu's voice. For a second they hesitated, but they were used to obeying Kalyanu, and once they paused a strong natural inclination came to the aid of his instructions. They shouted abuse and threw stones but kept their distance. The bear paused, grunted, then slowly made off towards the wild raspberries. The two brothers returned to pick up their wounded and take home the dead.

The youngest brother had a cracked shin-bone which needed nothing but rest. Kalyanu's case was more serious. His left leg required to be set before nature could begin the work of healing; and more serious still was his mangled thigh, with multiple wounds from the bear's teeth. He and his brothers knew well enough that a wound can go septic, but their only means of preventing this was to apply cow-dung to exclude the air and in this method they had, rightly enough, no great faith. Kalyanu lay tossing in agony while the two brothers who were still whole debated with the women of Bantok what they should do. No one really had any plan, until one of the outcast Doms mentioned that the day before he had met another Dom from ten miles down the river who had come their way in search of a stray goat. He had heard that the Deputy Commissioner would soon be coming to camp on the other side of the river, near the bridge thirty miles down stream which was their only link with the outside world. Everyone's face lightened; they were not used to responsibility but to doing what Kalyanu told them, and here was someone else on whom the responsibility could be placed.

'We will take him to the District Sahib,' they said. Kalyanu was lying on a bed, made of tough oak roughly shaped with the axe and strung with hemp string they had twisted themselves, but it was too wide for the paths they would have to follow. They must make a litter hardly wider than their own shoulders or it would catch on the cliff walls and throw them all over the edge. The women set to work quickly to make a hammock which could be slung from one stout pole, whilst the two brothers worked feverishly to get in what they could of the millet and to leave the farm in such trim that the women could manage without them. Ten or twelve miles on a hill path is a good day's stage for a loaded man, but they could not afford to take three days to reach the bridge. They must hurry, because they had to get back to see to the harvest and because if they were to save Kalyanu he must be in better hands than theirs as soon as possible. And before they went they had to burn Autaru.

It was not till the morning of the second day after the disaster that they started, taking with them food for three days only. They could get more on the other side of the bridge and they took with them some of their precious store of silver, a hoard into which they usually dipped twice a year to pay their few rupees of land revenue; once every year or two when one of them went across the river and down towards the plains to Chamoli to buy salt and iron; a few times in a generation to buy a bride. They started very early, after a drink of milk and no more, meaning to get as far as they could before they stopped for food. The women watched them move away, their reddish-brown legs naked to the thigh, their sturdy bodies square in the dark homespun blankets draped across the shoulders, Kalyanu swinging in his hammock between them. Then the women turned to get on with the work of the farm, the feeding of the children, the animals, and Darshanu the youngest brother, and the harvesting of the millet, their life-blood for the winter.

The path the brothers had to take followed the river and, since the river for most of its course ran in a precipitous rocky gorge, it was not an easy path. It went down to the river for an easy crossing of a tributary torrent where there were stepping stones, renewed every year after the autumn spates, and then across the shingly debris brought down from the hills in the course of years. The roar of the river here was deafening. You had to put your mouth to a man's ear and shout to make yourself heard. The water was milky-green with the ice-ground dust of glaciers and melted snow; it swept and churned and stormed, spouting high where it dashed against a bastion of the cliff, breaking with the shattering weight of Atlantic rollers over a rock in mid-stream, rolling and grinding the boulders in its bed, a stream of ceaseless, furious energy, seeking the centre of the earth with swifter force, but the same remorseless purpose, as the upthrusting green of trees and grass and corn.

Then the path went up, zigzagging up a narrow edge between two arms of the tributary torrent, then out on to the face of the sheer rock cliff over the main river, following a crack that led up and up for two thousand feet; then on to a long grass face, so steep that if one stretched out a hand to the bole of a pine below the path, the fingers touched a point twice the height of a man from the roots. Across this face the tiny track made by the feet of goats and men lay like a single hair. Down again, to a tributary crossing and a stretch of shingle; up, to go over another bluff with an impassable face; a long, long, tiring journey in which the mind after some miles could not disentangle the steady succession of cliff and torrent, corrie and grass slope, rock and pine.

The brothers kept going all day, except for a halt in the middle of the morning to eat. They had fresh water to drink at every torrent, ice-cold, and they were in hard condition, but they were very tired by the evening, for they had covered twenty miles, a long march over such country and with such a load. They gave Kalyanu water; he wanted nothing else; they put him by their side on a bed of leaves in the shelter of an overhanging rock, much used by goats and shepherds, where they rolled themselves up in the blankets that had covered their shoulders by day.

They reached the bridge at midday on the third day after the disaster. Near this point on the northern bank, there was a village, not an isolated homestead, for a larger tributary had made a valley in which there were slopes that could be terraced and ploughed. Here the banks of the river approached each other in two leaning cliffs, on each of which there was a convenient ledge on which a man could stand. From each side had been thrust out three pine trunks lashed together, the butts firmly wedged in hollows carved deep in the cliff face, the angle of the ledge pushing them steeply up, so that the space between the tips could be bridged by a pair of lashed trunks. The drop from the bridge was two hundred feet to the frenzy of the milky torrent below. It was not easy to walk over the two pine trunks with such a burden as Kalyanu in his hammock, but the two brothers did it. Fortunately Kalyanu was conscious at that point and they made him understand that he must lie quite still, for a sudden movement would destroy them all.

When they got him over, they looked at each other and grinned.

'That was worse than the bear,' said Amru, the elder.

They went on to the first village and began to ask questions. It was true. The Deputy Commissioner's camp was only five miles away up the hillside. In two more hours, his tents were in sight, but their hearts sank. They would have to talk and explain, to superior people, who would laugh at them because their hair was long and their speech barbarous. But their luck had turned. They met the District Sahib himself as he was coming back to camp and he stopped to ask them questions.

At first they were speechless, shifting from one leg to another. Then Amru said:

'Lord, it is our brother. It was a bear. We have brought him to you.'

And after more questioning at last the strange man understood them. His face was strange, sharp and light coloured, but kindly; still more strange was his speech; but he had understood. He would look after Kalyanu. They could go back to the farm.

III

MR. BENNETT, the Deputy Commissioner of Garhwal in 1875, was an amateur surgeon and physician of some repute. His methods were simple and usually drastic but they suited the people with whom he had to deal. Castor oil was the basis of his physic, warm water and carbolic of his surgery.[1] With a people who did not wash much and lived in highly insanitary villages, the moderate degree of surgical cleanliness he was able to achieve worked wonders, for, when it was released from the great majority of the foes it was accustomed to deal with, the injured flesh flourished and clove together with startling rapidity.

It did not need great skill to see that Kalyanu's left shin-bone would have to be set and Mr. Bennett set it and bound it to a splint of oak, an unshaped branch that happened to be the right shape and size. The bitten thigh was more difficult. The bone did not seem to be broken but was probably bruised; the flesh was terribly lacerated. There was really nothing to do but to clean up the oil and cow-dung which the people of Bantok had applied, wash the wounds generously with hot water and carbolic and tie them up again, continue the treatment, and hope for the best.

So Kalyanu's pole and hammock joined the considerable assemblage that moved round with Mr. Bennett's camp. Rest in one place would of course have been much better, but the business of the district could not be held up for one man and Mr. Bennett could not trust anyone but himself to look after the patient. The addition of a load that was now usually carried by four men made little difference to his arrangements, because his

---

[1] Lister's discoveries were only ten years old, and Mr. Bennett was somewhat ahead of the average of medical practice at this date. He owed his knowledge to a regular correspondence with a medical friend of his year at Oxford, a keen disciple of Lister.

tents and bedding and gear and that of his many servants were carried by the people of each village to the next halting-place. This was an ancient feudal service due to the Rajas which had been continued by the Commissioners of Kumaon because there was no other way of getting about. Kalyanu was moved every two or three days and the journeys were not pleasant, but then he was not used to anything pleasant and he was being looked after better than ever before in his life. Mr. Bennett's orderlies were charged with the duty of feeding him at Mr. Bennett's expense and, being hill-peasants only one degree less unsophisticated than Kalyanu himself, they did as they were told. It never entered their heads to underfeed him for their own benefit, or to overcharge their master. Once a day Mr. Bennett himself came and took off the bandages and washed the wounds. After the first day or two, as he began to mend and his mind grew clearer, Kalyanu tried to struggle to his feet when this strange ruler came to see him but it was made clear to him that this was forbidden. His first feeling of surprise and fear at being waited on by someone who was practically a king was gradually replaced by veneration and a deep devotion. If it is love to wish ardently for an opportunity to serve and be near the object of one's devotion, then Kalyanu loved Mr. Bennett.

Mr. Bennett in his turn felt an increasing liking for the man who grew to health under his care. For a generous nature, there is a natural inclination towards affection for anyone to whom a kindness has been done; and to this was gradually added an interest in Kalyanu himself. It was difficult at first to get him to talk. 'Yes, lord,' and 'No, lord,' and 'It was a bear, lord,' were the most that could be got from him, but gradually he told more and more of the story. His dialect was difficult to follow, for speech differs from village to village in Garhwal; but Mr. Bennett had been ten years in the hills, and he had applied himself seriously to the dialects when he first came. And Kalyanu himself gradually acquired a rather more sophisticated vocabulary. When his story had been fully explained, an impression was left of courage and initiative that was enhanced by his cheerfulness in pain and his obvious gratitude.

Mr. Bennett was not ambitious for an outwardly successful career ending in high office and many decorations, but he was by no means an ordinary man. He was a solitary, a poet, and a mountaineer. Had he been ambitious in the conventional sense, he would not have exerted himself in his early days to get on the Kumaon Commission, which could lead to no great post; had his recreations been those of most men, he would have preferred to his present loneliness the life of the plains, where there would be polo, pigsticking and racing, and brandy and soda at the club. But he loved the hills. He would perhaps never be the kind of mountaineer who writes books, or of whom books are written, but his love for mountains had guided his life. His long vacations in Oxford days had been spent in Switzerland, and it was to Switzerland he went on his first leave. He taught himself to climb in the Alps without a guide and he then began to experiment in the Himalayas, not with any object of making a name for himself or of achieving what had not been done before, but because the silence of the snows in high places raised his clear spirit to a wordless delight which nothing else could equal. As for poetry, every mountaineer is a poet at heart, though few have been poets in execution. Mr. Bennett might have been called a poet by virtue only of his pleasure in singing water, rock and cliff and flower and icy peak, but he was also a lover of the English poets, and of a most catholic taste. He read them all, and not the old masters only, for he had a standing order with his booksellers in Oxford for the latest works of his contemporaries. He might perhaps have been called uncritical, for he did not take sides in the controversies of his day, but found a stimulating pleasure in wrestling with Browning or Coventry Patmore and yet turned with an equal anticipation of happiness to the smooth melodies of Tennyson and Matthew Arnold.

But this argued wide interests, not lack of standards; for he burnt his own efforts remorselessly.

Mr. Bennett did a good deal of reading in his lonely evenings in camp but he was conscientious in allowing himself only a limited amount of time for his other recreation of mountaineering. His duties as Deputy Commissioner of Garhwal need not have been exacting, for although he was judge, policeman and chief executive officer in one, the administration could really have been suspended for a few months without anyone noticing much difference. Crimes against property were unknown, murder and assault were rare. There were so few Muslims that communal trouble was not even thought of. The only local official of whom the villager had any knowledge was the patwari, who with the help of one servant collected the land revenue — almost a token rent — and administered criminal justice for some sixty to a hundred villages, with no sanction but the authority of the Government and the possession of a shotgun. There was not even much scope to the patwari for rapacity, for every villager paid him annually a gift of grain which was a fixed proportion of his crop. Although this amounted to ten times the trivial wages paid him by government, neither the patwari nor anyone else regarded the practice as dishonest, as indeed it was not, for, since everyone paid regularly, he was on the whole as fair as his intellect and training permitted him to be.

For Mr. Bennett, therefore, the constant effort to prevent extortion which in those days made up most of the life of his colleagues in the plains hardly existed. His checks of the work of minor officials were little more than a formality. He could have spent his winters shooting tigers where the hills break down into the plains, his spring and autumn fishing, and his summer mountaineering, without anyone being actively the worse. Indeed, this was just what some of his predecessors had done. But he was a man with an essential goodness of heart who believed with no shadow of doubt that he was where he was for the good of the people he ruled. He made no attempt to change their way of life beyond putting an end so far as he could to certain practices which were repugnant to Christian morality and which orthodox Hinduism would have disowned. But he did think deeply about the welfare and the administration of his people and he came to the conclusion that, since most of the troubles which came to him were disputes about the ownership of land, the most beneficent boon that good government could bestow would be maps of the fields and a record of every man's rights.

After some months of correspondence he managed to convince his government that this was so and a survey expert was sent to make experimental maps. The expert made an accurate trigonometrical survey of one village and took two months to do it. His maps showed every terrace and every field. But he calculated that to cover the whole district would absorb four times the annual revenue received from the district for ten years. Government shook its heavy head.

So Mr. Bennett invented an ingenious form of survey of his own, which could be carried out with no equipment but a few ropes for measuring distances and which concerned itself with no trigonometrical pedantry. By this means he could make sketch-maps that would serve his purpose in one-eighth of the time taken by the expert and at one-thirtieth of the cost. And to this, after more months of correspondence, his government did agree; and so Mr. Bennett camped in every village of the district, worked ten hours a day to make his maps, and was happy.

When Kalyanu was well enough to walk, he felt no desire to go back to Bantok. Life there would not be the same without Autaru, and they seemed to be getting on fairly well without him, for Amru had developed unsuspected powers of leadership. Also, Kalyanu had tasted something of a more varied and on the whole rather less arduous life. But behind these superficial reasons was a warm positive desire to be near the man who had

41

saved his life, and for whom he felt a real devotion and affection. He could not formulate these wishes to himself, much less tell them to anyone else. He hung about the camp, trying to bring himself to go to the District Sahib and ask to be allowed to serve him; but he was too shy to come to the point.

He was brought to the point, however, by external circumstance. And this happened at the one moment most opportune for himself. Had it happened on any other day, Mr. Bennett would have told him he had no place vacant and advised him to go back to Bantok; and Kalyanu and his son and grandson would have lived out their lives in the yearly struggle to harvest enough grain to feed the homestead for another year. But the chances of this one day were to lead to the uprooting of himself and his family from Bantok and to the complex revenge which his grandson Jodh Singh was to take on society for uprooting him.

There were three threads of chance that twisted together into a pattern and altered Kalyanu's life. The first was that Mr. Bennett changed the plans for his march without warning, a thing he did from time to time to make sure that he saw what was normal and not something specially prepared for the occasion; the second was that having varied his plan he made a further variation within it because he was a mountaineer and felt he deserved a holiday; and the third was that Keshar Singh, one of his orderlies, had a friend in the village of Marora.

Mr. Bennett was moving eastwards along the south side of a steep ridge which varied between nine and ten thousand feet in height. There was a well-established route along the south side about three thousand feet below the crest of the ridge, with regular halting-places. If you went three days' march along it, everyone assumed you would take the next step and go on to the fourth halt. It was for this very reason that Mr. Bennett decided that he would leave it and go over the ridge to look at some map-making which was going on among the lower villages on the north side of the ridge. The locals shook their heads when he told them he was going to cross the ridge.

'There is no path suitable for your Honour,' they said.

'But there is a way?' persisted Mr. Bennett.

'There is a way that goats and shepherds take,' they admitted, 'but it is not a suitable path and there will be snow.'

Mr. Bennett pointed out that there was not much snow yet, only a sprinkling, and that where a shepherd could go, so could he. He gave orders that next morning his camp should cross the ridge by the goat-path.

They had packed the first loads and the first porters were moving off when he started next morning. He came out of his tent and stamped his feet and clapped his hands for warmth in the diamond sunshine. The breaths of men and mules came in puffs of steam. There was still frost in the shadows of the bushes and behind the tent. To the south, the hillside was cultivated right down to the stream; every arm and root running downwards and outwards was wrinkled by the terraced fields like the skin of some very ancient and scaly beast. Looking down on them from above they were as regular and orderly as the rings in the stump of a great tree, or the scales on a butterfly's wing. They were ploughed and sown for the winter crops.

Mr. Bennett turned and looked up to the north. From about the level of his camp to the crest, there was thick forest, from which, here and there along the ridge, peaks of rock or grass-clad domes stood out, sprinkled with the first powdering of snow. There was no wind and the smoke from the village to the east hung in a blue mist over the pines and oak scrub, sparkling with refracted light. A frosty, sparkling, diamond morning, thought Mr. Bennett, and his spirit rejoiced at the thought that he would see the snows of the main range when he reached the crest.

His three orderlies approached, Amar Singh, the senior, with his square competent face serious, his black pillbox hat tilted over one eye as he had pushed it when considering some problem about the loading of a tent; Keshar Singh, humorous, his crinkled brown face waiting to widen to a grin at the first excuse; Bharat Singh like a small boy unexpectedly grown up, with his ears standing straight out from his head, and his terrier air of wanting to be taken for a walk. No one had ever got more than 'Yes, lord' and 'No, lord' out of Bharat Singh, Mr. Bennett reflected. He smiled at them all with affection.

'Who is coming with me to-day?' he asked.

'Keshar Singh, lord,' replied Amar Singh. 'Bharat Singh is going on ahead as quickly as he can, and I shall see the last loads off and come with the coolies to see they do not rest too much.'

Mr. Bennett nodded and turned to go. The path at first was not difficult, for it was the way to one of the main village grazing grounds and led on to another village. It ran through patches of pine forest, where the reddish boles of the long-leaved pine stood up like the straight limbs of prehistoric animals, coated in plates of scaly bark, and the sun lighted the brown floor of needles; then through patches of evergreen oak scrub and rhododendron; and then began to climb, the long-leaved pine giving way to the blue pine and a few deciduous trees appearing. In one glade, Mr. Bennett stopped for a moment entranced. Through a tangle of rusty bracken and patches of bright couch-grass ran a little brown stream, tinkling happily over a dozen tiny falls. Alone in the glade stood one chestnut-tree, naked against the wintry blue of the sky, in a pool of its ruddy fan-shaped leaves. There was an autumn smell of dying leaves and frost and moisture. It was home, the English autumn, the English woodland. Mr. Bennett shook his head and went on.

Keshar Singh had enlisted a local man to show the way, whom he now led forward to introduce. He pointed out with his usual crinkly grin that here they must leave the main path and begin to climb. It was not easy going, overgrown with trees and scrub and extremely steep. All three men had to use their hands to pull themselves up and there was no more walking. After about two hours of this, they were on the saddle. The ground was comparatively level for a few yards and then began to descend. The path, if it could be called a path, for it needed some skill to see where it ran, led straight on, and by that road the porters and the camp would go. But Mr. Bennett wanted to see about him and on the saddle he was still among trees which obscured his view. He had noticed before starting that to the west of the saddle there was a sharply pointed peak, which seemed to be about ten thousand feet or rather more, with a rock face which might have possibilities; and he felt he owed himself some recreation, for there were no Sundays in camp. So he turned sharply westward.

In another hour he was out of the trees and only a few hundred feet below the little peak. It would be possible to walk to the summit if one kept on the north side but Mr. Bennett wanted some exercise on rock to keep him from getting rusty. He sent Keshar Singh and the local man by the easy route and himself spent a happy half-hour clinging by toes and fingers to the rocky southern face. There was a refinement of pleasure in this, because as he climbed he could not see the snows of the main range. He saved them up, like a child with sweets, until they burst upon him when he reached the summit. There they were, icy dome and snowy cliff, fluted ridge and needle, blue and white and silver, clear and hard in the diamond air, calm in the gay sunshine. Mr. Bennett held his breath in wonder and happiness, as he had done the first time he saw them, as he would do the last. Keshar Singh and the local man also sat and gazed.

After eating some sandwiches, Mr. Bennett began to discuss the way down. Keshar Singh and the local man wanted to go back to the saddle as they had come and follow the goat-track. It was the obvious route and Keshar Singh was particularly anxious to get into camp early because he had a friend in Marora village, an old comrade who had served with him in the 3rd

Gurkha Rifles.[1] But Mr. Bennett disliked doing the obvious, partly from temperament and partly because if he went by the obvious route everyone he met was expecting him. He favoured following a spur which ran due northward and reckoned that once they got down from that spur to the level of their camp they would find a lateral path that would take them the right way. Keshar Singh argued that the spur would end in precipice and the local man backed him, but had to admit he had never been on it and did not know the villages below it. Mr. Bennett was not to be persuaded and they started along the spur.

It was fairly easy going at first, through open country rather like a Westmorland fell, except for the forest immediately below them on all sides. But where the spur broke its smooth line, at the first knobbly knee, Keshar Singh and the local man both registered expressions which plainly said: 'I told you so.' For ahead to the north was sheer rocky cliff, and to the east, the side to which they wanted to turn, was a grassy slope on which none of the three would have trusted themselves. The only way down was to the west, and this they took.

The slope of the ground brought them into a side glen with cultivation among the trees. There was the smoke of a village up the glen to their left. They found a path leading downwards and out of the glen to the north and hurried along it, hoping for a more frequented path that would take them eastwards. Their path was little used and they met no one till they turned a corner and saw a small figure weeping in an utter abandonment of grief, one arm raised to lean against a boulder the size of a cottage, her forehead bowed on that raised arm, her whole body shaking with her sobs. She wore the uncomely blanket dress of the hills, which conceals the figure, and of her head nothing could be seen but matted dark hair, bleached here and there to auburn.

Mr. Bennett approached her gently. It would be very difficult

[1] Two companies of this regiment formed the beginnings of the Royal Garhwal Rifles twelve years later.

to find out what her trouble was. If Amar Singh had been with him, he would have deputed him to find out, but Keshar Singh, who was kept on as an orderly mainly for his humorous expression, was unreliable. He was in a hurry, and if he were left to find out the truth, he would put words into her mouth and report them as though her sobs had confirmed them. Mr. Bennett must talk to her himself and try not to frighten her. He sat down on the ground, not too close, not too far away.

'What is the matter, daughter?' he asked.

There was no answer, and he repeated the question gently.

'She is only a Dom, lord,' said Keshar Singh. Mr. Bennett told him to be quiet, and repeated his question.

'My master,' she sobbed. She meant her husband, and Mr. Bennett felt it was going to be more difficult than ever. But for once Keshar Singh was helpful.

'He has been beating her,' he said with a grin, in a voice which might just pass as an aside to the local man.

'No, no,' sobbed the girl, raising her head and showing a smooth round chin and a snub nose that would have been attractive in a face less disfigured by tears. She was young, almost a child. 'They are going to kill him.'

'Why are they going to kill him?' Mr. Bennett asked gently.

'The rope festival,' she wept, her head falling again on her raised arm.

'When will it be?' Mr. Bennett asked still more gently. He was very near something important, and he silenced Keshar Singh with his hand.

'To-morrow, in the afternoon.'

'And where? Here in this village?'

Between her sobs came a just distinguishable yes.

Mr. Bennett rose to his feet.

'Do not tell anyone you have seen us,' he said. 'Do you understand? If you tell no one at all, I will save your husband. Do you understand?'

She was lost in her sorrow and did not answer. Nothing would save her man. But Mr. Bennett judged she would not be likely to talk, while if he took her with him, the cat would be out of the bag and things might later be unpleasant for her. He left her and pressed on. It was after dark when they found the camp.

The girl by the rock stayed on. She was hardly conscious that they had been there; if she had been asked she could only have said that she had spoken to strangers, without knowing who they were, for there was no room in her heart for anything but her grief. At any other time, she would have been tongue-tied in the presence even of men from another village, but her defences were down, she reacted without resistance. She had given them the one thought in her mind — 'My master' — and then Keshar Singh's lucky brutality had stung her to protest. For her husband was kind to her. He did not beat her and she loved him dearly.

She stayed there by the rock with her grief till she suddenly realized that she was cold and it was getting dark. She had come out to get sticks and had only collected a few when her sorrow suddenly became more than she could bear. She dabbed at her eyes with her blanket skirt, pushed back her hair, blew her nose with her fingers, picked up her sticks and started for home.

Her husband was in the house and had begun to cook the cakes of millet flour.

'You are late, Padmini,' he said.

She did not answer, but turning her face away from him, put a pot of porridge on the side of the fire and squatting down beside him, took over the patting and tossing and roasting of the coarse pancakes.

Sohan Das himself was less disturbed than might have been expected by the thought of the ordeal he had to face to-morrow. It was not true that the villagers had decided to kill him. What they had decided was to hold the rope festival. This had been

forbidden by the British Government but they felt sure that no
one would come to hear of it. Theirs was a lonely and isolated
glen, which the patwari did not often visit. He had been there
recently and now he was busy in the villages down by the river
where the maps were being made. He would not be in their
village again for a month at least. So it would be safe to hold
the festival, which was exciting to watch and fun for everyone
but the victim, and was besides a sure way of making the fields
fertile. Everyone knew that the fields used to be more fertile
when the festival was held every year; nobody remembered
that there were then fewer people and more land and the fields
were left to lie fallow occasionally. So the villagers decided to
hold the feast and the young men were sent up to the top of the
cliff above the village from which the victim began his descent.
They looked at the tree to which the rope had always been tied.
It was still quite firm and strong; they fixed a post in the fields
below and began to make the rope, two hundred and fifty yards
long, and the wooden saddle on which the victim would sit.

It was a form of human sacrifice which combined the pleasures
of a simple exercise in geometry with a sporting gamble, a free-
for-all rough-and-tumble in which nothing was barred, and a
lucky dip. The top of the precipice was about five hundred feet
above the level of the fields and the post to which the lower end
of the rope was fastened was about the same distance from the
foot of the precipice; the rope when tied at both ends therefore
made an angle of about forty-five degrees. The victim sat on a
piece of wood shaped like an inverted Y, the inner angle of the
fork being polished till it was smooth and slippery. He held
the upright in his hands and put his legs over the branches of the
fork. Stones were tied to his feet and to the lower forks of the
saddle so that it should not overturn. There was a simple ritual;
his forehead was marked with a splash of colour in which a few
grains of rice were stuck. Then he was released. He would
shoot down the curving rope with growing speed, and one of

three things would happen. The rope might break, which happened seldom; it might catch fire, which happened frequently; or he might reach the lower end with nothing more than a few bruises or a broken leg, which happened less often. If the victim fell, the crowd at the lower end of the rope raced for his body, each man eager to pluck a fragment of his hair or beard, even his clothes, to bury in the fields and bring fertility. If the victim reached the ground alive, there was no race, but there was an added zest in the struggle for fragments of his hair or clothes, partly because there was less that was detachable and partly because the detaching was painful to the victim.

The prospect of being the victim was not one which would have much general appeal, but to Sohan Das it did not seem more unusual or alarming than the birth of her first child seems to a peasant woman. His community, a sub-caste among the aboriginal Doms, had always provided the victim for this festival and they were rewarded at the time of the festival by gifts of grain from all the shareholders in the village. It had hit them hard when the festival had been forbidden and they had been the most eager that it should be held again. They chose the victim on each occasion by lot, but a survivor, like the member of a jury, was exempt from service until there was no one else available. Sohan Das regarded the whole business as part of the course of nature, something which ought to happen and which must happen to him sooner or later. The fact that the festival had not taken place in the last few years seemed to him something impious, an interference with the seasons and the ways of God.

But it was different for Padmini. She was younger, and she came from another village where the festival had stopped earlier. She had only seen it once. She had seen the rope smoke and break into flame; she had seen her father falling, slowly, slowly, it seemed for a protracted second of time, his hands clutching at the air above his head; she could remember the distorted angles of his limbs when the villagers had left him and she followed her mother to what remained. To her, the warm kindly man with whom she shared her life was already broken, stripped and lifeless. She lay down in sorrow and her young face was wet with tears when she fell asleep.

Mr. Bennett, on the other hand, lay down to sleep with a pleasurable anticipation of excitement next day. His only fear was that Keshar Singh or the local man who had been with him might give away the fact that it had been the girl who had told him the secret. The local man, however, lived on the other side of the ridge and he would send him back first thing in the morning. Keshar Singh was more of a problem; either of the other orderlies could be trusted to keep their mouths shut if they were told, but not Keshar Singh. Mr. Bennett wondered whether he should send him back to headquarters and get another man in his place, as he had often wondered before, only to forgive him for his impudence and grin. He fell asleep without making up his mind.

It was next morning that the affairs of Padmini and Sohan Das impinged on those of Kalyanu. The latter shared a tent with the three orderlies, and it was a small tent in which the presence of an extra man was an inconvenience. Nobody minded much as a rule, but on the morning when the rope festival was to be held Keshar Singh had a hangover. As soon as he had been dismissed the night before, he had slipped away to see his friend in Marora and they had sat up over a bottle of spirits till far into the night. He woke up in a bad temper and grumbled at Kalyanu because he was in the way.

'Why does this son of a bitch live in the tent with us?' he said. 'Who asked him to stay on in this camp for ever?'

'I have a petition to the District Sahib,' said Kalyanu, on the defensive, for the same point had been on his conscience for some time.

'Then why don't you give him your petition and go?' Keshar

Singh spoke with ill-humour because that was how he felt about everything this morning, but there was confirmation for his point of view in the silence of the other two. Kalyanu saw that he must bring the matter to the touch at once.

The orderlies knew that camp was not to be moved that day, and on a halting day no specific duties were assigned to the man who had gone with Mr. Bennett on the day before. Keshar Singh was therefore justified in assuming that he would have nothing to do that day. Ordinarily, he would have asked Mr. Bennett before he went to see his friend. But to-day he was afraid that if he showed himself the traces of his carousal would be evident; besides, he was very anxious to get back for the opening of the second bottle, which he thought might make him feel better, and he did not want to risk being stopped. He took a chance and slipped away.

Mr. Bennett meanwhile was just ready to start. He calculated that the sooner he got to the village in the glen the better. The girl by the rock had said the afternoon; he would get there by noon, which was as soon as he could without arousing interest by a specially early start, for it was between three and four hours' march. By that time the situation should not have developed to a stage at which it would be difficult to stop. If he arrived when the victim was decked and on the altar, so to speak, things would be more likely to be awkward. He did not anticipate any difficulty, but it would be as well to take the patwari and two orderlies, instead of the one who usually came with him. It was Bharat Singh's day, and Bharat Singh presented himself. The patwari was also standing by.

'I want another orderly,' said Mr. Bennett. 'Whose day is it to look after the camp?'

'Amar Singh's, lord.'

'Then call Keshar Singh.'

Bharat Singh looked exactly like a small boy asked to sneak on a pal.

'He is not here, lord,' he said.

'Where is he?'

'He has gone to the village, lord.'

At this moment, Kalyanu arrived. He came forward sheepishly and stood first on one leg and then on the other, with that air of one about to ask for something with which Mr. Bennett was familiar. Mr. Bennett was irritated and was about to snap angrily at Kalyanu, as the first object within reach, but he restrained himself with an effort and remembered that Kalyanu had never asked him for anything before. It was a point of conscience with him that he should force himself never to be in too much of a hurry to listen to anyone who had anything to say. He swallowed his anger, counted ten and produced an encouraging smile.

'What is it?' he asked.

'I am better now, lord,' said Kalyanu.

'Yes, I am glad. What is it? Do you want to go back to your village?'

'No, lord. I want to stay with you.'

'What, doing nothing?'

'No, lord. I want to be your servant. With you. To work for you. Not for anyone else,' said Kalyanu, swallowing hard several times, and with long pauses.

Mr. Bennett was about to say he had no place for him, when he remembered the story of the bear and thought Kalyanu might be a useful man to have with him at an awkward moment. Then he remembered Keshar Singh's absence from duty.

'Well, you can come with me to-day,' he said, 'and we'll see later on. Bring a stick. You'd better both bring sticks. Have you eaten? No, of course not. Get something you can eat on the way. You give him something, Bharat Singh. Be quick, and catch us up. I am starting, with the patwari.' And he was off.

Kalyanu went with Bharat Singh to the orderlies' tent and

53

collected a handful of roast barley, a lump of molasses, and a stick, and a few minutes later was following the path Mr. Bennett had taken at a slow jog-trot. He was in a private heaven of his own. He was going to be Mr. Bennett's servant.

Soon after the party from the camp had started, a council of war was summoned at the village in the glen. The news that the District Sahib was camping only three hours' march away had reached the shareholders of the village, though they did not know he had actually been through part of their own glen. Ought they to go on with their plan of holding the festival? The priest had said very clearly that this was the one auspicious day, so that there could be no question of postponement. It was now or never. They had not told the surrounding villages, so there was no reason to suppose the District Sahib would hear of it, and everyone knew he was going down to the villages near the river to look at the maps. Yes, they decided they would hold the festival. But to make quite sure there was no interruption, they would hold it earlier than they had planned. They would hold it at noon. Someone was deputed to tell Sohan Das.

Both Sohan Das and Padmini took the news with calm. A few hours one way or the other made little difference, and indeed to Sohan Das there was even a feeling of relief. It would be the sooner over. For Padmini it was another knife into a heart numbed with grief. They finished cooking the morning meal and ate it together in silence. Then they started for the temple of the little godling who ruled the glen. Sohan Das was led before the godling's house and decked like a ram or a buffalo for the sacrifice. Then he was led away by four men, younger brothers of the shareholders who would stay below and who would make sure of a portion to bury in the fields they owned jointly. Padmini watched him go in stony misery. For her he had died already when the lot fell upon him.

As Sohan Das's procession went into the thicket by the side

of the cliff, through which a path zig-zagged to the top, Mr. Bennett and his three companions were coming up the glen and nearing the village. Their path was strewed with stones, winding along the course of the brook, which was attenuated by many irrigation channels. The slope was not steep, and the terrace-walls were low; but the fields were small because of the many rocks, huge boulders among which the little terraces wandered like paths in a petrified maze. It seemed an unfriendly and inhospitable landscape as it lay deserted under the bright sun, and Mr. Bennett quickened his steps. He ought to be in good time, but he did not like the absence of men and women from the fields, of smoke from the village.

He had marked the night before the cliff from which the victim's descent would obviously be made; there was only one near at hand; and he found his way without difficulty to where the villagers were standing, between the house of the godling and the post to which the rope was fastened. He noted the rope and the group of villagers, and realized at once that the sacrifice had not yet taken place. But there was another small group at the top of the rope, where Sohan Das's attendants were adjusting the weights of the saddle; it was just the situation he had hoped to avoid. The victim was decked and laid upon the altar, the priest's hand raised to strike.

He stepped forward and said:

'Who is the headman of this village?'

For the first time since he had been in the hills, the eyes turned towards him were sullen and hostile. There was a murmur in the crowd and a tall man of middle age stepped forward.

'You are trying to hold the rope festival,' said Mr. Bennett. 'It is forbidden. You know that. You are to stop it.'

A young man sprang suddenly on to a boulder by the god-ling's house. In his hand was a coloured scarf, such as is used in the village dances.

'Stop that man!' said Mr. Bennett, over his shoulder.

Kalyanu, Bharat Singh, the patwari, moved in that order. Kalyanu got there first. He brought the young man down by clutching his leg and pulling as he began to raise his arm. The signal was not sent.

The crowd surged forward angrily, sullen, undecided, wanting a lead.

'Stop!' said Mr. Bennett. 'Listen to me!'

He spoke to the headman, but in tones that all could hear.

'If that man slides down the rope, I shall make a new headman from another village. And if the rope breaks, I shall hang you, and the men up there. All of them. Do you understand? I shall hang you. And you will no longer be headman unless you stop this at once. Do you hear?'

The headman shifted from one leg to the other. After a long pause:

'How am I to stop it? They are too far away,' he muttered, sullenly and rudely. But Mr. Bennett knew that he had won.

'You can make them hear well enough if you want to,' he said. 'You know how it can be done. Tell them now.'

There was another moment of indecision. Then the headman said to a villager:

'Tell them it is stopped and they are to come down as they went up.'

There was another pause, while the villager wondered whether to obey. But he felt it was better to do as he was told, and moved to another tall flat boulder, three times his own height. He leaned his back against it, made a funnel of his hands, and sent a long call up to the top of the cliff. The patwari moved over to his side as he called. Wild echoes rang from cliff to cliff, and as they died away, an answering hail came from above. The caller below made his words very slow, he drew out the vowels of each syllable and waited till the echoes had died before he sent the next.

'It is stopped. Come down by the path.'

56

There was a pause and discussion at the top. Then the group withdrew from the edge of the cliff. Someone officiously untied the rope at the bottom.

'I want that rope,' said Mr. Bennett. 'Bring it to me, cut in pieces please.'

Then he sat down and began to talk to the headman.

He left the village some hours later, when he had seen the rope cut to bits. He knew it would take a week to make another, but to make sure he ordered the patwari to stay in the village for a few days. As he went down the glen, he turned to look back. Smoke was rising again from the village; people were moving about gathering sticks. Perhaps for this reason, perhaps because the sun was lower and the trees and boulders now stood in variegated patches of shade, the whole look of the valley seemed to him more friendly and human than it had in the stony glare of noon. It might on the other hand be due only to his own gratifying consciousness of something done. It would, he reflected with a smile, be something to put in his fortnightly report, a document over which he always felt difficulty, for nothing positive ever seemed to be achieved, one struggled eternally with intangibles.

He stopped to rest as he turned eastwards below the spur down which he had come yesterday. The snows of the high range were there, softer now in the evening light, rising serene, ineffably lovely and remote, against the dark glowing indigo and scarlet of the nearer hills. He wondered whether when he left it all he would be able to remember the beauty he had seen and recapture the happiness of the life he had lived, sunshine and snow and wet, the fatigue and responsibility, his gipsy wandering, the smell of cows and woodsmoke. He tried to remember his days in the Alps, and concluded with a wry smile that memories were a poor substitute for the actual. As poor a substitute, he thought, as the artist's achievement when it is compared with his dream. His own attempts at verse had taught him this before he burned them; and surely it must be so even with the masters. He thought:

> Oh how feeble is man's power
>   That if good fortune fall
> Cannot add another hour
>   Nor a lost hour recall!

When he got back to camp, Keshar Singh presented himself. He was very much the old soldier in the orderly room. Mr. Bennett however had made up his mind. He said:

'You are going back to headquarters. Kalyanu Singh is my orderly now.'

Kalyanu slept happily that night. So too did Padmini, her head on her husband's breast and his arms about her.

IV

KALYANU was now Mr. Bennett's orderly, and he wore a short coat of serge, trousers, and a black pill-box hat instead of a folded homespun blanket. He was gradually learning to speak a language which would have been moderately intelligible to a visitor from the plains. But his son was still at Bantok and his prospects of ever getting away depended on his father. So avid is man of his own unrest that neither of them would for a moment have questioned the desirability of leaving the home-stead for any job in the world outside. Kalyanu thought much about this, but it would have cost money to bring Govind Singh to headquarters and send him to school there. Kalyanu himself seldom stayed at headquarters more than a few days and it would have meant setting up house separately there as well as in Bantok. Besides, Govind Singh's mother was a unit of labour at Bantok and could not be spared. There really seemed no way of getting the boy educated until Kalyanu had saved some money, and that would take a long time, and by then it might be too late.

But the opportunity to get what he wanted did come, about a year after he was taken on as an orderly. It was due to no planning on Kalyanu's part, nor to blind chance, but to his own character and Mr. Bennett's. Mr. Bennett, as has been already explained, was troubled by conscience about his mountaineering. He did not like to give himself what amounted to leave and disappear into the snows on a long expedition; even when he did concede himself a few days, he liked to feel that he was carrying out an exploration of some practical value. He was therefore deeply interested in the persistent stories that there was once a direct route through the snows between the two great shrines of Badrinath and Kedarnath, to which people come on pilgrimage from all over India. Each is well within the high range, several days' march up a side valley from the main stream of the Ganges. It takes fourteen ordinary stages for a loaded coolie to walk down the valley from Kedarnath, up the main river, and up again to Badrinath. Yet on the map they are quite close. To find a way across through the snow might not have much practical value, for few would be bold enough to follow such a path; but it was a very attractive idea to Mr. Bennett.

He decided accordingly to make a reconnaissance from Kedarnath, in the west. It would be no more than that, the first day. He would go up and see how far he could get and gather some idea of what lay in the way; and he would come back to Kedarnath in the evening and decide whether or not to make a determined attempt. No local man would be any help to him, for they had no knowledge of anything above the snowline. He decided to take with him Kalyanu, to whom he had given some elementary lessons on snow and ice during the summer. It did not look as though there would be any rock work.

They started next morning an hour before dawn, and walked over peaty turf that by midday would squelch with water at every step but now was frozen hard. They made for the snout of the glacier, but before reaching it they turned eastwards on to a long slope leading to a cup-shaped corrie far above. At the foot of the slope they came on to snow. It was late in the season, and the snow was old. It had been melted by day and frozen by night a hundred times, and was like rough frosted glass. Their nailed boots rang on the snow. It was not bad going at present, while the slope was easy, but they moved slowly, for they had only just come up, and at first even twelve thousand feet should be treated with respect. It was a clear night, but there was a mistiness about the waning moon which Mr. Bennett did not like.

Kalyanu was a perfect companion for such an expedition, for he had utter confidence in his leader and in his presence would never show fear; he did exactly as he was told; and he did not

speak unless spoken to. Mr. Bennett revelled in the feeling of
release from the responsibilities and decisions which usually
beset him. He savoured every sniff of the frosty air, and rejoiced
in the sweat which soon began to trickle down his spine beneath
the sweaters and leather jerkin he wore.

It grew lighter. The world of moonlight, where there is an
unreally simple choice of black or silver and no half-tones, began
to give way to reality, with its infinite gradations of colour and
meaning. Rocks ceased to be shadows and took on shape. The
line of the crests above grew clear; the peaks to the west were
suddenly gay with sunlight. Mr. Bennett and Kalyanu were
still in the shadow of the eastern heights, a shadow which ran
across the cliffs and glacier to the west, and moved slowly downwards and towards them. Suddenly, unbelievably, a rim of
molten metal appeared above the eastern crest. The glassy snow
at their feet was dimpled with sun and shadow; for a few magic
minutes the tiniest hummock threw long blue fingers of darkness
towards them. Then the sun was up and all was glittering
light.

The first gentle slope was now ended and they were on the
floor of the corrie, at about fifteen thousand feet. It was almost
level here, but on three sides the cup-shaped walls rose about
them. To the west was the least abrupt slope; it was not too
formidable and would bring them up on to the rim in about a
thousand feet. They roped up, and proceeded to climb steadily,
cutting shallow steps as they went, each with a single cut of the
axe. Mr. Bennett led. They were on the rim in an hour and a
half.

This was one of the moments for which Mr. Bennett lived.
The valley with the temple was far below them, far and tiny,
the torrent from the foot of the glacier twisting like a green and
silver thread down the glen. Westwards the snow ridge stretched
on above them to the sky; north, there was a valley whose
depths could not be seen and beyond it a wall of rock reaching

up to twenty thousand feet, over whose edge the snow bulged in a gigantic cornice like the thick icing dripping over the side of a rich black Christmas cake; to the east, peak and glacier, needle and serrac, a fantastic tangle of ice and rock in frozen loveliness. This was really what he had come for, to gaze, and fill his memory with beauty; but he did want to see if he could get any farther. He must think whether any way led through all this to the east.

The rim of the cup on which he stood could be followed eastward without difficulty. At the point where he stood, what had been from below the skyline and had seemed the top was only a change in the angle of slope; but farther north it was a true rim, a col leading to a dome-shaped snow peak to the east from which he would be able to see farther. The first step was a traverse to the col, and from there it looked as though it should be easy to reach the summit of the dome, which he reckoned must be about eighteen thousand feet.

The slope above the rim was not acute and the traverse to the col was easy going. They could kick steps in the snow without much exertion and they made good progress, the chips of snow that they dislodged slithering down a few yards to the rim of the corrie and then dropping a thousand feet to the floor of the cup. Mr. Bennett thought of the possibility of establishing a hut on the col, as the first stage in the route he hoped to find. It would certainly be a good place for his own first camp, if he made a serious attempt, though rather a short first stage. If there was another easy col beyond the dome, it might be possible to push on to that; but that might make rather a long first stage. A short one was better to begin with.

Mr. Bennett glanced from time to time at the sky while he thought of these possibilities. There was cloud about, but it was high, and it did not seem to be moving fast. His view of the western sky was blocked. He judged that the weather might break next day, but that it would hold for at least another twelve hours. It was not till they were beyond the col and making their way up the dome that it began to look alarming. Clouds from the west at their own level began to drive down the main glacier towards the valley and the temple, shapeless wet nimbus that came with frightening speed in ragged wisps. Drifts of it curled round the mass of rock and snow to the west that had concealed the evidence of what was coming. It swept over their heads and hid the sun. In ten minutes, a world of glittering snow, sunshine, and blue sky, had turned to a grey and chilling landscape, full of menace to men with neither a tent nor a blanket. Mr. Bennett turned round and began to go back. He had led on the way up, mainly from natural exuberance, meaning to make Kalyanu take a turn when he grew tired of kicking steps. Now he had to lead, because he was much the quicker and it was important to get across the col and down the steep slope before the clouds came down on them. He regretted that he had not saved himself at the start.

But they were still on the col when the clouds came, and with them snow began to fall. It was not a blizzard. The wind was not strong and the snow fell lightly. The cloud was intermittent, and they could always see a few yards, sometimes more. After a few moments' reflection, Mr. Bennett decided to keep moving. He was doubtful whether either of them would survive a night on the col without a tent. There was no climbing worth the name by the route they had followed and it should not be difficult to find; nothing but care was needed on the steep thousand feet down to the floor of the corrie. The danger was fresh snow on top of old; but at present it was only a light feathering. He pressed on as quickly as he could, feeling his way along the rim of the cup which lay on their left hand.

The film of new snow made it more difficult to find the firm old snow beneath the boot and kick a step. And the step had to be a better step now than it had been coming up, because of that treacherous slippery coating. They did not get on so fast as he would have liked and he was getting increasingly anxious about the point at which to turn and cross the rim to the steeper slope below that led to the floor of the corrie. There was only one place where the slope could properly be tackled by two men in a hurry, and he began more and more to fear that he might pass it. There was no way of comparing the pace at which they were now moving with that at which they had come up, and he could not reckon with any accuracy when they ought to be at the top of the one negotiable slope. Half a dozen times he moved down to his left to the rim and peered over, only to find that he was peering over a cornice that would have been dangerous for anyone, out of the question for Kalyanu and himself. Reason kept assuring him that he could not have passed the place, but the nagging fear was there. If they did pass it, they would find themselves on an impossible rock face, and much time would be wasted in getting back; and they could not afford to waste time. In the best case, it would be dark before they were off the snow.

The seventh or eighth time that he peered over the edge, he found the slope definitely less steep. A few paces farther on and there was an improvement. He moved on till it began to get worse again. When he was sure he had found the best place, he turned to speak to Kalyanu.

'We shall go down as we came up,' he explained. 'I shall lead and cut the steps. All you have to do is to be careful. Make quite sure each foot is firm before you put your weight on it. Use your ice-axe all the time. If you do slip, drive it into the snow at once. Keep the rope tight and do not come down to me even if I am slow. Remember I have to cut the steps.'

That was Kalyanu's only fault. He was inclined to come on too fast and Mr. Bennett had more than once turned to find Kalyanu close behind him with the rope dangling uselessly between them. But he seemed now to be sufficiently impressed by the seriousness of the situation and he kept his distance, paying out the rope as Mr. Bennett went over the cornice and following slowly and carefully at the right distance. He did not find it easy because it was difficult to see in falling snow and wet mist; most of the time he had to watch the rope and move as soon as its tightening showed that Mr. Bennett had moved.

Coming up, one action had been enough to cut a step; one swift blow of the axe at the right angle nicked out a slice of snow just big enough to take the boot placed sideways. Now, three movements had to be made; one, to scrape away the fresh snow where the step would come and clear the firm frozen snow beneath; the second, to make the step; a third short one, to make it deeper because they were both tired now and it was slippery. It was slow work. Mr. Bennett wished he had not led in the morning and he told himself he ought to have waited another day at eleven thousand feet before doing this. His head was aching. He ought not to be so tired; it was the height, and coming up so soon. Scrape, cut, half cut; step; scrape, cut, half cut; step; scrape, cut, half cut; he went on mechanically, but he knew he was very tired.

They were still about two hundred feet above the floor of the corrie when they reached the steepest part of the whole slope. Mr. Bennett did not remember it on the way up; but in that light he could not see whether it could be avoided by traversing either way and he simply had nothing to spare, either time or energy, for a fruitless traverse. There was about twelve feet of almost sheer snow, and then again the steep but negotiable angle on which his scrape, cut, half cut, had been sufficient. This twelve feet would need more than that, but it was very hard snow. He decided to take it. He shouted to Kalyanu to come down to him, but the wind took the words from his mouth. They had never been out in a wind together before and had developed no system of signals by tugs on the rope. He began to cut deep steps. He panted at every blow of the axe and his head throbbed worse than before, much worse. When he got to the bottom of those twelve feet, he relaxed; he felt they were safe now. Just a little more of the old scrape, cut, half cut, and they would be able to walk. His head was throbbing less, but it felt as though it was full of hot liquid, hot blood and nothing else. He laughed. The Vikings used to drink from skulls. He wouldn't mind a drink from his own. Nothing like a warm drink. A minute's rest, he thought. He drove the axe into the snow, took off his glove and put his hand in an inner pocket for raisins.

At the other end of the rope, Kalyanu was worried. He had been following the steady tighten and dip of the rope, tighten when Mr. Bennett took a step, dip when he took a step himself. It went to the rhythm of the leader's scrape, cut, half cut, step. Tighten, step, dip, tighten, step, dip, was Kalyanu's slower tune. Suddenly it stopped. Mr. Bennett was considering whether to traverse or go straight down the steep place. Kalyanu shouted to ask what was the matter, but he heard no answer. Then the rope tightened, Kalyanu took a step, it dipped, but there was a long pause before it tightened again, while Mr. Bennett hacked the next difficult step. Kalyanu was worried. The pauses seemed to grow longer and longer. At last there came a pause that seemed to last for ever. Kalyanu now felt sure that Mr. Bennett had suddenly become exhausted, had managed to pull himself together to cut a few more steps very slowly, and was now collapsed, anchored by his axe. He went down to see what was the matter.

Mr. Bennett had eaten some raisins and was wishing he could give some to Kalyanu. Quite light-headed he had been for a moment, he thought, but he was better now. And now it would all be plain easy work, and in less than two hours he would be drinking hot rum and cocoa in his tent. He heard his name called and looked up to see Kalyanu peering down over the steep place. Mr. Bennett gave him a kindly smile, and quite simply stepped back into space to get a better view.

He had his hand on the axe, and the moment he felt himself

falling he came out of his temporary loss of reason and grabbed it with his other hand. It came away, and he found himself slithering and rolling with increasing speed down the slope of glassy snow at an angle of more than fifty degrees. He tried to turn over on his face and make his axe bite into the snow. There was a sudden tremendous jerk. He had come to the end of the rope. Kalyanu had braced himself for the shock and driven his axe in as far as he could, but he could not have been in a worse place nor in a worse position, peering over a twelve-foot drop. The jerk was too much for him and he came over the drop and hit the slope beyond with a jar that knocked all the breath out of his body. But the momentary check had been enough for Mr. Bennett to get his axe into the snow; he rolled over on his face and kicked his toes in as deep as he could, bracing himself for the moment when Kalyanu's weight should come on him. But he had not time to get sufficient grip. He too was torn away and both went down the slope, each desperately trying to get a purchase with his axe and slow up his fall.

Kalyanu was more successful. He did get his axe to bite and he reached the floor of the corrie, ploughing a deep furrow behind him, without serious damage. But Mr. Bennett, a few yards to his left, had not managed to brake his descent at all and he was stopped by a crevasse, not a wide one, at the foot of the slope. His axe jammed across the top of it and he was clinging to the axe when Kalyanu came to pull him out. When he was out, he could not put one foot to the ground and there was a pain in his side which could only be a broken rib. Kalyanu propped him up against a boulder and stood waiting for orders.

'Leave me here,' said Mr. Bennett. 'Go back to the camp and fetch men to carry me down.'

When he had said this, he lost consciousness.

Kalyanu reflected. It would be dark before he got to the camp. He was doubtful whether he would be able to find the place again. By the time he did, the Sahib might be dead. He decided

to disobey him. He picked Mr. Bennett up and managed to get
him on to his back, although Mr. Bennett was two stones heavier
and six inches taller than he was; he brought his arms over his
shoulders and held them firmly at the wrists with his left hand.
He took his axe in his right hand. Then he saw Mr. Bennett's
axe; it did not occur to his frugal peasant's mind to leave it and
with some difficulty he burdened himself with that as well,
passing it below the injured man's arms and across his chest.
Then he started to go down.

It was an hour before midnight when he got off the snow.
There were men there with lanterns; Amar Singh had brought
them out, but they could not go any farther because they did
not know which way the party had gone. Kalyanu could not
speak, but they helped him to the camp, where Mr. Bennett's
bearer took upon himself the responsibility of giving them both
rum and hot milk and sugar.

Kalyanu was himself again next morning. About midday,
Mr. Bennett sent for him. Kalyanu went rather guiltily, conscious only of his disobedience. Mr. Bennett was propped up
as well as he could be in a camp bed. He said:

'Kalyanu, I think you saved my life. What would you like
me to do to reward you?'

'Lord — ' said Kalyanu, and was silent.

'Yes? What would you like?'

'Lord, my son — ' Kalyanu was silent again. What he wanted
was too much to ask.

'Something for your son? What?'

Then it came in a rush:

'Lord, please make him a patwari!'

Mr. Bennett laughed.

'Very well,' he said. 'I will send him to school, and if he is
good enough, I will make him a patwari.'

So Govind Singh, the son of Kalyanu, left Bantok and went
to school.

PART TWO

THE UPROOTED, 1923

I

JODH SINGH, son of Govind Singh, son of Kalyanu Singh of Bantok, was coming back to Garhwal in a complicated state of mind. His father's sudden death was not the most important element in his emotions, because he had never been able to feel any deep affection for that careful and narrow soul. His real love had gone to his mother and his grandfather. Nor did the fact that he would be too late for the funeral rites worry him so much as it would have done had he been entirely orthodox in .his beliefs. The hill peasant, at heart the servant of older gods, is less concerned with the externals of Hinduism than the plainsman; and he only becomes deeply interested in rites and ceremonies when he is the victim of a snobbish desire to show that he is really just as good a Hindu as anyone else, an affliction which usually attacks the first generation removed from the peasant. The second generation is inclined to look at such things with tolerance or contempt; this had certainly been the effect on Jodh Singh of his English education at Lucknow University.

No, he was concerned with thoughts of himself, not of his father, and at the same time he was excited by the prospect of smelling the hill air and drinking hill water again. At school and college, Jodh Singh had been a disappointment to himself, though not to his father or to his teachers. Outwardly he had been moderately successful. He had taken his B.A. with second class honours in philosophy and English literature; he had played football for his university and hockey for his hostel; he had held office, though not the highest, in debating societies; he had been a scout and a patrol leader. The tin trunk under the seat of his intermediate class compartment contained a generous bundle of certificates from his teachers saying that he bore a good moral character, had taken part in all forms of college life, and had

71

every right to look forward to a brilliant career. But he knew himself that his achievements were in no way distinguished; and he thought they should have been.

It was not so much with the results of his examinations or with his games that he was dissatisfied. He felt that he ought to have cut more ice with his contemporaries. He was sure that none of them experienced the burning zeal which often filled him, the intense desire to put something right, no matter what, the ardent love for the idea of India, the indignation at her wrongs. If only some magic could press the catch and release the spring, he would soar above them all. If just that something would happen that would put him in the lead, everyone would follow him and recount with bated breath what he had said and done. But somehow it had never happened. Like most hill-boys, he was later in developing than is usual with Indians and he had been handicapped because he looked younger than he was. He was rustic and unsophisticated when he first went to school in the plains, compared with other boys of his age, and they laughed at him. And the diffidence born of that laughter had never quite left him. When he spoke at the debating society, his eyes wandered over the faces before him, searching for a look of derision, and he had never been able to lose himself in his subject and speak without self-consciousness, from his heart. And so he had never carried conviction.

All this would be very different in Garhwal, he thought. There were not many young men from the district with a college education and those few were almost all in government service, away in the plains. If he stayed in the district, he would have few rivals and no fear of laughter. Should he not make this his object, to be the leader of the district and guide his people from their backwardness and ignorance to something higher? He ought perhaps to qualify as a lawyer, but he did not intend to practise regularly. He could leave that to lesser men who had to earn their living.

His father, Govind Singh, had been rich by the standards of Garhwal, for his career as a patwari had been a long one. For forty years he had lived on the bounty of the villagers in his jurisdiction and had saved much. And every penny of his savings had been put to good use, being passed to a younger brother who had carried on a conservative and very profitable business as a money-lender under Govind Singh's direction. Govind Singh had been very wise and had avoided making enemies. No one had ever thought it necessary to tell the Deputy Commissioner about the money-lending. None of this worried Jodh Singh. It had simply never occurred to him to think where the money came from, although he was filled with burning indignation when he thought of the Government's failure to prevent corruption and put down malpractices, their connivance at the spoliation of the peasant. All that his father's wealth meant was that he had not to work for his bread but could devote himself to righting wrongs. Yes, that was what he would do! He would give his life to the district. His eyes filled with tears as he thought of the devotion with which he would toil for the simple peasants of his native land. But he could not afford to be sentimental, he told himself. Energy and courage were what he would need. He knew he had energy: he was burning to begin the fight at once. And he was sure he would have courage. He would be ready to face anything, torture, starvation, prison, death!

The train slowed up to stop at the junction from which the narrow-gauge line took off for the hills. As Jodh Singh sprang down from the carriage and pulled out his tin trunk and roll of bedding, he became for a moment the universal schoolboy coming home. He could see the hills from the station, but it was more important to him that the people on the platform were many of them hill-folk. Merely to look at them brought memories of clear running water, rock and pine and gravel, the smell of wood smoke and rotting leaves and frosty mornings. All these things he wanted, as every hill-man does when he is in the plains. But he reminded himself that he had a purpose, an aim in life. He must not be deflected by thoughts of simple homely things into forgetting his mission. There was nobody on the platform that he knew, but he was going to be their leader and impress them from the start. He would travel first-class for the few miles of his train journey that remained. Nothing would impress them so much as that.

But rich though he was by his own standards, Jodh Singh was too close to the peasant not to be careful about money. He had bought an intermediate ticket as far as the junction, rejecting the third class as fit only for peasants and the first and second class as recklessly extravagant. After the junction there was only upper class, consisting of first and second class ticket-holders; and lower class for the rest. It was, therefore, obviously a waste of money to buy an intermediate ticket right through; you were no better off in the last stage of the journey than if you had a third class ticket. At Lucknow, it had been his intention to get a third class ticket when he reached the junction and travel lower class. He now decided to buy a third class ticket and travel upper class. This he would do by the simple expedient of getting on the train at the last minute, knowing well that no one looked at tickets on this line once the journey had begun and that the ticket-collector at the other end would not notice what sort of carriage he had got out of. It occurred to him that the ticket-collector would probably hear in the evening, when word went round the little town at the terminus that young Jodh Singh had travelled upper class; but then, he reflected, no official would talk about that because it might get him into trouble. So he bought his third-class ticket, and hung about on the platform with his two pieces of luggage till the train was just starting; then with an air of lordly impudence he strolled forward with one in either hand to the empty carriage he had marked. There were always several upper-class carriages empty on the line to Garhwal. He settled down in his corner with a grin on his face that was purely boyish.

At the terminus, two miles inside the district, he got out sufficiently slowly to let any idlers on the platform see him, but did not delay long enough to attract the attention of officialdom. It was perfectly timed. He decided again to do something lordly, although this time he would have to pay for it. He strolled up to the lorry that would carry him ten miles farther into the hills, giving one anna to a coolie to carry his bundles, and bought a place on one of the two front seats, where he would be divided by brass rails from the common herd at the back, just as though he were an Englishman. Then he bought something to eat from a shop kept by a Brahman, for he was not sufficiently emancipated to disregard caste prejudices about food.

They drove the first stage of the journey up a savage and precipitous gorge, to a village where the traffic for the higher hills changed its motive power from petrol and steel to grain and muscle. You had the choice of walking or riding, your goods went on a mule's back or a porter's. Jodh Singh hired a porter and started to walk.

The valley up which he went was not beautiful. A stream boiled and foamed below him, but the channel through which it ran was a gutter into which poured from the hills on either side the debris of many landslides. The slopes of shaly rock were tortured and broken by the action of water as though by the explosions of a battlefield. Here and there a few fields hung together, shored up by the moraines of two converging scars of scree, but it seemed strange that such a country could support human life. The principal vegetation was the fantastic and inhospitable cactus.

The path wound slowly upwards and the ground became firmer, the slopes less extreme. Cactus began to give way to pine, there was grass and oak scrub, and fields became more frequent. About the middle of the afternoon, when heat and fatigue had begun to suggest a rest, Jodh Singh came on a dejected-looking group of villagers. In the steady toil of the ascent, he had almost forgotten that he had a mission. Now he remembered. He would talk to them and find out why they had assembled and why they looked so cheerless.

They would hardly have understood the patois of Upper Garhwal, but he had no difficulty in making himself clear in a dialect of Hindustani which would pass throughout the district. What were they doing, he asked, and why were they gathered here on a fine morning when there was so much to be done in the fields?

Their leader, a disreputable figure in an old army tunic and a pair of shapeless black cotton trousers, pushed a greasy black pill-box hat farther on to one side of his head and spat. He took a long pull through a funnel made by his hands at a clay pipe-bowl and passed it on to his neighbour.

'That sod of a patwari,' he said, 'has ordered us to be here. The tahsildar is coming on tour, and we are to carry the tents and gear.'

'But when is he coming?' asked Jodh Singh.

'God knows. He was to have come yesterday. The villagers from Deokhal were to bring the stuff here and we are to take it on to Dwarikhal. He will camp there. We waited here all yesterday. We may have to wait all to-morrow.'

Jodh Singh's blood began to boil. Indignantly he said:

'But this is a great hardship.'

They all began to talk at once.

'It is a great hardship. We lose three days' work on the fields for one day's pay. And it is beggar's pay. We are not coolies, we are shareholders in our village and the land belongs to us. It is not our work. Why doesn't the Government pay coolies to do this work? It is not for us.'

'It is a great tyranny,' said Jodh Singh. 'It is like the days of the Gurkhas. Why do you not refuse?'

They looked at each other. They had not thought of this; it had simply not occurred to their submissive natures. But the leader, rather shamefacedly, knew the answer.

'It is written in the settlement,' he said, 'we are to pay so much land revenue and work for the Government for pay whenever we are ordered. All but me. I am the headman. I do not have to work. But it is just as bad for me, this waiting. I lose three days' work in the fields, just like the rest.'

No one thought much of this.

'The settlement was fifty years ago, in the time of Mr. Bennett,' someone said.

'Times have changed,' said another. 'We are not coolies. It is a great tyranny.'

Jodh Singh had listened with growing anger and excitement. Now he began to talk. They were all squatting on the ground, and he did not rise, but spoke eagerly and earnestly, as he would have done to his friends, sitting in a circle. The words poured out, driven from his heart by the anger he felt. He spoke of the wrongs of India and the tyranny of the British, the wealth and corruption of tahsildars and patwaris, the poverty of the peasants, and now this, a burden not to be borne, an intolerable insult to their dignity.

'Are we not men?' he cried, 'Are we different from the tahsildar? Is there not blood in our veins too? Are we animals and beasts of burden? Why should we live on coarse millet bread while the Deputy Commissioner eats meat every day and drinks wine and lives like a Raja? He should be the servant of the people but it is we who are his servants. We sweat in the fields to pay him land revenue and he loads us like beasts and does not care what becomes of us.'

He had never spoken like this before, forgetting himself and his dignity and the fact that people might laugh at him. The villagers listened breathless with interest, anger rising in their hearts as they shared his emotion, his own passion feeding on the power this new gift of speech gave him, the sense of mastery, the unity of his whole self in the endeavour to persuade them of what he knew was right.

He ended on a note quieter and more intense.

'Why do you not refuse?' he asked. 'Show that you are men. Go home to your village. Let there be none here when he comes.'

Then he rose to his feet and the villagers rose too, all talking confusedly. They began at once to pick up their belongings and to go. The headman made no attempt to dissuade them, but stood by dejectedly.

'What am I to do?' he asked, 'I shall be dismissed.'

'Go back to your village,' said Jodh Singh, still in the flush of his new-found authority. 'Be bold with the patwari and tell him you are none of you going to be coolies any longer. Soon every village in Garhwal will say the same. They cannot dismiss all the headmen.'

Jodh Singh watched the last man start back for the village and then he too went on his way. It was eight stages to his home and he did not hurry but spent the full eight days on the journey, asking questions of the villagers as he went. He heard everywhere the same tale of discontent at the way the corvee was levied. If it had been one day's work and one day's pay, that would have been no grievous burden, though even so there would have been grumbling. But it was often two days' hanging about for nothing and then one day's work for one day's pay, and sometimes, if an official changed his mind, two days' hanging about for nothing at all. And it might come at the time of harvest or sowing, and the corn would be spoilt in the fields or the right moment pass for scattering the seed. Nobody liked it; but so strong was the habit of obedience that no one had thought of refusing the service till they heard Jodh Singh talk. It was not often that he found a gathering like the first, which he could harangue; but he spread wherever he went the tale of the village which had refused to give the service and he hinted that every other village where he had been had declared their intention of doing the same. The word spread outward from his track like water through thick dust, here slowly and doubtfully, there faster, but everywhere gaining ground, turning the powdery white dust to a paste of mud, colouring and changing men's minds.

On the eighth day, he reached the big house which Govind Singh had built on the south side of the river, below the bridge leading to Bantok. It was a very different house from the cabin where Kalyanu had lived originally, two-storied, with deep eaves to shoot the snow clear and leave a warm path round the house, with balconies on the upper floor that would be cool in summer, with deep carving in the wood round the door and intricate ornament on the under-side of the eaves. But Jodh Singh did not stay long to take possession of his patrimony. It was a pleasure to see the familiar fields and hills again and to be greeted with respect by his relations, but he had never had any intention of settling down among ignorant villagers; and now he had a mission. He greeted his mother with affection and explained that he must be away at once on important affairs. He did not explain what they were. He knew he could safely leave the money-lending business to his uncle and cousins, and to them also the management of the land, the shares in surrounding villages in which Govind Singh had from time to time invested. In three days, he set out again, taking with him as servant and companion one man to carry his blankets for the night and to cook his meals, a second cousin who was one of the exports of Bantok, where the holding could not be extended to keep pace with the population.

Jodh Singh and his cousin went north-eastwards up the river, and then struck off south and west up a tributary stream. Here in the upper hills his success was less obvious than nearer the plains; discontent there was at being kept hanging about, but time was on the whole less precious, and there was the compensation that when an officer did come their way, they were glad to see him. They were all ready to agree with Jodh Singh that the Government ought to employ coolies but they did not fire at his talk of the injustice of life in general. It was only right, they felt, that the Deputy Commissioner, who was a kind of Raja, should live a very different life from theirs. It was part of the nature of things. And at his talk of refusing the service they shook their heads and went away considering.

So he turned south, to the lower hills, where he would, he knew, be able to find more enthusiastic audiences. But he realized before long that it was no good merely stumping the country. He could fire a village in the southern areas to a state of fervour when they were ready to defy the authority of the patwari and would do so at once if he should arrive while Jodh Singh's glowing periods were still hot in their minds; but the mood would not last long after he left them. In a few days, the habit of centuries would reassert itself, and whatever discontent they might feel, they would do as they were told. Even if he could contrive to be in the village just before one of the tahsildars and persuade the villagers to leave him stranded with no one to move his tents, he would not have achieved a decisive blow. He must do something more than this. He must make things uncomfortable for the Deputy Commissioner, the District Sahib himself. Only by this means would the Government be made to feel their discontent and the grievance be righted.

Once he had reached this conclusion he sat down to think out the best way of tackling the problem. Should he be there himself at the moment of crisis? If he were not, the villagers might weaken before the authority of so great a man as the Deputy Commissioner. On the other hand, he might be arrested. He did not stop to consider whether this would be legal or not; he assumed it could be done if the Deputy Commissioner wished. He was not afraid of arrest, he told himself, but he did not want the work he had begun to be stopped. Perhaps it would be better to keep just one stage ahead of the Deputy Commissioner and not actually meet him. But the more he thought of this course, the less he liked it. There would be no doubt everyone would say he was afraid; and once that story went round, his influence would be lost. No, he would meet the danger. It was the course that appealed to his youth and fervour, when an older man would have prepared the way more carefully, waited, and not brought all to the touch at once. He would make for a village where the District Sahib was expected, incite the villagers to passive resistance, and stay there, come what might.

Having decided on his general course, he proceeded to make a more detailed plan. It was easy to get information of the Deputy Commissioner's next tour, for the present head of the district believed in advertising his tours and sticking to his plans. He argued that by this means people knew where to find him and could come and tell him anything they wanted. If no one knew he was coming, they might not hear of his presence till he had gone. And his methods would be much more convenient to his staff and to the villagers who had to carry his gear than the erratic and unexpected excursions of a genius like Mr. Bennett. Jodh Singh studied his programme and chose a large village, not far from the plains, where a large proportion of the population had been employed outside the district and were thus more sophisticated and volatile material than the peasant who had never left home. He decided to arrive some ten days before the Deputy Commissioner was due and sow the seed; he would go away and let it mature; and he would return on the critical day. And having made his plans, he went ahead with them.

Jodh Singh was very happy. Action and excitement brought out the best in him; he was delighted with the new power that came to him when he faced an audience, the thought that he was in danger and defying authority was a perpetual and agreeable stimulant. And at the same time he was sustained by the consciousness that he was doing something noble and striking a blow for his oppressed people. Add to this the physical well-being that came from living in the hills, walking from village to village, sleeping and eating where he could, and what more could a young man want, except to be in love as well?

II

HUGH UPTON, Deputy Commissioner of Garhwal in 1923, looked at his watch. Half past four, and the last appeal of the day finished. Very satisfactory.

'Anything else, Gobardhan?'

'No, Sir, nothing that requires your attention.'

He left his court room with a sense of deep contentment. He was well abreast of his work and for the first time in his service was without the gnawing irritation of knowing that he had a pile of arrears with which he could never catch up because he was doing three men's work. He was fitter than he had ever been in his life and the immediate prospect of tea by the fireside with Margaret on a frosty November evening was as pleasant as anything he could visualize. He put his hands in his coat pockets and strode steadily up the steep and narrow cobbled bridle-path, that was the main street of his headquarter town — by courtesy, but it was really only a village — of Pokhra. He passed through an avenue of spruce, cedar and pine, planted fifty years before by Mr. Bennett, through the little bazaar of thirty or forty shops, which sold headstalls with scarlet tassels and bells for mules, brass pots and pans, grain and sweetmeats and vegetables, and cloth from the plains for those who had become too sophisticated for the native blanket. The shopkeepers squatting by their wares rose to their feet and saluted him reverently as he passed, all but one or two who were politically minded and ostentatiously ignored him. He regarded this ceremony as a bore, because it meant taking his hands out of his pockets to return the salute; but nevertheless noted carefully who omitted it. Any such knowledge might be useful one day.

In a few minutes he was out of the bazaar and he turned aside, from the bridle-path which led westward over the hills, to the

winding path which led up through the forest to his house at
Pokhrakhal. It was a path he took every day when he was at
headquarters and it was therefore in good order, but automatically his eye looked for drains that would need repair if a big
bill for repairs after the rains was to be avoided, for shrubs that
needed cutting back, and boughs that might cause damage if a
heavy fall of snow brought them down. He was a practical man
with a tidy mind, no visionary or reformer. He had seen most
of his service in the big cities, where his level-headed competence
had saved much bloodshed, and he regarded a short spell in the
hills as a well-earned respite from heat and riots.

He turned into the big pleasant sitting-room with bay windows
on two sides and found Margaret kneeling before the fire, doing
things with the copper kettle and spirit stove which she always
managed to produce in the most unlikely places. The tea things
were on a low table. There was a blazing wood fire. Hugh was
not an emotional man, but as he saw her kneeling there, her
cheeks rosy from the fire, her blue eyes between black lashes that
always seemed to be smiling, he felt, as he always did, a sudden
quick excitement, somewhere deep in his body a pang of wonder
and joy, and sorrow too.

She looked up and regarded him, big and smiling, his face red
from the frosty air, with the scar running down his face from a
stone in a riot at Cawnpore, a nice ugly face, she thought, nicer
and uglier than when she married him. She thought for a
moment of Ronald, and put the thought from her like a dutiful
wife.

'Tea?' she held up the cup to him. 'Anything interesting this
afternoon?'

'Usual sort of stuff in court,' he answered, sipping at once while
it was still scalding hot and thinking that Margaret was the only
woman in India who seemed able to produce a decent cup of tea.
'But there's a rather interesting thing happening in the district.'

'Do tell me,' she said.

'Yes, I think you should know about this. It may affect our next tour and make things rather uncomfortable.' He settled into an arm-chair. 'Do you remember the story I told you about the man who beat a bear to death with sticks?'

'And afterwards he saved somebody's life, didn't he? Who was it? I forget.'

'Somebody's life? It was Mr. Bennett's — the great Mr. Bennett, who made the maps we curse for being so inaccurate — but it was a good job he made of them all the same — and planted all the trees and made the house. Well, Mr. Bennett rewarded the man who saved his life by making his son a patwari, and the son was a success and made money and sent his son to a university in the plains; and now the grandson has come back and he's raising hell.'

'Doesn't his grandfather tell him to behave?'

'The old man's dead, and so is the father. There's no one to control the boy. He seems to speak well and he's calling meetings everywhere and asking the villagers why the Deputy Commissioner should be better off than they are — when Adam delved and Eve span — that kind of thing.'

'But no one in Garhwal would listen to that,' said Margaret incredulously.

'They seem to be listening in the lower hills. And he's got hold of one genuine grievance that he's having a lot of success with. You know the villagers carry our tents and baggage on tour?'

'They always seem very cheerful about it. Don't they get paid?' she asked.

'They get paid all right, at least they do in my camp, and I don't think they mind doing it for me very much, because I always say in advance where I am going and when, and I stick to it. But the tahsildars make a plan and then change their minds — sometimes they can't help it, something else crops up. Anyhow, the patwaris collect the villagers and keep them hanging about, sometimes for two or three days, and of course they don't get paid for that, and they hate it. And in the lower hills they're beginning to think it's beneath their dignity to carry a load at all. I've tried to make the tahsildars be more considerate, but it doesn't work. It's no use trying to make water run up hill, or a tiger go the way he doesn't want to.'

'And what exactly do you mean by that, you old cynic? Have you got a cigarette?'

'I mean, it's the way of the country and it's no use trying to tell junior officials to be thoughtful for peasants. They won't, unless you're there to make them. The only thing is to change the system.'

'Well, how can you?' Margaret settled herself again on a cushion on the floor, leaning back against the chair opposite Hugh's. She looked idly at the smoke of her cigarette as he talked; she had learnt long ago to keep him talking about the things that interested him; it did not need much effort.

'Oh, it would be quite easy. We could run a transport company. We might get a contractor to take it on and find the coolies. Or perhaps it might be difficult to get a contractor up here. In that case, we could do it ourselves and hire coolies for the whole tour. But of course that would cost money to begin with.'

'It sounds easy enough.'

'I've suggested it before, but Smith wouldn't put it up. He didn't like suggesting anything that would cost money, and he said anyhow it was all nonsense — they've always done it and why shouldn't they go on? I wish now I'd put it stronger.'

'Do you think there'll be trouble?'

'I think there will. This boy — Jodh Singh his name is — has persuaded one village to refuse to carry the tahsildar's camp gear, and he's telling them all to refuse. In fact he's trying to organize a sort of general strike.'

'But will he be able to do it?'

85

'Not a general strike perhaps, but he'll get some villages to do it. I've done what I can to discourage them, but there's not much I can do. Even dismissing the headman will take months — he'll have to be given an opportunity to give his reasons and he'll engage counsel and make as much delay as he can. When we go into the lower hills next month we may have some trouble.'

'Well, that'll be fun,' said Margaret. 'Couldn't you beat him by just not going to the villages where he was expecting you? Then you could finish your tour quite happily and everyone would laugh at him.'

Hugh shook his head. He said:

'That would be no good. He'd have scored. Everybody would know that I'd run away from Jodh Singh and that I couldn't go where I wanted in my own district. The real trouble is that I agree with him about this, but I mustn't say so till I've convinced Smith and the Government that I'm right. Lucknow will probably begin by advising me to hire bullock-carts. They never seem able to realize that we haven't any roads or any carts.'

'Having to go on being loyal about something you don't agree with always seems very hard to me. However, I suppose you must.'

'Of course we must,' said Hugh. 'If we weren't loyal we shouldn't be here; and if we didn't go on being loyal, we shouldn't stay.'

'Have you time to come for a walk, or must you do your old files? Do come.'

'Yes, I can manage a stroll round. I'll write a report on all this after dinner.'

'Cheers. Come on.'

They went out on to the narrow lawn in front of the house. They could see clear across through a gap in the pines to the snow peaks forty miles away, flushed with rose in the last light of evening, a few tiny puffs of cloud high above them still a tender lucid gold. The nearer hills were warm scarlet and orange;

86

the distant loveliness of the snows swam up from deepest glowing blue.

Margaret caught Hugh's arm.

'If I could only paint that!' she said. 'But no one would believe it. Hugh, do you think we shall be able to remember it? The lovely things we've seen and the fun we've had?'

'When we're playing golf at Cheltenham, d'you mean? We shall be able to remember that we've had a good time, but you can't live it over again. Memory's a poor thing. I've often tried to live over again a good day's shooting or fishing. You can't do it.'

'No,' she said, 'you're right. I can remember England in May, the bluebells and the primroses, and the hedges white with may. But I can only remember it and want it. I can't really see it.'

She sighed, and they went on. He said:

'I must tell them to cut back the undergrowth along this ride. These brutes of hill pheasants won't get up unless you make them. They creep right up to the open and then scuttle across, and you can't get a shot. If we cut it back ten yards they'd have to fly.'

III

JODH SINGH had chosen the village of Chopta in the south-eastern part of the district as the scene for his crucial test of strength with the Deputy Commissioner. It was in the right area, only two days' march from a railway station, it was a large village for the hills, with over a hundred families, a post office and primary school, and the younger brothers usually made their way to the plains to take service of some kind, the humbler as messengers or private servants, the better educated as postmen or typists. And there were many Brahmans, who would offer better material on the whole than the Kshatriyas, the Rajputs, the warrior class. The village was too close to the plains to be favoured by the army, who preferred the simpler peasant from the higher hills, the man whose knowledge of the outer world was all learnt in the regiment; and to Jodh Singh this was an additional recommendation. He did not want any danger of an opposition party of old soldiers whose life-long habit of obedience to authority would be hard to break. It was of course impossible to find any village in the district in 1923 which had not sent someone to the army, but from Chopta they would be hospital orderlies, mule-leaders, and the like, not riflemen from the infantry. And if the soldiers did venture on criticism of his ideas, the sting would be drawn by the fact that they themselves were exempt from the corvee.

By the time Jodh Singh reached Chopta, he had already made a good deal of progress in the technique of his approach to a new village. He had found that if he began his propaganda among the villagers without first going to the headman, almost invariably the full weight of traditional authority was turned against him. The headman more than anyone else had something to fear, for his post depended on his behaving as officialdom thought he should, and he could be dismissed. Whereas, if he comported himself correctly and his heir was not obviously disqualified by deformity, idiocy or bad behaviour, the appointment was hereditary. It brought him slight material advantage but much honour, and he did not want to lose it. He was, besides, himself exempt from the corvee and the headman was therefore in every village liable to be distrustful of Jodh Singh's persuasions. If to this natural disinclination was added jealousy because his influence was being undermined, he would usually turn hostile. It was true that by approaching him direct, Jodh Singh risked an initial rebuff, for the headman might commit himself to an opinion before he realized the weight of popular feeling and it might then be difficult to make him change. Jodh Singh, however, had by now decided that the risk was almost always worth taking, although, with a foresight beyond his years, he would make inquiries at the next village before he arrived and suit his approach to circumstances.

In the case of Chopta, he learned nothing from his preliminary inquiries to make him vary his usual method and he went straight to Ram Dat Naithani, the headman. Ram Dat, being the eldest brother, had managed the land and taken over the duties of headman from his father and he had never been far away from the village. Being a Brahman, he could read and write Hindi and had some knowledge of Sanskrit, but he knew that both in education and knowledge of the world he was a long way behind his own younger brother, who was a sub-assistant surgeon in the plains, and many other younger brothers who had served as postmen or clerks. This made him cautious and suspicious and increased his Brahmanical preference for the indirect. He had of course already heard rumours of Jodh Singh's teachings and thought the matter out with some care. He was not a man of impulse who would be guided by his heart. He had made up his mind as to the line he would take before he saw Jodh Singh.

As a Brahman, he was naturally suspicious of a Rajput, for in the old days the Brahmans had enjoyed a monopoly of learning, and had held all the civil posts. Now the Rajputs were claiming a share and every Brahman resented it, the more so as the army still preferred the Rajput. Again, as an old man he regarded with reserve the arrogance of a youth straight from college who was telling his elders what to do. But already everyone in the district was talking about Jodh Singh and he might perhaps stand for election as their representative in Lucknow. If he was successful in this he would indubitably be a great man with whom it would be well to be in favour. If the Brahmans decided to support him, and they might, for they had no good candidate of their own, and the sitting member was a militant Rajput who hated Brahmans, it would more than ever be desirable to have helped him in his early days. He would have to reward the Brahmans and naturally the best he had to give would go to old friends. All this, perhaps, was looking a long way ahead, but it touched on the immediate problem, which was the line to take about compulsory labour. It would be no use going all out against a movement to end the corvee. It was bitterly unpopular, particularly so in such a village as this where there were many unused to bodily labour. To oppose the movement wholeheartedly would kill the headman's influence in the village. On the other hand, to support the strike openly might mean dismissal from being headman; of course, if refusal to work became general, it would probably be impossible to dismiss all the headmen — but it would be remembered against him always. No, everything led to one conclusion; he must avoid offending Jodh Singh and let both him and the villagers know that he was on their side, but outwardly, he must appear to help the patwari.

Jodh Singh greeted Ram Dat respectfully. He placed his hands together in the attitude of prayer and addressed him as 'Pandit', the Brahman's title of respect. He treated him with the deference due to an older man and asked for a blessing. All this increased Ram Dat's suspicion of him as a Rajput, but he responded graciously, and the conversation proceeded with extreme courtesy and goodwill.

When Jodh Singh at last came to the point and asked Ram Dat whether he would mind if he arranged a meeting in the village — he was careful to explain that he did not expect the headman himself to call the villagers together — the Brahman began to explain his difficulties. He was after all the headman, and he had to think of his son as well as of himself. He saw the justice of Jodh Singh's arguments and sympathized entirely with his point of view. He would do everything to help him but he had to think how this could best be done. If he were to act openly, the patwari would report against him and much of his influence would be lost. To give the maximum help, he must seem to be acting with the patwari. It might perhaps appear as though he were not being entirely helpful, but everyone would know he did not mean anything he might say in the presence of the patwari. He would take good care of that. Privately, he would be using his influence the other way.

Jodh Singh was accustomed to this attitude, though it was not usually stated so explicitly. The first time he had met it, he had exploded with anger, for his nature was impetuous and direct; but that had got him nowhere, and eventually he had been forced to regard that village as one of his failures. He had learnt to curb his impatience and contempt at an expedient which he regarded as cowardly, because he knew it was the only way he could get what he wanted. He felt his anger mounting as Ram Dat talked, it seemed almost to choke him; but he would not give way to it. He must force himself to be calm. He nodded wisely as Ram Dat made his points and it was with all the courtesy and deference at his command that he said he entirely understood and agreed that this would be far more helpful than open support. He knew that the real struggle with Ram Dat would be over the amount of secret support that he could get.

Whatever the Brahman might decide as a matter of policy, he would never get over his suspicion of Jodh Singh as a Rajput, and he was perfectly capable of playing a game with three tiers of duplicity — in public, supporting the patwari, and in private appearing to encourage the villagers to refuse the customary service, but qualifying all he said with hints of evil consequences that would undo much of Jodh Singh's work. And this, reflected Jodh Singh, was almost certainly what he would tell the patwari he was doing. He would know that the patwari would not be such a fool as to be deceived by his public utterances, and so he would probably explain to him that while he would uphold his position and satisfy the decencies in public, in private he would not be able to declare himself strongly as a supporter of government, or he would lose all his influence. So in private, he would say, I shall pretend to be backing Jodh Singh, but everything I say will be so craftily qualified . . . Jodh Singh could see it all, and his anger again began to rise, but again he beat it down. He felt that it would take someone very clever indeed and far more experienced than himself to know what the old man was up to. Much, he felt, might depend on the impression he made and he tried, therefore, to be not only polite and deferential but to give an impression of judicious calm and a reason and understanding beyond his years. He had to do this mainly by silence and by nods for he could not trust himself to speak. Inwardly, he boiled with impatience to get out and to talk to the villagers.

The upshot of his talk was that Ram Dat agreed with him that he should call a meeting, at which the headman would ostentatiously appear and tell everyone to go home; but no one would take any notice because the word would have been privately passed round beforehand that they should not. And what else would they be told at the same time, Jodh Singh wondered; but he was not really worried, for the headman's hold on the shareholders of the village was tenuous. Apart from his government post, he was only the first of equals, the president and managing director of a board. His influence depended on his never cutting directly across the popular will; he must guide rather than command; and Jodh Singh felt sure that Ram Dat had seriously underestimated the power of his eloquence and his ability to fire the villagers to action in a cause to which they were already strongly inclined.

When he rose to go, Ram Dat suggested that he should stay with one of the Rajput shareholders, but Jodh Singh politely declined an offer which he knew to be a trap. If he stayed with a Rajput, all the Brahmans would believe that they were plotting together and Ram Dat would use the suspicion to throw further confusion into the minds of everyone as to which side he was really backing. No, said Jodh Singh, he would sleep in the village school, which was commonly used as a guest-house. No one could question the right of the villagers to use it in this way, as they had built it themselves, the District Board having undertaken to pay for a teacher if they would do so. He would sleep in the school and perhaps the shareholders would be so kind as to send him some food; he realized that with his position to consider, the headman could not be expected to send food from his own house. But perhaps he would see no objection if some of the others did. Ram Dat gravely agreed and so it was arranged.

Next day Jodh Singh went with confidence to the meeting, which was held in a field close to the village. All the shareholders were there, Brahman and Rajput, elder brother and younger brother, for all were in theory equal in the management of village affairs, although in practice one had authority in the village and one in each family above the others. There were no women. The Doms, such of them as had come, were in a separate group, on a higher terrace above the main gathering. As arranged, Ram Dat appeared and in a loud voice but with a very unconvincing manner told everyone to go home and not to listen to this dangerous and seditious person. No one took any notice and

Ram Dat then went home himself. One of his brothers however remained.

By this time, Jodh Singh had his speech perfect and it slipped off his tongue very smoothly, with impressive pauses at the right places, with mounting emphasis as he completed a point, a quiet resumption of the argument as he started a new one. But beneath his perfected technique was real emotion, which mounted steadily as he spoke. His heart burned within him and the fire spread and warmed his audience. He began by speaking of all the district had done in the war, how their blood had been poured out in generous response to the appeals of the British, of how freedom had been promised to India in return for her help and of the falsity of every promise made.

'Has freedom been given us, now that the war is over?' he cried. 'No, the British are laughing at our simplicity. They know us for the simple and credulous fools we are. They know that they can go on, living in luxury while we toil in the fields, sweating to feed them with wine and meat and to clothe their women with costly silks, while we live on millet bread and porridge and wear blankets.'

He went on from the general to the particular and to the grievance of the corvee. Here was something which would show whether the British were sincere in what they said of freedom. Would they go on forcing the peasant to toil for them, carrying camp gear as though they were mules or coolies, instead of free shareholders, Brahmans and Rajputs, twice-born? There would be no difficulty in arranging for coolies; it was simple for the Government, with all the power and the money and the prestige in the world at their disposal, to arrange anything they wanted. But they would not do it. Their devilish policy was to oppress the peasant and debase his spirit by making him carry loads. Thus he would show the world that he was a slave and would keep for ever the slave spirit; and so long as he knew he was a slave who had to carry burdens he would never rise against his oppressors.

So it went on. Jodh Singh believed every word of it. As he spoke, his hearers became more and more moved; and when he ended they crowded round him asking him what they should do. He told them that their duty was simple. They had nothing to do but to refuse politely when the patwari told them to carry the Deputy Commissioner's camp gear.

'I shall be here to help you,' he said. 'I am going now to all the villages near by, to make sure they do not come to the Sahib's help; but I shall come back the day before the Deputy Commissioner comes and I shall be here if there is trouble. There is nothing for you to fear. If anyone is sent to prison, it will not be you, for you are too many. I am the only one who is in danger and I shall be here if they want me. But there must be no violence. Not yet. No violence, that is what our Mahatma has said.'

His eye was roving round among the crowd as he spoke. He wanted to find the natural leaders, the men of energy and character to whom the others would listen. He must take those men aside and talk to them, he must leave behind lieutenants working for the cause with something of his own ardour and determination. He picked on three, one of whom was Ram Dat's younger brother, and he detached them after the meeting and talked to them long and earnestly. In the evening, he paid a polite and ceremonious call on Ram Dat, but he came by night, and explained very tactfully that he had taken care no one should see him come. This would make it possible for Ram Dat to tell the patwari that he had reproved Jodh Singh at their first interview and refused to have anything to do with him. Next morning he saw his three lieutenants again and satisfied himself that they were solidly behind him. Then he left, to spread the word among the neighbouring villages and make sure there were no blacklegs.

ON the same day that Jodh Singh first arrived at Chopta and talked to Ram Dat, Hugh and Margaret Upton started on their tour to the south-east. Their road lay in a huge half-circle round the end and side of a wide shallow valley. Below the road the ground fell steeply, mostly rough pasture on which only a hill beast could find sustenance, with patches here and there of pine or oak scrub, remnants of the forest that had once clothed all the hills but had been gradually eaten down to the few surviving areas, jealously preserved now by villagers who began to realize the value of what they had destroyed. Below the pastures, where the slope became gentler, the cultivation began, terrace on wrinkled terrace, writhing over every fold of ground, outlining every contour, a finely reticulated net over the whole floor and lower slopes of the valley. Not a yard of land was wasted here, for the population was three or four times what it had been in the days of the Rajas and Gurkhas.

Above the road, the hillside swept up to low down-like crests, with outcrops of rock here and there among the short, golden grass, and here and there the dry bed of a stream, its sides clothed in dark scrub. Hugh had to stop several times on the way to deal with people who wanted him perhaps to check the monstrous tendency of the next village to encroach on their preserves of grazing-land or forest, perhaps to restrain one of their own shareholders from defying the village community and taking more than his share of the common land. When she saw that familiar sight, a figure standing by the side of the road, petition in hand, Margaret looked round for a convenient seat and settled herself to rest, looking back to the north at the snow peaks, or watching the faces round her husband. Sometimes sketch-book and pencil would come out and she would try to catch the look on a wrinkled face, or the angle of a gesticulating arm, but quite as often her eyes would rest in endless wonder on the serrated line of ice and snow. Those who knew her superficially would have said she was a brisk practical woman, for all her beauty emphatically a Martha; but it was not because the externals of life were her only interest that she was concerned with them, but because she was determined to let no one know that life had not given her what she had dreamt of and what she had now decided she could never have. She would make a good job of her marriage and her life, and she would enjoy both.

There were fewer interruptions and discussions than usual on the road to-day, because it was near headquarters and almost everyone who had anything to plead had already come in to see Hugh and tell him about it. As they came to the last stretch of the journey, for about a mile the track lay in the shadow of the hillside. All morning the sun had blazed upon it and the surface had been beaten by the feet of mules and men into powdery white dust, two inches deep. In the late afternoon, when the shadow of the hill fell on the path, a fine covering of dew had formed over the dust; and an hour later this had frozen. The road before them stretched shining and dimpled, like old snow in the early morning after a frost; but with every step they broke the thin crackling surface and plunged into dry feathery white dust.

They were not using the tents the first night, but were to sleep in a rather dilapidated bungalow built in the old days by the Deputy Commissioner as a rest-house for travellers and now maintained intermittently by the District Board, to whom it had been transferred as a measure of self-government. Margaret had sent a servant ahead and he was waiting for them by a blazing wood fire, with her inevitable copper kettle and spirit stove. The water was hot already and she had a cup of tea in Hugh's hands within five minutes of arrival. While he was drinking it, she moved quickly about the room, putting up brightly coloured curtains and throwing cushions on the chairs.

'There!' she said, coming back to the fire-side, 'that's a little more cheerful and homelike. And may I remind you once more that the proper place for your boots when you take them off is neither the table nor the chairs. At heart you're still a bachelor who happened to get married. I ought to have caught you younger.' And that, she thought, is true, oddly enough. If I had met him first — she brushed away the thought, and went on:

'Well, there wasn't any trouble with the porters to-day, was there?'

'Not actual trouble for us,' said Hugh, 'they did the job all right. But the patwari says he had a difficult time getting them together. There was a good deal of argument and discussion and he had to use all his influence.'

'What are you doing about it?' Margaret asked.

'There's nothing I can do, except tell the patwaris to persevere and do the best they can, and at the same time tell the Government about it. I've written to Smith again, and I'm expecting the letter for signature this evening. We shall run into trouble in a few days and that will convince him that there's something in it. Nothing else will. Ah, here's Tara Dat with my letter.'

The lamps had been lighted, and Hugh read over the letter he had dictated that morning before starting. He had said:

'I hope you will forgive me for writing again on this subject so soon after my official letter, but all my reports indicate that Jodh Singh is having very general success with his propaganda and I think I should be failing in my duty if I did not warn you of what I fear the results may be. You are of course aware of all the facts about this agitation and I know that there is nothing new that I can tell you about the district, but I think it is worth restating some obvious points which have a bearing on the situation.

'The main point I want to make is that there are no police and we hold the hills entirely by bluff. There is one patwari for every sixty villages on an average — about one to every eight thousand of the population. The headman is a shareholder in the village first and a Government servant second — a very poor second. Our only assets are the prestige of the Deputy Commissioner and the patwaris, and the habit of obedience. Once that habit is broken, things would be very different. In other words, with the present arrangements, we can only carry on the administration if we have the general goodwill and backing of the people. This we still have, as we always have had in the past, because we have never done anything they regarded as seriously unjust or unfair and because we started with the initial advantage of being their deliverers from Gurkha oppression.

'I do not mean by this argument that we ought to give in to anything which the people of the district might demand. But I do wish to suggest that if it ever did come to a show-down, we ought to be on very firm ground. In this particular case I do not think we are. There would not be so much objection if it could be ensured that the system of forced labour would be administered considerately and with a minimum of inconvenience to the villager, but as I have explained in my official letter, I do not think it will ever be possible to make sure of this. And even if this difficulty could be overcome, I venture to think there would still be an objection to the system. Forced labour does not sound well in modern times. It is a feudal survival and I think it would be very difficult to justify calling in outside force to maintain it.

'If it is decided to continue the present system, I have no doubt that it will be necessary to call in force from outside. Perhaps not much would be needed. We might arrest Jodh Singh for obstructing a public servant in the execution of his duty, though I have not taken legal advice, and we might restore the situation in a few villages with the help of say a hundred armed police. But I think that this would leave behind a legacy of mistrust and dislike which would lead to more trouble before long, and would eventually mean that the cost of administering the hills, at present very low, would be increased considerably, with no corresponding increase in revenue. I advise most strongly against it.

'I sent you with my official letter a scheme for starting a transport company, with an estimate of cost. This does not include any estimate of receipts, but I see no reason why the public should not come to use such an agency, which might then in a few years become self-supporting. The outlay should therefore be small and I believe that if it could now be announced that we were about to introduce such a scheme, all the sting would be taken out of Jodh Singh's attack. His general political propaganda is dangerous because it is associated with a practical grievance, which I venture to think is genuine. Remove the grievance and I believe the political propaganda would fall on deaf ears.

'Once again, I hope you will forgive me if I seem to press my own views strongly. But I think it is essential you should be in no doubt of what I fear the consequences may be before you take a decision. If it is decided that I am wrong and that Jodh Singh should be arrested, he will undoubtedly get the best lawyers he can, for he has money, and they will probably come from the plains. In that case, the whole business will get into the press and I think the matter is certain to be brought to the notice of government by questions in the legislature.'

Hugh read through what he had written and made some alterations. Margaret said:

'May I see? Or is that being an interfering wife?'

'Of course,' he said, 'I'd be glad to hear what you think of the last paragraph. Does it sound too much like a threat? You see, I know Smith, and he doesn't like putting anything to government at all. He thinks that the best district officer is the one you never hear of, and he believes everything will always come right in the end provided you're firm but not provocative. And he

will say of course that my arguments cut both ways. If everything in the hills depends on the prestige of the patwari, then
you should never give in to agitation or the habit of obedience
will be lost. His instinct on getting my letters will be to say I'm
belly-aching and to do nothing about it. But if he thinks government are going to hear about it anyhow, he may be forced to
tell them in advance. I hope that my last paragraph will make
him send on copies of my letters to Lucknow, with his own
opinion in a covering note. But I'm afraid his covering note
will be against what I advise.'

She read the letter through.

'I think you're right,' she said. 'Though I don't expect he'll
love you. You're not quite such a fool as you look, are you, my
funny old ugly?'

He grinned cheerfully.

'Oh, I don't expect to be loved,' he said. She was sure there was
no second thought behind his words. She was sure he had no inner
problems of his own and was not aware of hers. She did not even
glance at his face to see what he was thinking when he used that
ambiguous phrase. He sent for the clerk to dispatch his letter.

They moved on next day towards the south-east and for a
few days marched through low hills, rolling down-like country
with steep short valleys in between. The tops were short golden
grass; there were few trees; a windy, open country, in which
there were many disputes for Hugh to attend to, because the
pressure on the land was great and the few remaining trees were
quite insufficient for a people whose inherited way of life was
built on inexhaustible forests. It was only occasionally that Margaret caught a glimpse of the high snows, for the view to the
north was blocked by another range, the same Mr. Bennett had
unexpectedly crossed to find the rope-sacrifice preparing on the
other side. But it was a country which had many attractions;
little tinkling streams which they would cross after a steep stony
descent, friendly corners where the fields, beautifully terraced and

faced with stone to make a level surface for irrigation, made clear clean patterns below the rounded golden tops, villages clustered in a huddle of tiled roofs and a blue mist of wood smoke, on which you looked down as if from the air, stacks of golden straw, a pond with willows round it from which the buffaloes rose slowly one by one, a hundred little intimate pictures to be sketched.

As usual, the porters turned up to carry the loads, villagers came out with petitions, schools lined the road and sang songs of welcome; but there was a difference, difficult to define, but noticeable. There was not the usual air of spontaneous pleasure in their coming; in camp at evening everyone had come strictly for business; there was no cheerful crowd of spectators and those who clustered round Margaret for medicines and plasters were fewer. And everywhere the patwaris reported that it was only by the exercise of all their powers of tact and patience and persuasion that they had collected porters.

On the tenth day they reached Chopta. Their gear had been brought by men from the last village and the tents were pitched, but Dewan Singh, the senior orderly, came to meet Hugh as soon as he arrived, his round face serious.

'Lord,' he began, 'the villagers here will do nothing for us. I got the men from the last village to stay and put up the tents, and they helped us to get wood for the fires and water for the baths; but there was nearly a fight because the Chopta people tried to stop them, and I had to call the patwari. Now the men from Deora have gone and these men from Chopta will not help us at all. We shall not be able to move on to-morrow.'

'Then we must stay here,' said Hugh cheerfully. 'Where is the patwari?'

'He is in the village, lord, trying to persuade them. Shall I send for him?'

'No, he will be coming to report when he is ready. Don't hurry him.'

He went on to the tent where Margaret was already making tea. There were two tents, each just so big that you could stand up in the middle if there did not happen to be a lantern swinging from the ridge-pole, as there generally was. At the far end of each tent there was an alcove within the outer fly, divided from the main tent by a curtain. This made a pantry for one tent, a bathroom for the other. In the living-tent were two small tables, two canvas chairs.

'Tea as usual is the first thing I want,' said Hugh. 'I never really knew how good tea could be till I came here. After a day scrambling about these hills, it's meat, drink and tobacco in one, the staff of life, absolutely. Well, the trouble has come.' He told her what he had heard from Dewan Singh.

'What are you going to do?'

'I shall stay here to-morrow and talk to them. I've plenty of written work to keep me busy in between. I shall ask Master Jodh Singh to come and have a chat. It will be much better to do nothing at all to-night. I don't want to seem excited or worried. Calm and good-humoured and rather amused, that's me. Meanwhile, I shall have a bath. It may be the last we'll get for a day or two. Mind if I go first? Then I shall be finished by the time the patwari comes up to report.'

He shouted for his bath and went into the other tent. It was cold at five thousand feet in November and the business of bathing needed careful timing. He undid his boots but waited till he heard the bath being poured before he tore off coat and shorts as quickly as possible and crept through the flaps into the little alcove, which smelt strongly of the damp straw on the floor. It was just not possible to stand up here and it was essential not to waste a minute between the pouring of the bath and getting in, because the water cooled so quickly in a tent; for the same reason, it was very important to get into the flat zinc tub when the water was just a little hotter than it could be borne. Having adjusted the temperature of the almost boiling water by

adding cold from an old paraffin canister, Hugh stepped in delicately. It was agony, the water was so hot; and the part of his
flesh not in the water was like a newly plucked fowl from the
cold air. There was a band of deep mahogany colour round
his knees and on his forearms to the elbow, from day-long ex-
posure. Drying was difficult, because it was necessary to crouch,
and there was a penetrating wind that blew down one side of
the tent between the outer and inner fly and through the bathroom. But once it was over, he was in a happy glow and he
hurried to pull on warm clothes, long felt boots, and a dressing-
gown over everything, which gave him the appearance of a
gigantic Tibetan.

He was on his way back to the living-tent when the patwari
arrived, to confirm Dewan Singh's report. He had done everything he could to persuade the villagers but he could not shake
them. The headman was pretending to help him but in secret
he was certainly using his influence in quite a different way.
Jodh Singh himself was here and he had managed to get
considerable influence.

Hugh smiled cheerfully, thanked him, and told him to come
back in the morning with any fresh news; he said that he was
going to invite Jodh Singh to come and see him. When he lay
down two hours later in the narrow camp bed by the side of Margaret's, he fell asleep the moment his head touched the pillow.

Next morning, Hugh had a talk with the patwari, who told
him there was no change in the attitude of the villagers, and then
he wrote a letter of invitation which he sent to Jodh Singh by
one of the orderlies. Next he sent a telegram by a special runner
to the nearest office for dispatch to Mr. Smith.

His telegram said: 'As expected villagers of CHOPTA have
refused to carry my camp gear or fetch wood and water for
camp. stop. My advice is still to announce immediately Government's intention of forming transport company. stop. If decision
is against this consider only alternative course will be to arrest

Jodh Singh if he proves obdurate and request immediate dispatch ten repeat ten armed police. stop. Consider this may lead to situation demanding dispatch one hundred repeat hundred armed police. stop.'

When the telegram had gone, Hugh considered again very carefully for a few minutes. He decided it would be no use talking to the villagers collectively himself. If they had' made up their minds to this extreme step and the patwari could not shake them, it was unlikely he could persuade them to change. And if he tried and failed he would only make things worse. He must make alternative arrangements, and accordingly he wrote another letter and dispatched another man on urgent business to the west. He settled down to a morning of correspondence, dealing with various questions he had put aside while travelling. He felt he was unlikely to be interrupted until after lunch and could allow himself the rare luxury of working slowly and thoughtfully. He had considerable powers of concentration and in any case he was in no way excited by the crisis which had arisen, for he felt himself quite detached from what was happening. He had given advice which he was sure was right and now the decision lay with someone else.

Jodh Singh's frame of mind was very different. This he was sure was the big crisis of his life. He was sitting on the veranda of the school house, where he was lodging, when one of the Deputy Commissioner's orderlies came and asked if Jodh Singh was there. His heart pounded and his stomach turned to water. Perhaps this man had come to arrest him. It must be that. He was not going to resist arrest, but he would go slowly, and collect a crowd, and address them before he was bundled away to he knew not what dreadful torments. But all the orderly did was to hand him a letter. He took it with surprise and confusion. His hands still trembled as he opened it. There would be threats in it and anger. But he would not be browbeaten or frightened. What he read was this:

'Dear Thakur Jodh Singh, I hear that you are in the village of Chopta and as there are one or two things I should like to talk over with you, I wonder if you could come up to my camp and have a cup of tea with me this afternoon about four o'clock. I hope you will be able to come. Yours sincerely, Hugh Upton.'

Jodh Singh was so taken aback by this that when the orderly asked him if there was an answer he replied automatically:

'Say I will come.'

But as soon as the orderly had gone, he began to wonder whether he had done the right thing. He had always heard that Englishmen were haughty and contemptuous and usually angry; those he had seen, it was true, had usually appeared utterly careless, seeming not even to notice the crowds about them, talking to each other as if in their own homes. The only Englishman he had really known had been a professor at the university, a shy grey man whom the students regarded with affectionate contempt. But everyone said he was not really like an Englishman at all. Jodh Singh's picture of the Deputy Commissioner was of a stout red-faced angry man; he had expected a letter either abusive and threatening or curt and official. This polite note, written as if to an equal, and as if there were nothing of importance in the air, was the last thing he had imagined. It did not even ask him to come at once. It was probably a trap. The English were cunning behind their careless appearance. The sahib would try to melt Jodh Singh's heart with tea and kind words. Would it be better even now not to go?

The danger in going was not physical. They could arrest him when they wanted. It was that he might melt. Well, he would steel his heart and make up his mind not to melt. Was there any other danger? He could not see it. And to be asked to tea was a score; there was no question of that. He was negotiating on equal terms — but would it appear like that? Would the district say that the Deputy Commissioner had called him, and he had gone at once, like an obedient spaniel? Ought he not to try to make the Deputy Commissioner come to him? His imagination quailed at this stupendous thought. It will come to that, he told himself; one day I shall make him come to me; but for the present, it is enough that he has asked me to tea. Yes, I will go.

He passed the rest of the day in a fever of excitement. He had to meet a man older and more experienced than himself, and of a race whom his forebears for several generations had regarded as masters and superiors. And he had to play on his adversary's ground. He would be hampered by social problems. He would not know what to do with his cup and saucer. And he would be talking a foreign language. It was as though a boy from a labourer's cottage in Victorian England had been asked to sit down to tea with an earl and discuss important affairs in which he alone had to use Ciceronian Latin, while the earl spoke his mother tongue. At a quarter to four, he began to walk up the hill. He said to himself:

'I will not give way. I will not be worried about my tea-cup. I know I am right. I will remember India's wrongs. I will not give way.'

He was sweating when he arrived and ran his hand over his hair, which he wore long and well-oiled, cut in a European style. An orderly, with a faint air of wondering what the world was coming to, led him to the two larger tents, and Hugh came out to meet him, grinning cheerfully, and unbelievably large. His face was not red but a clear healthy brown, not much lighter than Jodh Singh's own; and he was neither fat nor angry.

'Come and sit down,' he said. 'This is my wife.'

'How do you do, Mr. Rawat,' said Margaret. She was wearing a magenta silk shirt with a dark blue skirt, fitting closely to her hips and flared out at the knees to suit her slim figure and to free her movements. The colours brought out her vivid colouring, dark hair, eyes of a sunny blue, cheeks flushed with the sun and the hill air. To Jodh Singh she was unbelievably beautiful, and his confusion was increased.

107

'I am very well, mem-sahib,' he replied, bending over her hand as he had seen Europeans do in the cinema. It immediately occurred to him that he should have said Mrs. Upton, not mem-sahib, as though he were a servant, and his shyness increased. 'I hope you are well.'

She gave him tea and asked him with a friendly smile whether he was glad to come back to the hills after the university in the plains. They talked of Lucknow for a little. He thought she must be insincere in saying that she was happier in Garhwal; she could not like this rough, lonely life. He was very shy and stilted, but spoke with an obvious desire to please and to be polite. She liked him. At last she said:

'Well, you want to talk business, so I must leave you. Good-bye, Mr. Rawat; I hope we meet again soon.'

She had been kind and friendly and it had delighted him to look at her, but he was more at ease when she left, though his emotion increased. His heart beat fast and painfully, for now the moment had come.

'I must not give way,' he said to himself. 'I must not give way.'

But Hugh did not come to the point at once. He spoke of the high esteem in which Jodh Singh's grandfather had been held and of his father's good record as a patwari. It was a great thing for the district, he said, that there were now more educated young men; and he asked Jodh Singh what were his plans for the future.

This put Jodh Singh in a difficulty, for he did not want to be rude. His every instinct was to repay courtesy with courtesy, for he had been charmed and flattered by his reception and he liked this big man. He did not wish to say that he was going to devote his life to driving out the English. It was haltingly, therefore, that he began to explain that he meant to lead the people of the district to higher things and a better way of life, but as he spoke he warmed and spoke more fluently. Hugh made encouraging noises from time to time and suggested that there could really be nothing more helpful than persuading the villagers in those areas where they still had forests to preserve them carefully. They might thus avoid the fate of the lower hills, where they not only had no fuel but were beginning to see their fields swept away by torrents because there were no forests on the hilltops to act as sponges, to soak up the rain and release it slowly. Jodh Singh cleared his throat nervously and began to say that this was really work for an official; but his courage came back to him and he said:

'But we shall make no real progress in that or anything else until we are free. We must have a government of our own.'

'I agree there's a great deal to be done that only an Indian government can do,' said Hugh. 'We only differ as to the date on which an Indian government will be able to take over from us. But surely there's a great deal of progress that can be made in the meantime and much on which we should be agreed and on which you could help.'

'But it is the first duty of every Indian who is not an official to work as hard as he can to bring the day of freedom to birth. Other things must wait,' said Jodh Singh seriously, and so the argument proceeded.

At last Hugh began to talk about the corvee. He told Jodh Singh that he thought he understood his case and explained very fully what he believed that case to be.

'Now, in the first place, is that your case and have I put it fairly? Is there anything I have left out — apart from the political background?'

Jodh Singh agreed that as regards the forced labour, nothing had been forgotten.

'All right. Now I have told the Government that that is what you want and why you want it. I have told them what I think it would cost to run a transport company. What I have to ask you now is to wait patiently for their decision and meanwhile not to make it difficult for me to get on with my job of running the district. After all, what I do on these tours of mine is all for the benefit of the peasants, you know. Now, will you help me? Call off your strike now and let me get on. If the decision is as you want it to be, well and good. If not, our bargain is ended and you start again, and then it is my job to stop you. I don't want to threaten — but in that case I should have to do whatever I could to restore discipline and it might be unpleasant for you. To be frank, I should probably have to arrest you, much as I should dislike doing it.'

Everything in Jodh Singh warmed to this man. He wanted with all his emotional nature to be friends with him and help him. He wanted to accept this offer at once, though he knew he had not had time to think about it. But astonished and distant, as if he were far from his body, he heard himself say in a small obstinate voice:

'No, I will not give way.'

Hugh paused. Then he said:

'Are you quite sure, Jodh Singh? I should like to be friends and we could do a lot for the district together.'

Jodh Singh shook his head. He was almost in tears. He could not trust himself to speak again. He shook his head, stretched out his hand to the Englishman in friendship, and walked away.

'I take off my hat to that boy,' said Hugh to Margaret. 'I was really very unsporting and did everything I could to make him take the wrong decision. But he stuck to his guns, though he wanted desperately to be friends. He's an emotional creature. They all are, of course, particularly when young. That's the mistake we make. Too cold. But it's our nature to be aloof with them, just as it's theirs to need that emotional appeal.'

They are like women in that, thought Margaret, and you make the same mistake with women. She said:

'But why do you say you tried to make him take the wrong decision?'

'From his point of view it would be wrong. They'd start a

file at Lucknow and argue about the thing for a year. Nothing would be done. And if he tried to start it again, he'd have lost the right moment. He'd have no way on his ship and you know what it's like trying to bring a boat round into the wind once you've lost way.'

'Then why did you try to make him take it?' she asked.

'I had to try every means of taking the pressure off government. It's my job to advise them, but I must do everything I can to give them the chance of an unforced decision. It would be disloyal not to. I had to try it.'

Margaret looked at him seriously.

'Oh, dear, how public-school we are,' she said. 'I liked him. I hope you won't have to arrest him. Do you think you will?'

'I don't know. Fifty-fifty chance, I should say. The Government seem only to think of money and in the long run I believe it would be cheaper to start a transport company. And morally it's the right thing to do. If it wasn't for Smith, I think they'd take my advice. But he's a pugnacious old devil. He loves a row and hates giving way, and he has this idea of prestige on the brain. Give way on one thing and they'll ask for another; that's what he'd say, I know. I don't say he's not right; it's a point of view. But our feet are on the slippery road of giving way already. We've said we're going, and it seems to me much more dignified to go with a good grace and meanwhile to carry on loyally, doing what we feel's the right thing for the future.'

'Can't you do anything else? I'm sure there's a lot of good in that boy.'

'I don't see that I can do anything more. I've put my views as plain as I can.'

'Why not go to Lucknow and talk to them?' Margaret asked.

'Well, in the first place, we seem to be stuck here. In the second, I can't short-circuit Smith and rush off to Lucknow to talk to the Chief Secretary direct. It would be frightfully disloyal. Of course, if it was the summer — they'd all be in Naini

Tal in the hills. I could go to talk to Smith — and I'd be in duty bound to call on the Chief Secretary and he'd be sure to ask me what I'd come for.' He grinned. 'No one could complain about that. But it isn't the summer. Smith's in Naini Tal and the Chief Secretary's in Lucknow. It can't be done, I'm afraid. I must go back to work.'

He thought how beautiful she looked in that shirt, the dark hair swept back from her temples, her lovely slim figure standing at the door of the tent in the last sunshine. But he did not say what he thought. He went to his files.

Half an hour later he was back, a letter in his hand.

'Funny what you said about Lucknow,' he said. 'Here's a letter, a week old of course, telling me that Smith has been suddenly called to Lucknow for a conference of all Commissioners about the political situation. He must have got there to-day.'

'Then you could go to see him? Oh, do go. It would be grand to save that boy and make him see reason.'

Hugh was doubtful.

'I suppose I might. I shouldn't have thought of it myself. I don't quite see that anything new has happened to make me want to go. Seeing Jodh Singh hasn't really changed the situation.'

'You could pretend it had.'

'Yes, I suppose so. I've never been much good at pretending. But you're right. It would disturb the district for a long time if they went wrong on this. It's the district I'm worried about, not the boy. All right, I'll go. You'll come, of course?'

She shook her head. She knew who was in Lucknow. She was not going to tear her heart again.

'I should only be a nuisance. You go by yourself. But how will you get away from here?'

He was disappointed. It would have been fun to have gone together. But he did not argue about that. He had made it a rule never to ask her for anything twice.

'Oh, I've got a scheme which may come off for getting away from here. We might get away to-morrow night and it's only three marches to Ramgarh. I could get a slow train from Ramgarh and then catch the night mail from Ramnagar, stay Thursday and Friday, back in Ramgarh Saturday morning. You could stay in Ramgarh.'

'Yes,' said Margaret. It wouldn't be a very happy two days she thought, as Hugh went off to send a telegram to the Commissioner. There was one phrase in that last letter that to her seemed scorched on steel, something she could never forgive. She hadn't thought of that for a long time, consciously. Funny how this came in waves, like a headache, only there wasn't any aspirin. Sometimes you'd hardly know it was there, and then it would suddenly start again. Wonder what started it this time. It began before there was any talk of going to Lucknow. Something Hugh had said, perhaps. Nice old Hugh. He might see Ronald and know nothing. She would paint like mad for those two days; it might help her to paint a decent picture. Hugh said memory was a poor thing. Well, it didn't do her much good.

Next day towards evening an old gentleman, from two days' march to the west, came to see Hugh. He wore narrow trousers of white wool and a full-skirted white woollen coat, falling to the knees, collarless and fastening right up to the neck with tape. He had been born before the Mutiny, and his grandfather — they were a stock who seemed to beget eldest sons late in life — had been one of the barons to whom the Rajas had delegated feudal power before the Gurkhas came. When the British sent the Gurkhas back to Nepal and took over the country, Raghubir Singh's grandfather had been in hiding with his peasantry; he reappeared and the British restored his lands, but they took away his feudal powers and he no longer exercised the high, low and middle justice. But he kept much of his influence. Among Raghubir Singh's most cherished possessions was a parchment dated 1857, addressed to his father, signed by the Deputy Commissioner of the day and sealed with his seal, which, when shorn of elaborate formal phrases and imposing calligraphy, said quite simply: 'If any strangers come into your villages from the plains, kill them.' Raghubir Singh was far from a man of blood, being a very gentle old person indeed, but he mourned the simplicity of those days when an order was an order.

He placed his small hand in Hugh's large grip and left it there affectionately. It was the wrinkled hand of old age, the skin still fine because it had never driven a plough or carried a load, but it was warm and alive.

'Have no care, sahib,' he said. 'My villagers will listen to me before they hear the words of an orderly's grandson from the upper hills. They will be here to-night, and they will come after dark as you say, and they will leave to-morrow before it is light. They will take you all the way to Ramgarh. They will do it for love of me and of the Government.' He paused and laid his left hand on Hugh's, which still enclosed his right. His gentle old face became sad. 'I am old and you are young,' he went on. 'Bring back the old ways.'

Hugh too was sad, because there was nothing he could do for him except betray him to the new age he did not like.

It was barely light next morning when Jodh Singh was wakened by a villager who came to tell him that the Deputy Commissioner's camp was already on the move. The first porters had started already and soon the whole long bobbing line would be winding in a string of dots towards the plains.

'Shall we stop them? We could easily catch them for they are loaded and we should have nothing to carry but our sticks.'

'Wait,' said Jodh Singh, scrambling to his feet. He must think for a moment about this new problem.

He had left Hugh's camp two evenings before, deeply stirred by the necessity for refusing an offer that seemed to be made in friendship. He had wondered whether he had been right, but not for long. Only his previous resolve, impressed on himself till it was stronger than his conscious mind, had stopped him from giving way to his emotions and saying yes. But as he went down the hill, he had time to think and he saw as clearly as Hugh had done that he would have been wrong. And his feeling of friendship for the big man who had seemed so friendly, but had really used all his charm of manner and his social prestige to deceive him, turned to anger, a sick envious anger that made him unhappy. For he envied Hugh his ease, his certainty, his wife, the possession of everything whose use had almost undone him. His anger had grown yesterday and he had talked with much bitterness to his lieutenants in the village. But he had made up his mind once more to resist sudden impulse and the pull of his heart.

Now the sahib had again deceived him and escaped him. His anger rose and choked him. He would stop him! He would send the village to beat up his blackleg porters, found by some lickspittle. But he stopped himself. I must think what would happen then. We should all be prosecuted. The village would suffer and be punished. We should be in the wrong. And there is to be no violence till we are forced to it. He told me he had written to the Government. We must not fight till they have decided against us. Then we will fight to the death.

But his anger rose again; he wanted to show his power, to stop this superior being from escaping him and laughing at him. But if he struck, it would really be a victory for the Government. They would be in the right and the villagers in the wrong. And as it was, the Deputy Commissioner had had to run away. That was the important thing to remember; he had had to run away. Jodh Singh decided to let him go. Of all he did in this matter of the corvee, nothing showed so clearly as this decision the possibilities of wise leadership that were in him; but it cost him much, more than his youth could afford.

He went outside the school house and looked towards the village. There were others hurrying down the path to ask for

115

instructions. He told them to wait, and would not let them know his mind till a small crowd had collected. Then he spoke.

He spoke well, as he always did now, with passion and bitterness. He spoke bitterly of the sahib who had tried to deceive him once, and had now sneaked away in the night, though even as he spoke he saw again the brown kindly face, the beautiful lady who had smiled and given him tea, and a pang of regret mingled with his bitterness. He brought in much of his stock-in-trade, now familiar to his hearers, though still capable of stirring them, and he stressed again and again the fact that by making the Deputy Commissioner run away they had scored a victory.

'Let them go,' he said, 'let them go. Soon all the district will think as we do and the Government will give in and put an end to this tyranny.'

And at that moment he saw on the edge of the crowd Ram Dat the headman. Ram Dat did not speak, but in his face Jodh Singh saw all the cynicism and indifference of age, the contemptuous knowledge that the young cannot make the world to their own pattern; and something seemed to snap within him and he forgot his wisdom and patience, worn thin by the effort of his previous restraint.

'Yes, we shall win,' he cried, 'we shall win, whatever you may think, Ram Dat, and whatever you and your kind may do, lickspittles, trencher-hounds, cowering before the hand that beats you.'

As he began to speak, Ram Dat turned to go, but the crowd turned too at Jodh Singh's abuse and looked at the Brahman with hostility. He turned on the defensive, and in a moment of panic, cried:

'I have done nothing. All the world knows the part I played.'

' "I meant to be virtuous, said the mule's mother",' mocked Jodh Singh, and he quoted another proverb: 'Yes, we know the part you played. You were the washerman's dog, that belongs

neither to the house nor the washing-place. You eat at both if
you can.'

The crowd laughed. Ram Dat went home. Jodh Singh
finished his harangue and felt better. But he had made the first
of the enemies who were to undo him.

When Hugh came back to the district five days later, Jodh
Singh was moving northwards, back towards his own country,
revisiting the villages where he had been most successful in his
journey south. Although he had rejected the Deputy Commissioner's offer of a truce he could put no heart into further fiery
preaching. He was exhausted by the strain of the last few days,
and needed the relaxation of going back over ground already
broken. He was in a particularly friendly village when the news
came through that government had announced that the corvee
would be ended and a transport company started in its place.

Jodh Singh could hardly believe it. It was ended. It really was
ended. He had won. He had won against the English government and the Deputy Commissioner. He had killed his bear.
His face suddenly lighted:

'Let us dance the dance of *Bakhtawar Wins* to-night,' he
cried. 'Let us eat raw game. Is there a home-fed sheep in this
village that I can buy?'

Among those who circled that night in angular dance among
the flaring torches, in a tiny patch of flame and movement against
the dark stillness of the hills, none was so wild as Jodh Singh.
When the time came for the madness to enter the dancers, it
seemed as though he was indeed possessed by that drunkenness
which the gods send on men who venture into the high places,
when the snow has melted and the flowers are in their first
glory.

V

IN the months immediately after the corvee was remitted, Jodh
Singh's mood was very like his grandfather's after killing the
bear, allowance being made for difference of age and upbringing.
He too was like a young man in love who knows himself admitted to favours shared with no one else and believes he has
every woman at his feet. There was nothing he could not do;
but while in his grandfather there was no outward manifestation
of the inner feeling of mastery, because he had to get in the
harvest and had no time to waste, the grandson did not wait for
them to come but went out looking for bears. He went from one
to another of the larger villages of the district, preaching the
wrongs of his country and looking for a concrete grievance to
which they could be linked.

As a triumphal progress his reception was gratifying, but as a
basis for further achievements, it was disappointing. He was
successful in interesting his audiences and he was everywhere
greeted with great honour as the man who had ended the forced
labour; but that was usually as far as he got. No one was going
to be enthusiastic about mere words and until he could find a
genuine grievance no one regarded his talk as anything but
words. It was no use telling anyone in Garhwal about the fiscal
policy of the British in India in the nineteenth century; they
had never seen the sea or a train and many had never seen a
bullock-cart or a five-rupee note. As for the heavy burden of
defence expenditure, they prayed for war as others pray for
rain, so that employment could be found in the army for all
the younger brothers. No, their grievance must be local; and the
nearest approach to a genuine local grievance was that in the
north, where there were still plenty of trees, there was some
resentment that the Government was protecting them, while in

the south, where there were hardly any trees left, there was a strong feeling that they should have been protected sooner. In fact, Jodh Singh was beginning to despair of ever raising the district to political manhood, when at last he came on a bear, a small one, it is true, and one he could regard with contempt, but it had the advantage that it came from the headquarters of the district at Pokhra.

Pokhra was originally a village of no particular importance on a fairly extensively used route which ran east and west along a low range of hills. But the first British officers did not care for the old capital of the Rajas, which lay in a hot and steamy valley, so they chose as their capital the nearest hill village of any size, which happened to be Pokhra. The first Deputy Commissioner built his office and courts of justice by the side of the bridle-track round which the houses clustered. It would at the time have been strange and pointless if he had not. But as time wore on and the traffic on the road increased, there came a Deputy Commissioner to whom it seemed intolerable that mules with their bells should jangle past the door of his office, raising clouds of white dust and bringing flies and smells and the loud cries of muleteers, offending not only himself but the waiting petitioners and litigants, the lawyers and stamp vendors and the contractors who offered sweetmeats and tea to all these people. He built a wall in front of his office, enclosing a large space, and deflected the road in a detour down the hill. But at either end of the enclosure, where the old road used to enter, was a stile for pedestrians and an iron gate which was usually kept closed but could be opened for an official procession on the occasion of a Jubilee or the Coronation of a monarch. Everyone could remember that the gates had been open and a procession had gone through to celebrate the end of the war; and most people could remember a previous occasion, at the time of the coronation of King George V.

Now there was in Pokhra a small but fairly vigorous branch

of the Congress party. Its members, like Jodh Singh, found that most of their teaching fell on very stony ground and took no root at all, but they had a certain number of secret adherents who were afraid to come out in the open; the majority of the villagers, and of those who came in from the neighbourhood for litigation or the payment of revenue, were indifferent to politics of any kind. However, the party persevered with a fine persistence and they held a public meeting once a week on the one open space in the village, where they harangued each other and a sprinkling of schoolchildren and loafers who came from curiosity. It was usually a disappointing audience, because they seldom had anything new to say, and the figures of attendance sent in to their provincial headquarters looked bad, even though they were strikingly larger than those sent in by the patwari to the Deputy Commissioner. Their leader was one Ram Parshad Singh, a lawyer with a long narrow face and a drooping moustache who on six days of the week wore a check knickerbocker suit, while on the day of his weekly meeting he put on snowy homespun cotton, the uniform of the Congress party. His moustache and his knickerbockers would have automatically qualified him for the part of the squire's wicked son in a rustic melodrama. Ram Parshad Singh was worried about his poor audiences; he decided that he must attract a better house and it occurred to him that this could be done by organizing a procession through the village which would end at the meeting. If there were flags and drums, people would follow and stay to listen.

So a procession was organized. It assembled outside the village to the east and marched with beating drums and a host of flags, green, yellow and white, by the detour below the courts and along the bridle-path right through the village, and then turned down the hill to the meeting-ground. It was undoubtedly a draw to begin with and audiences increased considerably; but they soon dropped off again when people found that at the end of the march there was nothing to look at or listen to but Ram

Parshad Singh talking as usual about tyranny and fiscal policy and imported cotton goods. Ram Parshad Singh felt he must liven up the proceedings; and he thought he could best do this by being in some way openly provocative to the officials of the district. He was encouraged in this idea by the remission of the corvee, which he interpreted as having been conceded by a reluctant government solely because they were afraid of the agitation started by Jodh Singh. He knew nothing of the part played by the Deputy Commissioner. After some thought, he came to the conclusion that it would probably be a good way to begin the provocation if he took his procession straight through the court enclosure, making as much noise as possible on the way. No one could call the detour a burning popular grievance, but it could be worked up a little and it could be argued that if the route was available for an official procession it ought also to be open to the one political organization in the district, particularly as that organization claimed to represent the whole of India. Whatever the merits of the case, someone could be found to support it; and it would certainly annoy the Tahsildar. 'Anything to give pain', was really Ram Parshad Singh's thought.

Before he made up his mind to adopt this particular form of irritation, Ram Parshad Singh considered the method. He might write a letter asking, in words sufficiently insolent to ensure refusal, that the gate should be opened for his next procession. Or the next procession might climb over it, for it was a simple five-barred field gate of iron. If he chose to climb over, he would certainly get away with it the first time and there would probably be a show-down next time he tried it. If he wrote a letter, it would mean a show-down the first time.

He had come to this point in his deliberations when a letter reached him from Jodh Singh, who had not yet been to Pokhra since the decision about the corvee and wished to include the headquarters of the district in his triumphal progress. Ram Parshad Singh thought this over carefully. He was not an idealist and an enthusiast as Jodh Singh was; he was a careerist, a political adventurer. He wanted to represent the district at Lucknow and Jodh Singh was a dangerous rival whom it would be pleasant to discredit. On the other hand, he was a draw and his presence would send up the numbers at Ram Parshad's weekly meeting. How could he be used to the best advantage? Could he be connected with the gate agitation?

Suddenly a smile lightened Ram Parshad Singh's long sallow face, making it for the moment almost attractive. He would take his procession over the gate before Jodh Singh arrived. The Tahsildar would know nothing of this until they were right in front of his court-room and by then it would be too late for him to stop them. They would bring it off the first time. Next day, he would write to the Tahsildar complaining that his procession had been obstructed by a gate. 'A gate,' he repeated to himself with relish; he would write as though he had just noticed it for the first time, though he had lived in Pokhra all his life; he grinned at the idea, for a hill-man is seldom without a sense of humour. He would invite the Tahsildar to have it open for his next procession. The reaction, he could be certain, would be sharp; the Deputy Commissioner, who was a less predictable factor in any situation, was as usual away on tour and the Tahsildar in charge was a fire-eater. Then Jodh Singh would arrive. Ram Parshad Singh, with a fine show of deference to so successful an agitator, would hand over the situation to him. There would be a sharp tussle and Ram Parshad Singh did not think victory would be achieved quickly. Jodh Singh would not want to stay in Pokhra for ever; he would leave when nothing was settled and everyone was tired of the whole affair. Then Ram Parshad Singh would tidy it up. His friends could be trusted to use the incident to the best advantage in a whispering campaign, which would show him as uniformly successful and Jodh Singh as having fumbled. Yes, that would be how it would go. He wrote a letter to Jodh Singh cordially welcoming him to the headquarters, and a week before he was due to arrive led the procession over the gate and through the court enclosure.

Bhola Nath, the Tahsildar[1] of Pokhra, was a Brahman from the plains who regarded all hill-men as dirty, a condemnation which bulked so large in his mind that he was not impressed by their courage, simplicity and humour. He had plenty of courage himself, and a liking for the direct old-fashioned way of dealing with trouble. He liked a government to govern, no doubt for the good of the people, but as the Government conceived the good, standing no nonsense. He did not like conciliation. And he hated the Congress, partly because they were agitators and he was a ruler, and partly because he was a landowner in the plains and they made it difficult for him to collect rent. He disliked Ram Parshad Singh more even than he did other Congressmen, the reason he gave being that he liked a man to come out in the open and show himself for what he was; and he held it against Ram Parshad that he did not wear his Congress uniform every day.

When Bhola Nath heard the drums and shouts of the procession pass the door of his office, he was furious. It was the grossest impertinence to come that way at all, and for a few minutes he could not hear himself speak in his own court. His first impulse was to rush out and stop the procession at once, but a moment's thought convinced him that this would merely make him look ridiculous. A procession of avowed Congressmen could not stop at his bare word without becoming a laughing-stock themselves; and he could not in the time available collect enough force to ensure obedience. There was no police administration, but there were a dozen armed police at Pokhra who provided the guard for the treasury, a few hundred yards away, and he could muster twenty or thirty orderlies if he had a day's warning,

[1] Actually, the magistrate in charge when the Deputy Commissioner was away would have been a grade higher than Tahsildar. But the titles of civil officers differ in various parts of India and are all confusing. I have eliminated this higher grade for the purpose of this book.

but at a few minutes' notice, not more than five or six. He had no alternative but to sit and fume. All the same, he was not going to put up with this kind of thing. He published an order before he went home, prohibiting the taking of processions through the court enclosure, a practice which he stated was dangerous to public order and tranquillity. He had copies of this posted on both gates and gave instructions for other copies to be served on Ram Parshad Singh and his principal henchmen.

This order anticipated Ram Parshad's impertinent letter, which reached Bhola Nath next day and increased his anger, as it was meant to; he repeated phrases from it to himself all day with growing irritation.

' "Found his way obstructed by a gate," indeed! As if he hadn't lived here all his life! And I am to "be so good as to see that this obstruction is removed", am I? You wait till next Wednesday, my friend, and just try it on again. You'll see what you'll get.'

He would collect old soldiers as well as orderlies and his handful of police. They would soon knock the stuffing out of a handful of half-hearted Congressmen. He began at once to make arrangements to collect them, and it was not till the evening that it occurred to him that he ought to tell the Deputy Commissioner what he was doing. By this time, the patwari had ferreted out the news that Jodh Singh was expected during the week and Bhola Nath added this to his letter, which he sent off with the rest of the day's work by a runner who would hand it over by a system of relays and cover the four stages to the camp in a day and a half.

Hugh was fishing when the runner reached his camp and he did not open the bag till the evening. He was not a man to look for work, as Mr. Bennett had done, and since he regarded his time in the hills as a pleasant interlude in which to recuperate from the burden of responsibility he had borne in the plains, he was scrupulous to allot one day in seven to recreation. If there was no fishing or shooting in the neighbourhood on the seventh day, he went on working till he was somewhere more suitable, but he saved up every day due to him. There had been three days owing to him which he was working off in a fishing holiday, of which this was only the second day. He had not done badly so far and hoped to do better to-morrow; but even if he didn't it was a good river to fish.

Nothing released him more completely from the cares of the world than to see the arrowy curve of his line in a good cast, to feel his lure swimming home smoothly across the tail of a long pool as he wound steadily in; nothing gave him the same un-mixed thrill of excitement and pleasure as the tug of a heavy fish. Margaret too enjoyed the days by the river. Her enthusiasm for fishing was intermittent, but she revelled in the colour of the valleys in winter and spring, the translucent green of deep pools that glowed with inner light like chrysoprase, the silver and diamond of glancing rapids, the bleached white of little beaches of sun-soaked sand, the black of wet rocks and stranded drift-wood. She liked the scrunch of pebbles under her feet and the bobbing of the quick wagtails as they prinked and perked and flitted. And after vain attempts to paint wide hillsides and snow mountains, it was a joy to turn to the closer, more intimate pattern of glowing pool, dark bank, and glittering cascade.

They walked back to camp together to a late tea. Hugh opened his bag of mail at once, and looked through it quickly to see what could wait and whether there was anything he must look at now. Bhola Nath's letter was marked urgent. He read it with an expression of disgust.

'What's the matter?' asked Margaret.

'Bhola Nath and the Congress have started a quarrel at Pokhra and the old man wants to beat them up. It's the most trivial thing — but it might cause a lot of trouble if he did. Damn! It means I ought to go back to Pokhra to-morrow, I suppose.'

'Curse them!' said Margaret. 'Why can't they agree among themselves?'

'I suppose it would leave me out of a job. Let me see, I could take a horse most of the way. It's Saturday, I think, isn't it? Then I could be there Monday evening and I should have Tuesday to try to settle it. If anything happens it will be on Wednesday.' Hugh was thinking as he talked.

Margaret said:

'What's it all about? Or is it too secret to tell me?'

'It's really complete nonsense. Last Wednesday the Congress people took a procession in front of the courts, where we had the party to celebrate victory, making what Bhola Nath calls great uproar and intolerable commotion. He's forbidden them to do it again and they've formally applied to him to open the gate, in what he says is a highly scurrilous and impertinent letter. So they're both committed up to the hilt. He wants to collect an army and stop them by force. The trouble is I've just had a letter to say the Viceroy is engaged in very delicate negotiations with Gandhi and we're to do nothing to provoke the Congress just at the moment. It's the usual sort of letter of course; "while on the one hand", do nothing, "on the other hand" don't let anyone else do anything. Nice easy instructions to follow. Well, I'm not going to lose my day's fishing. I'll come back and have it later. Would you like to stay and finish your picture?'

'No, I'll come with you if you can arrange so that it won't slow you up. But I'm afraid that pool won't look the same to me when we get back. It's a pity because I was liking that picture. Are you sure you must go? It does seem silly. What can you do?'

'I'm afraid I must. They're sure to make a fuss about it if Bhola Nath does beat them up and I can't very well stand aside and leave him to take the blame later. Your old friend Jodh Singh's going to be in Pokhra too, which will add to the excitement. The whole thing's absurdly trivial, but it's the kind of

thing that does happen in India. Both sides are committed to
something they don't really mind about much in itself, but it
becomes a life and death affair because prestige will suffer if
either gives way.'

'Well, if it doesn't matter, give way and have your day's
fishing,' said Margaret flippantly.

Hugh shook his head.

'Bhola Nath would think I'd let him down, and not a patwari
in the district would have any confidence in me. Nor would
I in them. They'd always be afraid to do anything without my
written orders for fear I should let them down again.'

'Where do we sleep to-morrow?' was all she asked.

Four stages could easily be done in two days with the help of
ponies, but it was hard on the porters. Still, it was done, and
Hugh was in Pokhra on Monday evening.

Meanwhile Jodh Singh had arrived and found the tracks of his
small female bear. Ram Parshad Singh had used considerable
skill in leading him to them. The local leader had heard enough
to realize that he had to deal with an enthusiast, a youthful
idealist to whom it would be no use to present the issue as it
appeared to himself, a move in the game, a simple matter of
profit and loss. On the other hand, Jodh Singh could hardly be
such a fool that he would think it a matter of burning public
importance that a small procession should have to make a detour
of a few hundred yards. Ram Parshad Singh acknowledged that
the detour in itself meant nothing.

'But it's a principle that's at stake,' he went on earnestly.
'This is a test case. Are the British really sincere when they say
they are going to give us freedom and show us how to become a
democracy? They talk of giving us power when we're fit for
it — but actually they look on every political meeting as a danger.
Why is there a patwari at every meeting we hold to take down
what we say and report it to the Deputy Commissioner? They
mean to cling to every vestige of power and suppress every sign

of awakening nationhood. That's why they oppose it. They don't want my brave volunteers, who are ready to face prison and torture rather than be slaves, to corrupt the toadies and lick-spittles who hang round the courts.'

Jodh Singh agreed eagerly. This was the language he had been brought up on and used himself. He accepted without demur Ram Parshad Singh's suggestion that he should take over the conduct of the affair, and he made several fiery speeches. People came to hear him. They came the first time out of curiosity, to see the grandson of old Kalyan Singh whom they had all known, and to thank him for what he had done in the matter of the corvee. They came a second time because they found his speech exciting. He spoke with warmth and obvious sincerity, and what he said was dramatic; he lowered his voice at critical points till every ear was strained to hear him, he raised it again to heighten and then release the tension, and their emotions rose and fell as he intended. He did not talk about fiscal policy; it was simple but emotional stuff about freedom and tyranny. He told them stories (mostly quite imaginary) of oppression when the Gurkhas ruled the land and the courage of those who had fought against them, of brave Garhwalis who charged to their death, with the name of their great temple on their lips in the war-cry of 'Jai Badri bisal!'; and then skilfully he transferred to the present the ardour he had roused. But though it was good entertainment and a fine purging of the emotions, it led very few to think it worth risking either a broken head or arrest by defying Bhola Nath's order and taking part in the procession which was to march past the court-rooms. To the practical peasant, there seemed no point in it.

Jodh Singh came away from his first meeting in a glow of triumph. He had carried his audience with him; they would follow him anywhere. Ram Parshad Singh fed his vanity with compliments and the other local men picked up the cue and said the same. But talks next day with secret sympathizers who might have been expected to come into the open were disappointing. And when at the end of his second meeting he asked for a show of hands and promises of attendance, only the little band of regulars, mostly briefless lawyers and unemployed, showed their hands, while the body of the meeting began to melt. A stream began to flow out from the meeting-ground through the narrow lane that led steeply up to the bazaar.

Fury and disappointment filled Jodh Singh's heart. He sickened with disgust at the cowardice of men and the strength of custom and tradition. He forgot for the moment everything but his fury; he wanted to hurt, to smash, to revenge himself on the world which had disappointed him. He clenched his fists; his eye circled the meeting and it fell on the patwari Uma Nand Naithani who was standing quiet and observant at the back of the audience.

'It is you who make men cowards,' he cried, 'you and the likes of you, Uma Nand, dogs who are ready to lick any trencher, who will sell their own brothers to the English for fourteen rupees a month. Once you take up this shameful bondage of government service, there is no infamy too base for you. How much money did you take in the matter of Dewan Singh Rawat's house? And how much for Vidya Dhar's shop? Corrupt and faithless, will you stop at nothing?'

There was a thrill of horror among the crowd. It was a shameless breach of convention to speak in public of such transactions. It had never been done before. The flow to the lane increased. No one could tell what might come next. The patwari himself stood frozen and motionless. If his superiors heard such talk, something would stick whether they believed it or not. He dared not look on either side of him at the faces of the crowd. He stared fixedly towards Jodh Singh.

Jodh Singh recovered himself. He announced that the meeting was over, but that there would be another to-morrow; and on the following day the procession would take place. Ram Parshad

Singh and his friends said nothing about his outburst against the patwari. They felt it was in rather bad taste and the less said about it the better. But secretly they were glad because Jodh Singh's stock had gone down.

When he heard Jodh Singh say that the meeting was over, Uma Nand the patwari drew himself together and took a long breath. He turned and went up the steep lane towards the bazaar with the others, but he was careful to catch no one's eye. He looked at the ground and walked slowly. He had next to go to the Deputy Commissioner's house to meet him on arrival and tell him the latest position. He was a fattish man, with a long body and short legs; his long face was broad at the temples and jaw so that it looked oblong and blockish at first sight, but there was nothing stupid about his wrinkled eyes or wide sad mouth. His skin was greyish over its brown, as though dusted over with flour. He walked with his shoulders bent, slowly, thinking of Jodh Singh.

He had felt unfriendly to the young man before he saw him. He had recently had a short spell of leave and had revisited his native village of Chopta in the south-east, where he had talked much with his cousin Ram Dat Naithani, the headman. Ram Dat had spoken bitterly of the insults heaped upon him by Jodh Singh, on him, the headman, in public, in the presence of his own villagers.

'They are all the same, these Rajputs,' Ram Dat had said. 'They hate all Brahmans. Sometimes they try to hide it, but it breaks out like this. He is not to be trusted. He is plotting something against us. If he stands to represent the district at Lucknow, he must not have our backing.'

Well, Ram Dat was clearly right. Jodh Singh must be bitterly hostile to all Brahmans, and particularly against the clan of Naithani. He had done the same thing at Pokhra as at Chopta, hurled abuse at the patwari in public, before the people of his own area. Uma Nand was filled with horror and anger. Dirt had been heaped on his head. He could not be happy until he had put things right and he could only do that by bringing disgrace upon the boy who had injured him. He would do that in good time. He would think later what he would do. Meanwhile, he must consider what he should say to the District Sahib. If he said nothing of the accusations made against him, he could be sure that someone else would, and though there would be no proof — . He stopped and cast back anxiously in his mind. He was not a particularly corrupt or extortionate man, but the pittance he received from government of fourteen rupees a month (that is one guinea or four dollars) was much what it had been in Mr. Bennett's time. And while the cost of living was ten times what it had been, it was no longer the rule for every peasant to pay the patwari a fraction of his crop, except in some isolated parts of the high hills where life had not changed. The patwari now had to make what he could on disputes and reports. Uma Nand liked to take something from each party and send in a report that was substantially accurate, and he had therefore the reputation of being an honest man and a good patwari. But sometimes of course one had a more difficult course to steer and could hardly help oneself. As easy to pass through the eye of a needle as to be an entirely honest patwari. No, his conscience was reasonably clear and whatever gossip might say about those particular cases, he was confident there could be no proof. There was always a fear — but it was better in any case to avert suspicion in advance by making a clear confession of what had been said. If the Tahsildar had been a hill-man, he would have gone to him first, in spite of his orders to be present when the sahib arrived.

He was coming up by the forest path now and in a few more minutes he was at the house. He did not have to wait long before Hugh and Margaret arrived and he was able to make his report at once. He said that if Jodh Singh led the procession past the courts he would have with him the dozen or so of Congress regulars and perhaps thirty or forty others, not more. He ended by telling of the attack on himself.

'And at the end, lord, he said much against me. He gave me very bad abuse. He said I had taken bribes. What am I to do, lord?'

Hugh thought this over. At last he said:

'You need do nothing. I shall make inquiries. If you have not taken bribes, you need fear nothing.'

'No, lord, never, never.'

'Then do not fear.'

Hugh went to his desk and wrote a letter to Jodh Singh:

'I hear you are in Pokhra and are planning to defy the Tahsildar's orders. I hope very much that before you do something which will certainly lead to violence, you will have a talk with me on the subject. Your party and the Government both wish to avoid violence, so let us talk it over before it is too late. A talk can do no harm and may do good. So please come and see me to-morrow morning.'

That night the moon rose late and in the darkness Uma Nand the patwari went to the house of Ram Parshad Singh. He tapped quietly on the door and would not say who he was or show his face until the Congressman in person came to see him. When he knew who it was Ram Parshad Singh smiled to himself. Things were going his way and he was amused. He led the patwari into a very small side-room in which there was just sufficient space for an empty string bed. Both had to stoop to get through the low door. They sat on the bed side by side, uncomfortably; the room was lighted only by the yellow light of a hurricane lantern; the walls and beams were of wood blackened with smoke. They talked of nothing for a few minutes. Then Uma Nand said:

'You were at the meeting. You heard what Jodh Singh said to me.'

'Yes, I heard. He is young and hot-tempered and impetuous,' said Ram Parshad Singh soothingly.

'I think perhaps he is not altogether a good person to stand for the district,' said Uma Nand.

'He is my colleague. As to who will represent the district' — a modest pause — 'That rests with the public.'

'Still, I think it would be better if he did not. Perhaps you think the same. And if at any time you need my help — ' Uma Nand left the sentence unfinished and rose to go. 'I do not wish him well.'

'Of course, of course, I understand,' said Ram Parshad Singh. He did understand perfectly, and he was more amused than ever. The bargain was sealed, as firmly as it could be between two people who distrusted each other thoroughly.

Next morning at breakfast Hugh remarked to Margaret:

'I've asked your friend Jodh Singh to come and see me this morning.'

'Oh, have you? Do send him along to me if I'm here. I'd like to talk to him for a few minutes. He seemed so young and full of life and enthusiasm.'

'Yes, I like him too, but he's riding for a fall, annoying people unnecessarily. He's really too young, years too young, for the position he's got himself into.'

'What shall you say to him?' she asked.

'There's not really much I can say to him, except ask him to be sensible. I don't expect much from that, though I have to make the attempt. But there's just one fly I shall put down on the water over his head very, very gently, just within reach, which may appeal to his impetuous nature. And if he takes it, we might avoid a scrap. Otherwise, we'll have to have one, but there couldn't be a worse moment.'

'What's your fly?'

He laughed.

'I'll tell you later.' He went to his desk.

She watched him go with a smile. He's really quite subtle about his work, she thought. Odd that he should be so unsubtle in other ways. Is it because he's never loved anyone but me? Or is it just that he's a different sort of man? I suppose most men are that kind really, but you don't find out about that kind till you've married one. How very different. Much more worthy and reputable; the kind of man the world admires; and so do I admire him. Only — . Come on, woman, see the cook; order stores by post for the next tour; go down to that new women's hospital; would there be time to see that unfortunate girl guide woman? I ought to try.

Jodh Singh read his letter with mixed feelings. His mood of triumph and mastery was already beginning to alternate with one of irritation and despair when he came to Pokhra. Most of the time he was full of elation at what he had done, but the wonder was beginning to wear off, the almost stunned feeling 'Can it really be true? Have I, Jodh Singh, done this, pulled off this unbelievable triumph?' And from time to time he was plunged in the blackest depths at the strength of the forces of custom and inertia with which he had to contend. When his enemy seemed to be that abstraction, the foreign government, then he could be joyful in the fight; but when it was his own countrymen with whose muddy spirits he had to contend, there was no strength or joy in him, and all things beneath the sun seemed to him futile and pointless. He was in such a mood of despair now and it was coupled with irritation because he knew he had failed himself and made things worse by his outburst of fury.

But his spirit lifted as he read the letter. He was the leader, and the District Sahib wanted to treat with him. He was Jodh Singh, who had ended the forced labour, and on whose word all men hung. And here was a problem to be considered. Should he go? It could do no harm and he would like to see that big man again. And it was true that the Mahatma said violence should be avoided. He would be glad if it could be avoided by the other side giving in. But he would not give way himself. Yes, he would go.

He started at once, pleased by the prospect of action. He thought of his last meeting with Hugh, and how nervous he had been, and how he had said over and over again to himself that he would not give in. Well, he would not be nervous this time and there was no question of giving in. But he would like to know what that big man would say to him. He knew that last time he had done Hugh an injustice. When he went to Lucknow, the Deputy Commissioner must have spoken for the district and advised the Government to give up the forced labour; it was a fair deduction that they would not have given it up against his advice and in any case a certain amount of what he had said in his letters was now known, having leaked out partly from the camp staff in the district and partly from relations in the secretariat staff at Lucknow. But why did that big man not say that he was on the side of the people? If only he had said that, the two of them could have made a plan together. Jodh Singh's heart swelled at the thought. He could have worked with that man happily. But he had not been trusted and brought into partnership. He could not forgive that. It was quite outside his training and experience to perceive, or even to understand if it had been pointed out to him, that Hugh would have regarded it as deeply disloyal to his superiors to express his own thoughts fully to Jodh Singh.

This time Hugh came straight to the point with a directness that appealed to Jodh Singh's temperament. He expanded the point he had made briefly in his letter. No one wanted violence. Why provoke it over so trivial a matter?

Jodh Singh said:

'But if it is trivial, why does the Government insist? I agree, Sir, it is nothing, this matter of the gate. But it is the attitude to our party that is important. If we are to be a nation, we must develop political consciousness.'

Hugh could not say what he thought about the difficulty of carrying out a policy conceived in Westminster by means of officials in India who disliked it, nor could he say that with him the main consideration was that he must back up the Tahsildar. He said:

'We cannot get on with our work and administer the law if there is so much noise in front of the courts that we cannot hear what the witnesses say.'

'But it is only for a few minutes once a week; that cannot make any difference.'

'It would not make much difference if it was only that. But if we let one party and one procession through, we should have to let the others. We couldn't discriminate. And it wouldn't end with processions. The next thing would be meetings.'

'But you already discriminate. You let a government procession go through, to celebrate the end of a war into which we were forced without the will of the people being consulted.'

So it went on. They could get no further without one or the other giving way, and since neither had any such intention, no progress was made. At last Hugh said:

'Well, I see it's no use trying to make you change your plans. But about your future, if you will allow me to talk about it. I still think you could be doing far more valuable work for the district if you would turn to something constructive. I know you think politics must come first, but you could talk politics at the same time and they'd listen to you if you had something practical to talk about. Last time we talked I suggested you could help the district over forests; but there are lots of other things if that doesn't appeal to you. I'm sure the system of agriculture here could be improved if someone would really do some work on it. Or teach the villager some sideline that would pay him, such as bee-keeping. And look at all the work that could be done on primary education.'

'It is very bad,' agreed Jodh Singh.

'Now let me be frank with you,' said Hugh. 'You people want India to be free and manage her own affairs at once, but what sort of a showing do you make at managing a district, let alone a country? The deputy commissioners may not have been enthusiasts for education but they did keep roofs on the schools and see that the teachers were paid. How many schools are there that are falling down and how many teachers are there who are more than six months in arrears with their pay, now that the district board has taken them over? You could become a member of the District Board and make education your special subject. They'd make you chairman of the education sub-committee. You could do immense good. But it'd be real work, not just talking about national consciousness and freedom and tyranny, if you'll forgive me for putting it like that.'

He spoke with so cheerful and friendly an air that Jodh Singh could not be hurt. He went on:

'Or if it's social reform — what about the Doms? What are they but serfs? They're a feudal survival if you like. Your own Mahatma talks about helping the depressed, but no one else does anything about them. Which of your Congressmen here would stir a finger to help them? Would you dare to go and get Mangi Das, their leader, here, and put him at the head of your procession to-morrow riding on a horse? Of course you wouldn't. But that's something you could do at once, to-day, and it's something that only you can do, yourselves; I can't help in that, nor can any British government. You must do it. But you won't. No, Jodh Singh, I'll believe in your new India when I see you getting down to something practical.'

He stood up:

'Forgive me my long lecture. Will you come and speak to my wife? She'd be glad to see you again.'

'There is nothing to forgive, Sir. I am very thankful for your advice. It is very good, but I am not sure it is right for me. I must think more about it. Thank you very much; I am very thankful.'

They went together to the next room, where Margaret was

137

making out a list of stores. They both thought how lovely she looked, tall and slim, in a tweed riding coat and Jodhpurs, a dove-grey shirt, an emerald tie. Hugh left them and went back to see other visitors. Jodh Singh was desperately shy, but he thawed as she talked to him about the beauty she loved in the hills and showed him some sketches she had made near his home in the upper district. She told him too about the women's hospital she was going to visit, and the pathetic shortage of stores and equipment. There was not much he could say to her, because they had so little common ground. He thought the poverty of the hospital a reproach to the Government and therefore to every English person; she could only see the indifference of everyone about her, the fact that no one would help with gifts, or time, or interest. She would have said it was a reproach to every Indian. But each was conscious of the other's liking. He was shy because he did not know how long to stay or how to go; she perceived his embarrassment and at last said she must say good-bye as she had to go to the hospital. He left her in a mood of sadness. How could he find a wife like her among his own people, he asked himself. I shall always remember her and think more kindly of the English, he thought. She was kind to me, she liked me.

He was halfway down the hill before it occurred to him that he had no business to be thinking of a wife, for to-morrow night he would be in prison. He was overcome with self-pity and sat down on the boundary wall of the Deputy Commissioner's forest to contemplate his own heroism and wretchedness. If only there was someone near who loved him and understood him and would be sorry for him. But he was alone, for his mother did not understand him, and as for the mem-sahib—he used the word to himself with sarcasm—she would be sorry for him for a minute, but it would not make her lose her sleep. She must look very beautiful when she was asleep. He thought of her husband. He shook himself; he must think about other things.

It had been a very unprofitable talk with her husband. He had not got much there. But there was something in what he had said at the end. It is true that we are unpractical, visionaries, dreamers, he thought. It is because we put the spirit first, and these Europeans always think of the material. That is why they are our masters, but the things of the spirit are more important, and there they are children. But there was much in what he had said about the Doms. It is true that only we can help them. It would be a great thing, to make it my next mission to help the Doms. It was the teaching of the Mahatma. It would show her husband how wrong he was to despise Indians.

But it is too big for me, he thought in another wave of depression. There would be no one on my side. No one. No help anywhere. It was no use. His eyes travelled across forty miles of limpid sun-filled air to the square snowy tower of Chaukamba, the crown-shaped peak that stands above Badrinath and is called that name by Europeans. The home of the gods. His eyes travelled from peak to peak; thought left him; he felt more calm.

A man trudging outwards from Pokhra with a load on his back stopped at the top of the hill for a rest. He leaned back and let the weight of his load come on the wall, lowered himself gradually till he was sitting on top of the bank that rose to the wall's foot, and then allowed the load to slide down until it was resting on the bank. He looked up at Jodh Singh, joined his hands as if in prayer as a sign of respect for his sophisticated clothes and style of haircut, and said:

'Maharaj!'

Jodh Singh was miles away in the home of the gods. He muttered something impatiently, but the man with the burden was not to be deterred. He told with easy garrulity how he had come to Pokhra to pay the land revenue for his elder brother the headman who was sick and whose son was still small; he recounted the things he had bought for his friends and relations and the prices he had paid, and compared present prices with those before the war. Then he asked Jodh Singh who he was and what he did for his living and whether he was married and had any children.

'I am Jodh Singh Rawat, son of Govind Singh son of Kalyan Singh.' The man with the burden scrambled to his feet.

'Jodh Singh that stopped the forced labour?' he cried. 'Maharaj!' And he made a sweeping gesture of obeisance as though to touch the ground at Jodh Singh's feet.

It was more than enough to restore Jodh Singh's confidence. He came down from the clouds and talked to his admirer for a few minutes. Then he stood up to go. He looked again at the snowy crown of Chaukamba and muttered aloud the war-cry which he had invented for his Garhwali heroes in the Gurkha wars:

'Jai Badri Bisal!'

Yes, he thought, I will do it. I am Jodh Singh and I can do it. I will raise the name of the Doms and end their serfdom. I will show her husband that we can do something practical.

He did not delay but went straight down through the little town to the Domana where the Doms lived. He asked for Mangi Das, found him, and took an instant dislike to his dark skin, insolent manner and coarse appearance. However, he had made up his mind and there was no going back. He wasted no words but told Mangi Das that he was determined to carry out the wishes of the Mahatma and treat the Doms as brothers. He would begin by asking Mangi Das to lead his procession to-morrow.

'On a horse?' asked Mangi Das. He was lying on a string bed and did not rise but propped himself up on an elbow. The burning grievance with his community was that the Brahmans and Rajputs forbade the bridegroom to ride on a horse or the bride to go in a litter at their weddings.

Jodh Singh hesitated. Then:

'Yes,' he said firmly, 'on a horse. As far as the gate, of course. You'll have to get off at the gate. But the horse can be led round.'

Mangi Das reflected. He had become a leader because he was clever and insolent and had served in a labour corps during the war, but the root principle of his life was laziness. This might involve trouble and going to prison. He could avoid blows by giving himself up without resistance. He might avoid prison by saying he was only a Dom and knew no better. And in any case, he knew about prison, and there was plenty of food there, almost as much as in the army. And to have been in prison for one's politics gave one a distinct cachet. To ride on a horse at the head of a procession would be a great stroke, establish him firmly as a leader.

'Yes,' he said. 'I'll be there.'

Jodh Singh looked at his wrist-watch; he really did want to know the time, but there was also a consciousness that the movement would impress Mangi Das. He had to meet Ram Parshad Singh and his committee and would be late unless he was quick.

When he told the committee that Mangi Das was to ride at the head of the procession, they looked down their noses. Ram Parshad Singh exulted; it was all going far better than he had hoped and this silly boy was making every possible mistake. But his face was serious and deferential as he said:

'But are you sure that would not be a mistake? I know it is the teaching of the Mahatma that we should regard these people as brothers, but we have had no official orders from the party.[1] And here in this district which is so backward politically — we have so much to contend with. It will only turn people away. But of course it is the Mahatma's teaching.'

Jodh Singh flared up. This was time-serving; these mean-souled calculations brought the party into disrepute. They must do what was right, fearlessly.

[1] The Congress party did tackle this issue fifteen years later, and lost some ground in the district thereby.

Ram Parshad Singh paid a tribute to these high ideals and said that of course Jodh Singh was the leader. The other members of the committee were sullen; they did not like Doms, who were dirty and black and servile, and least of all did they like Mangi Das, who was insolent instead of servile; and they were sure this new move would alienate the public. But Jodh Singh had made up his mind; opposition merely infuriated him, and Ram Parshad Singh, while outwardly gently demurring, fanned the flame of his resolve.

Jodh Singh held another meeting that afternoon. The attendance to start with was poorer than at any he had yet held; it grew less and less when he began to talk about making brothers of the Doms. He came away with his chin up, determined to go on, but his boy's heart was once again in the depths. He knew it was going to be a failure.

Next day, at the gathering point for the procession that was to defy the Tahsildar, there were present Jodh Singh, Mangi Das with his horse, a handful of the Congress regulars and some twenty or thirty others who had come out of curiosity. A small boy brought a letter written by Ram Parshad Singh's schoolgirl daughter to say her father was sick with fever and could not come and so she was writing for her mother. Jodh Singh read it with a bitter smile. He knew what that meant. He began to arrange his procession.

When they saw that Jodh Singh was persisting in his intention of putting Mangi Das in front on a horse, the spectators began to melt away and the Congressmen became unaccountably shy. They found every kind of excuse. The procession that eventually reached the gate consisted of Mangi Das on his horse and Jodh Singh holding the bridle, his heart bursting, but his head still high. There was a crowd of small boys and loafers following to see what would happen, but they kept at a distance to show they were not part of the procession.

In silence Mangi Das dismounted and they climbed the gate

together. Together they walked in silence across the court enclosure to the gate on the other side. A way was left for them. Litigants, spectators, stamp vendors, onlookers, let them pass and laughed. Bhola Nath and his army stood on the veranda to watch, let them pass and laughed.

'Two does not make an unlawful assembly,' cried Bhola Nath. 'Let them go.'

So the sticks and handcuffs were idle and nothing happened to mar the negotiations between the Viceroy and Mr. Gandhi. Mangi Das enjoyed it all. He had seen from the start that with only the two of them in it there was no danger of blows or prison and his fears had gone. And it was amusing to be attended by a Rajput and walk by his side. He grinned insolently at the crowd.

Jodh Singh did not let a muscle of his face move but before he reached the second gate, big tears were forming one by one and rolling down his stony cheeks. Once over the gate, he turned in a fury on Mangi Das:

'Take that grin off your face! Get out of my sight! I never want to see you again.'

Then he ran as fast as he could to his lodging and burst into a storm of weeping. If only crying could help! There was no one who could help him. He was all alone.

'Roll up the bedding and everything inside. We are going at once,' he said to the cousin from Bantok as soon as the fit began to abate.

'Where to?' asked the cousin.

'North, north, to the high hills,' cried Jodh Singh. 'I don't know where. Yes, I do know, to Bantok. Yes, to Bantok.'

VI

IT was the sight of his cousin's face that made Bantok occur to the conscious part of Jodh Singh's mind, but the will to go which responded immediately to that slight stimulus came from something very deep indeed. It was only as a boy that he had been there and his memories of the place were vague. He had still been small when Govind Singh had built his fine new house to the south of the river and that was the home he remembered. He had not gone back to Bantok for the same reason that had made his father desert the place, because of that contempt for peasant mentality and peasant habits which usually colours the conscious mind of anyone of peasant stock who has recently found another way of life. But when he was hurt it was the place to go; it was the hole to which the wounded animal drags itself, to lick the rankling part in silence. No one would laugh at him there.

And he was hurt, badly hurt. He was not quite sure whether or not the Englishman had deliberately put into his mind the thought of helping the Doms in the hope that he would act on it and wreck his plans. Most of the time he felt sure that this had been the intention and then he was very bitter in his mind against the man he thought of as her husband. On the other hand, he was quite sure that Ram Parshad Singh had deliberately kept away from the fiasco and had rejoiced at his discomfiture. Therefore, he was bitter also against Ram Parshad Singh and against the Congressmen and the people of Pokhra; he raged against them because they were cynical and selfish and greedy. But his thoughts came back again and again to his own failure, his own lack of control. He had been ruled by his emotions. He ought not to have given way to bad temper and abused the patwari; he should not have given way to the wave of feeling that had made him decide to take up the case of the Doms. He ought to have considered the whole question carefully and rationally, but no, it had all been emotion. First he had been depressed and felt he could not do it; then a chance meeting with a stranger had filled him with confidence and he had committed himself immediately to Mangi Das without consulting anyone else first. He was not old enough to be a leader; he had failed and spoilt everything; he kept coming back to the thought, to torture himself as one presses with the tongue on an aching tooth. It was no use; he had failed himself by giving way to emotion and the people of this world had planned and plotted and conspired together against him, and the world had been too strong for him. Somewhere to lick his wounds where no one would laugh at him, that was his need.

When he could for a few moments get his mind away from its twofold bitterness, against himself and against the world, he reasoned that if he was ever to take up his work again, he ought to know more than he did know about the peasants of the district and their way of life; and that there was no better place to learn about them than the homestead from which he drew his being. But this was his reasoning; his reasons were quite another matter.

It was towards the end of March when he left Pokhra and the deep pools in the river still glowed a tender lucid green, the rapids still flashed silver. Soon the snows would begin to melt and the water to curdle with ice-ground dust, the torrent rise till the black rocks were hidden in a milky grey-green smother, but in March there was still the colour and beauty of winter. Jodh Singh marched steadily for ten days. He would not talk at meetings, he would hardly speak to the headmen of the villages through which he passed. His cousin had to make excuses for him, to explain that he was sick and tired. He would not even stop at his own home at Gadoli, but went straight past it to Bantok. He crossed the perilous bridge, unchanged since

Mr. Bennett's time, on the eighth day, and very early on the
eleventh he reached the homestead where his father and grandfather and his fathers' fathers had been born.

It was not long before he tired of living in the low smoky
cabins of the homestead. He was used to a diet that to a European
would have seemed simple and monotonous, but here there was
not even rice, only flat thick pancakes made from coarse millet
flour, or occasionally from barley as a treat, eaten sometimes
with porridge and sometimes with potatoes. There was meat on
feast-days only; and there was honey, mixed with grubs and wax
and bees' legs, such as a bear might eat; and sour buttery cheese.
He missed the rice and the rich spices to which he had become
used, but he could put up with the coarse simple food. What he
did dislike was the dirt and the communal life, a whole family
herded together into a tiny room. There were neither chimneys
nor windows and the smoke found what egress it could, by
leaks and cracks or in the day-time by the open door. There
were dungheaps within a few feet of the doors of the cabins,
and when it rained, the water that trickled under the door and
through the cabin was impregnated with farmyard manure.
Until the regular rains began, Jodh Singh decided to live out,
building a hut of leaves as a protection against occasional
thunderstorms.

There was practically no level ground except the fields of the
upper and lower farms, but he set out to look round the edges
of the crops for somewhere flat enough for a hut. The thin
straggly barley was not yet cut in the lower fields and would not
ripen in the upper for a month; he found the place he wanted in
the upper farm at the top of the bluff which made one side of the
narrow place where his grandfather had killed the bear. There
was a spring in the woods above and a stream ran down
through the narrow place which his kinsmen told him never
failed. The top of the bluff ran out into a flat table of rock ten
yards square; there was a sparse covering of grass and pine-

needles, but you came to the rock in an inch or two inches and so it had never been cultivated. One great pine had thrust its roots deep into crevices in the rock and drew its nourishment from some hidden source.

Jodh Singh and his servant-cousin cut a forked stick from the forest and prodded about near the pine till they found a pocket of earth in which they could make it stand upright. Then they lashed a pole from that to the pine and with that as the ridge of their roof they made a thatched hut that would keep out any but the heaviest rain. Autaru, the cousin — there are very few names in Garhwal and they are repeated from generation to generation — was good at this, for he had been brought up at Bantok and was well used to making such huts in the high pastures where they took the sheep and goats in the rains.

It was cold up there in April. There was still snow in the hollows, where there were clusters of pink and white saxifrage, like dwarf spires of horse-chestnut bloom on plump red stems, and here and there little purple primroses and earth-loving violets. The oak was only just putting out new leaves, tiny crumpled buds of pink and bronze and yellow. But the sun shone by day and at night they made huge bonfires from the inexhaustible forest above them. To Autaru it was madness, for they might have been warm in the smoky cabins a thousand feet below them; but Jodh Singh was happy, released from the bitterness that preyed on him, the fear of scorn and laughter. His cousins in the homestead treated him with deference, almost with reverence, for he had escaped from the hard bondage of the daily life that bound them, he was educated, a great man. But he did not see much of them, for when the work of building the hut was finished, he explored the forests by himself, coming back in the evening to the bonfire and the food Autaru had cooked.

In the mornings, when the water had been fetched and the fire lighted and the breakfast eaten, he would sit gazing across the river at the great hillside opposite. The river had begun to rise and the water was curdling to the milky green of summer; he could hear its roar above the silence of hill and forest; from here it was a little snaky streak of greyish-green showing here and there between the gorges. Across the river, the hill rose steeply at first, in rocky bluff or precipice or a velvet green side of grass. Then the slope grew less and there were villages and cultivation; brown fields where there would soon be rice, green fields of barley yellowing to the harvest. And above the fields, the forest stretching up to the sky-line, pouring down into the corries, between the fields, wherever the ground was too steep for terraces.

There was a great contrast between his own hillside and that other across the river. Here there was essential silence, and the noise of the river and the breath of the pines; the tiny evidence of man was an intrusion. Over there, man was everywhere, it was the forest which thrust down and intruded among the fields. But that world of men and defeat and laughter that hurt, was a long way from Jodh Singh in his eyrie, with the blue smoke of the fire curling up in the still morning air and the pines about him throwing back the sunlight from a million dancing needles.

Jodh Singh's was not a nature that could be idle long. After the work of making the hut and the first few days of solitary rambling and exploration, he made two decisions. First of all, he would not be beaten; he would not give up; he would go back to the world of men; he would be a leader and would represent the district in Lucknow; but before that he would go on to the District Board and he would work for a practical end as well as educating the people to want the nationhood that was their right. But not just yet; he would spend the summer here in Bantok and get to know the way of life here in the lonely homestead, and he would grow older, and give people time to forget his defeat at Pokhra. And perhaps he would forget it himself. The second decision was to build a house for him-

self here, on this rocky bluff, a house that would be all his own
and that he could come back to when the world of men sickened
him. And some day, but perhaps not yet, he would marry and
there would be a wife and a son to come back to. This idea of
marriage was only a vague intention. He knew that he needed
a wife, but where could he find a wife who was fit for him? For
was he not Jodh Singh, who was different from other people and
would one day be a great leader? He had met no educated girl
of his own people; he did not want to marry a peasant girl, a
cutter of grass and gatherer of sticks. He put the idea away as
something to be thought of later.

As soon as he had made up his mind about the house he wrote
to his uncle for money and carpenters and masons. Here in
Bantok they could build a house of a kind, but they could not
afford to be specialists in anything and it would be a rough affair
indeed; in any case, they were busy just now with the spring
harvest. He sent off Autaru with the letter, and while he was
away, busied himself with planning his house and marking out
the foundations; when this was more or less to his liking, he
set to work to make huts for the carpenters and masons.

The money-lending uncle was disturbed by the idea of building a new house at Bantok when there was already a house big
enough for everyone at Gadoli. He feared that Jodh Singh would
be a serious embarrassment to him and business was already not
so good as it had been in the days when Govind Singh was alive.
He considered whether it would not be a wise move now to
separate from Jodh Singh and partition the family fortunes which
were all held in common. But he had too much money out; he
could not find Jodh Singh's share if there was a partition. If it
were not for that bridge, he would go to the boy and try to make
him see reason. But he did not like the thought of crossing the
bridge, so instead he wrote a letter which he hoped would
dissuade Jodh Singh from the plan.

It brought Jodh Singh to Gadoli in a fury. He did the journey in less than three days; when he returned he took with him the money and the men he wanted. His energy and determination would have overcome his uncle's timidity and lethargy in most circumstances and he did not have much difficulty on this occasion because he had the whip hand. He could always demand a partition and his uncle dared not face one.

The days spent in building the house were very happy. It was warmer now and Jodh Singh, Autaru, and the four workmen camped together in their leafy huts in luxury. Autaru cooked and kept house for everyone. Jodh Singh made plans and altered them, but no one was irritated or minded how often he changed his mind; he learnt too, to shape a block of stone or a beam in the rough and he worked hard with the men. In the evening he joined them round the fire and they told stories, wonderful stories told simply, as a child tells them, without detail or emotion, but with an occasional vivid touch.

' — And his wife said to him: "I know you have the power to turn yourself into a panther. Let me see you do it." And he said "No", because he did not know what he was doing when he was a panther and he might hurt her. But she worried him to do it, and at last she worried him so often and so much that he took her out into the forest and told her to climb a tree to be safe, and watch. And then he changed himself into a panther. And she watched from the tree and saw him. And the panther saw the woman in the tree and climbed the tree after her. And it killed the woman and ate her up. And then it changed back into a man. And he did not know what he had done. And he looked for the woman everywhere, but could not find her. So he went back to the village and said he had lost his wife in the forest. And they came with him to look for her. And they found what was left of her body and they knew the man had turned into a panther and killed her, but he did not know what he had done. . . .'

They were happy days, and Jodh Singh was a boy again,

laughing and working and forgetting that people had laughed at
him. But the rains came before the house was finished, and they
were miserable in their leaf huts, and the masons could not make
mortar and the carpenters did not like to work with damp wood.
So the workmen went back to Gadoli, promising to come again
in the autumn and finish the job, and Jodh Singh and Autaru
went up with their kinsmen to the high pastures with the sheep
and goats.

They climbed up through the forest, winding about the line
of the stream that ran past the homestead, making a path as they
went, for last year's tracks had been buried for eight months and
the grass had sprung up under the snow. Blue pine gave way to
silver birch and spruce and silver fir and then to creeping rhododendron, with great blooms of purple and creamy white and
rose-pink. The slope grew less and the stream which had poured
over the boulders and mantled the cliffs with sheets of spray ran
more gently, a brook of clear water hurrying over brown
pebbles, fringed with rushes and fern. Then they were out,
above the trees, on grassy golden fells, with streaks of snow still
lying in the corries, and bridges of snow across the streams. The
flowers had burst into their first radiance, dwarf iris carpeting the
ground in sheets; blood-red anemones; primulas pale as lady's-
smock; potentillas, scarlet, white and purple; and great clusters
of the flowering thistle, five feet high, a cathedral spire of blossom, pink and white and gold. In the miles and miles of high
pasture, there were millions of flowers and butterflies of which
perhaps one in a thousand would ever be seen by the eye of man
or beast, surging upwards to life in a prodigal gaiety that proceeded from sheer joy in creation, the mood in which the stars
sang together. The grass was knee-deep and every armful was
rich in colour and scent, a heavy spicy fragrance. Jodh Singh
knelt and buried his face in it. When he stood up, he was dizzy,
his head swam in circles, his throat was constricted. One of his
kinsmen caught his arm:

'It is the drunkenness,' he said. 'It comes from the scent of the flowers. Sit down by a rock and rest. There will be pain in your head to-night and again to-morrow, but after that you will get used to it.'

In one place up there in the high alps there was a low cliff of grey stone, with the heavenly blue of the Himalayan poppy growing here and there in the crevices. Beneath this cliff were caves, not deep, but sheltered from rain and wind, with encircling walls built to keep off wild beasts and to throw back the warmth of the fire; it was here that the colony from Bantok made their headquarters. Here they sat at night with the sheep huddled round them, telling stories of ghosts and gods and godlings and warlocks who turned at night into bears or panthers. The fire shone back from the eyes of the sheep; it flickered on the ruddy faces of the men, their long hair hanging out from under round caps of unbleached wool. Men and sheep alike smelt of damp wool, and there was the raw bitter smell of wood-smoke, the drip of water outside in the mist, and the small sounds of the sheep stamping or changing their ground.

In the day-time, Jodh Singh wandered about with the sheep and learnt their ways. Sometimes the whole day there was white mist in wreaths swirling in the hollows and round the rocks, rain and mist and the sound of running water and the squelch of fine tussocky grass under the feet. The men would come back to the caves with the moisture standing on every hair of their woollen blankets like tiny diamonds, just as it stood in the sheep's wool, for the wool of the blankets held the natural grease of the sheep and kept out the rain. Sometimes in the early morning the sky was clear, the sun shone, and then you could gaze away to the south towards the plains, over ridge on scalloped ridge, hill and peak and forest, the dark green of the nearer hills melting to indigo blue, and then fading, fainter, to the smoky blue of the distance. Or you could look north to the icy majesty of Dunagiri and Nilkanta's graceful spire of silver, or east to the long ice slopes and snowfields of Nanda Devi and Trisul, or west to the square snowy crown of Chaukamba. They stood waiting, glacier, peak and snowfield, glittering in the diamond sun, icy, joyful, remote.

As the day grew older, clouds would billow up and their shadows play across the blue hills to the south; they would pile themselves in mountains of white radiance. Evening would stain them angry red, with long jagged bars of grey against the crimson, touches of glowing gold, orange and the pink of a flamingo's breast. And when the splendour died, the bloom would linger on peak and snowfield till it was lost in the enveloping night.

Jodh Singh was happy, he was a boy, he forgot his cares and bitterness. But it began to grow cold at nights as the rain grew less frequent and when the first frosts came at the beginning of September the men and sheep moved down again to Bantok. Jodh Singh sent Autaru to Gadoli to make sure the workmen returned and when they came, he finished building his house. Early in October, he went to Gadoli, planning to come back to Bantok again in the summer.

His uncle met him at Gadoli with a suggestion. Jodh Singh's mother had been worrying the old man to arrange her son's marriage. He did not feel he could do anything in the matter without his nephew's consent, but was it not time he married? He must have a son and now he was a man ripe for marrying. If Jodh Singh agreed, there was the daughter of a lawyer from Chamoli who had been to a middle school and knew a little English. Secretly he thought that a wife would be a steadying influence that was badly needed.

Jodh Singh felt that the world had come upon him again, at once. It had sprung on him the moment he showed it his face. He did not want a wife of his own people, for none of them were fit for him. If his father had been living and had been secure in a comfortable post, something better than a patwari, he might have been able to arrange a marriage with an educated girl from the city of Dehra Dun, someone who might have been a companion, but by himself he could do nothing. A wife who was beautiful, who could talk and paint and think, like the Deputy Commissioner's wife — but it was no good dreaming of any such thing. It is because of the foreign government that our women are so backward, he thought.

A sick numbness filled him at the grip of the world. It was no good, he must take what was offered. He agreed. His uncle could arrange what he liked. He would be there on the day. Meanwhile, he was off to wander about the district, to talk to the villagers about politics, to find out what their schools were like and to see what could be done to improve them.

He let it be known that he was going to stand for the District Board, and went into the villages in the neighbourhood. He was greeted everywhere with honour and gratitude for what he had done in the matter of the corvee. His failure at Pokhra had hardly been heard of here, and what they had heard meant nothing to peasants who had not been there. His confidence began to return.

He went through the ceremonies of his marriage and the beginning of his married life with indifference. His wife could read and write Hindi; she knew a little English of the standard of 'The cat sat on the mat'. She was a prodigy of female learning for Upper Garhwal but she had never been ten miles from her home and she had no understanding of the ideas in Jodh Singh's mind. She was shy in his presence and could not talk to him, but she was ready to love him and worship him as a Hindu wife should do. She was sturdy and not uncomely; she had the smooth skin and firm muscles of youth and health; he took her as he took his food and left her without regret. She made no impression on his mind. He went away to his self-appointed work. She could stay at Gadoli for the present; in the summer, unless she was expecting a child, she should go to Bantok and

start to keep house there. She might as well learn to cut grass
and gather sticks, he thought bitterly; she was fit for nothing else.

It was about the time that Jodh Singh came back to Gadoli
from Bantok that the panther began to kill in the river valley.
There were always a dozen ordinary panthers, of course, up and
down this stretch of the river, but they confined their diet as a
rule to wild animals, the barking deer, the little chamois or a
young pig, with an occasional goat or dog. But this was no
ordinary panther.

The first news came from a village called Bhainswara, twenty
miles from Gadoli, and it so happened that Jodh Singh was in
the village that night. One Deb Singh, a young peasant on an
isolated homestead above the village, had just married, and he
felt that with an extra pair of arms to cut grass from the forest
and help in the fields, he could manage to increase his stock by
another bullock. He knew the beast he wanted, in a village two
miles below Bhainswara, and one day early in November he
determined to go to see the owner and bring off the deal. After
the morning meal he said good-bye to his wife and sent her up
into the forest to bring back a bundle of grass. He thought of
her with pleasure as he went down the hillside with the easy gait
of the hill-man, loose at knees and ankles. She pleased him well,
for she was young and strong, smooth of skin and firm of muscle
and a child still who could laugh and play with childish things.
She was not shy with him. She laughed much, and when she
laughed there was a dimple in her cheeks, below the high cheek-
bones and slightly slanting eyes, a broad comely merry little
face. He had given her father three hundred rupees. Deb Singh
was very happy and he sang as he went down the hill, at the
top of his voice, a song with few words, a long and rather
mournful cadence, though he was singing for joy. He had done
his business by midday, but he sat some time smoking and talking with the seller and it was towards evening when he got back
to his own little homestead. Sita Devi was not back yet and he

was rather surprised, but he went about the work of the farm near at hand and did not trouble his mind till darkness began to fall. Then he became anxious; she would not fall, but she might have met a snake or a bear. He took a torch and went up the hill, but it was no use, for she might have taken any of a dozen branching cattle tracks. He came back without her and spent an anxious night; as soon as it was light, he went down to the village to get help. Jodh Singh had slept that night in the village and he came with the rescue party.

It was the vultures that told them where she was, what was left of her. Deb Singh wept bitterly. A panther had killed her, there was no doubt of that. They found blood on the path, for he had attacked her in the open, she had not stumbled on him in the grass by accident. He had dragged her up the hill into a thicket to make his meal. It was the deliberate murder of a man-eater, not the panic-stricken act of a beast suddenly disturbed.

Jodh Singh was moved by Deb Singh's grief and he determined to have revenge on the panther. He would sit up for it over a goat. He borrowed a double-barrelled muzzle-loader from the headman and made himself a platform of a few sticks in a tree near the place where the body had been found. He tied a live goat to a stump in a glade through which a cattle-path led and settled down to wait. But he was by temperament the worst person in the world for such a vigil. He was impatient and ex-citable; every movement of a bird, every falling leaf, was a panther; his hands would grow wet with excitement and his breath come faster. And he was physically restless and un-disciplined; he could not keep still when his leg was pricking where the blood was checked. There was never half an hour when his tree did not shake and the leaves chatter with a change of position. After two sleepless and tiring nights, he gave up. He put in one good night's sleep and then he resumed his wan-derings and moved on.

On the fourth night, the panther killed again, on the outskirts of a village ten miles away. This time the victim was a man; he had spent too long smoking with a neighbour before he went to fetch home the cattle. His wife had just been delivered of a child or she would have gone, but to-night he had to do it and he had forgotten until it was late. It was dusk when he passed the big rock outside the village and he got no further. The panther must have been on top of the rock; it sprang on him as he came out from the rock's protection, and dragged him up the hillside into the scrub. The frightened cattle ran on into the village and clustered round the shed. His wife heard them and managed to get up; when she saw they had come home without their master, she called the neighbours. They went out along the path towards the grazing ground with torches, but they did not go very far. They had heard of Sita Devi's death and no one would leave the path and venture into the scrub.

After that there was terror in the valley. The panther went from village to village; he never killed twice running in the same area; he seldom came back to a kill. For one thing the kill was seldom there if it was a human being, the relations being scrupulous to burn what remained and to throw the ashes in the river. And it was usually a human being, although he did not keep himself exclusively to man but would occasionally take a goat, a dog, or even a cow. Most often it was a woman, for it was the women who brought home the cattle and fetched the grass, and the kills were made in lonely places near the forest, not in the fields where the men did their ploughing. But the panther was very bold and its tracks were often found in the morning in the farmyard muck in front of the houses. Every three or four days the story would run up and down the valley of a fresh killing, ten, twenty or thirty miles from the last. Thirty miles up-stream from Gadoli, thirty miles down, in a wide belt from the river below to the forest above, men made for their homes before twilight and slept with barred doors and every living thing shut safely within.

Hugh Upton came up from Pokhra and spent some time in pursuit of the beast, until he had to move on to other parts of the district. Before he left, he wrote to men well known as good shots and keen followers of wild beasts, and asked them to take up where he left off. Several came at different times, but it was no use. They sat up over carcasses of animals and even over a human corpse if the relations could be persuaded to leave it; but the panther never came near a guarded kill. They lost their sleep and stiffened their limbs over live baits, but he seemed to know they were there. There are no hunting people in the hills and there was no one to track him, even if it had been possible in that precipitous country. They tried poison, but the panther seldom came back to a kill and when he did, he seemed to know that poison was there. Only once did he eat of the poisoned carcass of a cow and then, before he had taken ten paces from it, he vomited up every fragment he had swallowed and was none the worse.

The villagers baited their clumsy wooden drop-traps for him with live dogs, but he would not go near them. Hugh tried spring traps. But here too there was the difficulty that relations would not leave out a human corpse a second night, while goats and cows were rare victims and in any case were seldom revisited. A dozen times the big steel traps were cunningly hidden in grass and leaves; anxious hours were spent to make sure nothing was left that would betray them to eye or even nose, although the panther is almost without the sense of smell; but a dozen times, the work went for nothing, because next morning the tale would come in of a fresh kill twenty miles away. Three or four times the panther came to a trap, but he seemed to know it was there and they would find from his tracks that he had walked once round it and made off. Once and once only he stepped within the steel circle. That day there were half a dozen spring traps set on every approach and on the carcass itself. It did not seem possible for anything bigger than a cat to touch the meat and escape. In the night there was a sudden scream of fury, horrible to hear, yet the morning party of inspection found only one trap sprung, and that at first sight empty. The dust showed that the panther had leapt lightly over the traps and stepped delicately to his meal as though he had known where every spring lay; he had torn a few mouthfuls only, as if not in hunger and with the sole object of showing his scorn for men; but when he turned to go he had sprung one trap and left his toe in it. There was a blood track which they were able to follow with great trouble and patience for about a mile before it was lost, and this showed that he had travelled very fast, in great bounds.

Further news soon came in of that night when he lost a toe. In his fury he had gone through village after village, travelling thirty miles before dawn, going right up to the houses in his search for something on which he could be revenged. But every man and animal was behind barred doors, except in one village. There a traveller passing through had left the dozen goats he was driving in a pen below a leaning rock on the outskirts of the village. He could find nowhere else to put them and had not dared to stay with them. The panther had come through that village. He had sprung into the pen and slain them all. He had not eaten. The torn bodies lay there as witness of his rage.

As the tale of his killings grew, the story of his cunning and boldness passed from mouth to mouth. He seemed to have more than natural cunning, and whenever two men sat down to smoke and gossip, heads shook and the same word was spoken. He was more than a beast. A panther by night, he must be a man by day. There was a story of someone walking home in the evening hand in hand with a friend and suddenly he felt the hand in his grow furry, the nails grow sharp and long and cruel . . . All the better to grip you with, my dear . . . People began to look at their neighbours with sidelong eyes. Can it be he? But at first there was no name to which the horror could be linked.

Now at this time the patwari in the lower half of the panther's country was that same Uma Nand whom Jodh Singh had abused at Pokhra. Hugh Upton had made inquiries as he had promised. He had looked up the two cases of bribery which Jodh Singh had quoted. But there was nothing that suggested unfairness in the reports the patwari had made. The parties to both disputes had been questioned but though in both cases the losing party said the decision was unfair, neither had anything to allege against Uma Nand. He was exonerated, but all the same Hugh thought it better to move him. And he came to the area south-west of Gadoli.

It was he who first hinted who the panther might be. He had finished an investigation about a piece of grazing land on the borders of the forest which the owner of the nearest fields wanted to plough. The shareholders of the village objected; it was common land, and they were short of grazing. Uma Nand came and heard their story and wrote his report. When they had fed him, he sat smoking with the leaders of the village, passing the clay pipe-bowl to and fro, for there were Brahmans here with whom it was lawful for him to consort. Each man made a funnel of his hands and drew the smoke cunningly from the bowl; it would have been pollution to touch the clay with the lip. Talk turned on the panther, and who he could be. No one doubted he was a man.

'It will be someone who moves about,' mused Uma Nand aloud. 'No one who stays always in one village. Look how far up the river the killings go.'

There was a long pause, and the pipe-bowl passed. Heads nodded slowly. It sounded sense.

'It began at Bhainswara,' he went on. 'Was there a stranger in the villages near Bhainswara that night? I do not know. It is not my circle.' He rose to go. 'It is late. It is not well to be abroad in the evening these days.'

It was enough. The seed was sown. The whisper went round. It was Jodh Singh who did not sleep in his bed at nights. Everything fitted. He had more than human energy. He was restless.

He did not live quietly in his house like a reasonable man, but wandered from village to village. He did not even stay at home a week after his marriage. Everyone had heard of the sudden rages into which he would fly at the most reasonable remarks. He had been in Bhainswara the first night. And there had been no killing at Gadoli. It was Jodh Singh.

The last two people to hear this story were Jodh Singh himself and the Deputy Commissioner. To Jodh Singh the change in the attitude of the villagers came suddenly. One day men had crowded round him to thank him for what he had done in the matter of the corvee and had listened respectfully to what he had to say. Next day, in another village, there were sullen looks and averted eyes. As soon as the whisper reached them, everyone had accepted it; there was no one else but Jodh Singh who filled the bill. There were very few in the villages of the upper hills who had sufficient education to question the idea that a man could turn into a panther by night. Even those few were not sure. They might laugh deprecatingly if an Englishman asked them questions and say it was a superstition of the peasants, but they had heard tales round the wood fires in the evening too often to be sure. There might be something in it; queer things happened. And whatever they might think of the rumour, few of those with education had much love for Jodh Singh. He had not borne his honours meekly. He had not been patient with those who temporized and were ready to make a bargain with the world. His following was among the simple peasants, who knew only that he had sympathized with them and fought their battle and won; and it was they who believed the whisper without question.

When he saw the changed faces, Jodh Singh asked no questions. He went quietly to the lodging where he was to stay and, pretending to notice nothing, kept to himself as much as possible. But he sent to Autaru to find what was in men's minds.

It did not take Autaru long to get to the bottom of it. He was a simple peasant himself, simpler and less sophisticated than anyone brought up to the south of the river. His approach was blunt and direct. He met silence from a few but before long found someone as direct as himself, for the hill-peasant in his native state is direct, as the most illiterate plainsman is not. Autaru came back to Jodh Singh in fear.

'Yes,' said Jodh Singh, with his usual impatience, 'What is it?'

'Lord,' began Autaru. 'Brother.' He was silent. He could not say it.

'Come on,' said Jodh Singh. 'Tell me. You will get no milk from looking at my feet.'

The homely phrase brought it out. Autaru said all in a breath: 'They say you are the panther.'

Jodh Singh sprang to his feet. He was furious, astonished, incredulous, hurt, deeply hurt, all in a moment. His people. His own people. They could not believe such a thing. He would go and talk to them. Now, at once. But he stopped. He must think. He must hold on to himself and not act in a rage. He turned his back on Autaru and sat down to think. Autaru waited in silence and sorrow. And when he began to think, Jodh Singh saw how it fitted, how everything about him lent to the story. He had been at Bhainswara at the time of the first killing. There had been no deaths at Gadoli. And he was different from everyone else. It was true he was different from everyone else. They were tame and he was wild. He belonged to the forest not the villages. Then a new thought came to him. They said such men — warlocks — knew nothing of what they had done when they were beasts. Could one turn into a beast without knowing it? It was nonsense of course, a peasant superstition. No educated person would believe a man could turn into a panther. But science and common sense and the West did not know everything. And things were different in the hills. What was that story of the man who devoured his own wife and knew nothing of what he had done? It was all nonsense of course. But that they should believe it of him! His own people, whom he loved, who knew how much he loved them, who loved him because of what he had done for them. He had done so much and was going to do so much more.

Rage and grief and hurt pride, and a haunting ridiculous fear — but it must be nonsense — and then the odd feeling that it was somehow appropriate, for he was truly different from other people — chased through his mind in confusing and illogical sequence. For a moment he hardened his jaw; at least it was better to be feared than to go unnoticed. Then self-pity overcame him and he wept; but again he braced himself and tried to think what he should do. One thing was clear; it was no use trying to talk politics while this was in men's minds. He must leave his work in the villages till it had cleared. He would go to Gadoli first and on the way he would think what to do next. He turned and gave his orders to Autaru. Then he said suddenly:

'Have you ever known me go out in the night when I seemed to be asleep?'

'No, lord, no,' cried Autaru. 'Never.'

But there was a new look of fear and horror in his eyes.

It was two days' stage to Gadoli, and the way lay through the village which was the headquarters of the patwari. Uma Nand himself was away on one of his inquiries, for there were only two or three nights a month when he slept under his own roof. But his son Dharma Nand was home on half-term leave from the middle school fifteen miles away. Half-term was an important institution in the middle school because most of the children lived a full day's march or more away and the parents could seldom afford boarding fees in cash. So they sent each child with a sack of flour and he came home to replenish it at half-term. Dharma Nand was naturally feeling ebullient because of his holiday and since his father was away, there was no one to restrain him. He had heard of course the rumour about Jodh Singh and, though he did not know it had started with his father, he did

know that there was some enmity between them. When he saw
Jodh Singh and Autaru going through the village, he ran after
them, and with the instinct that makes little birds mob an owl
in daylight or a crowd stone a woman in the pillory, he shouted
as loud as he could:

'There he goes! There goes the panther, the man-eater!'

People left their houses and ran to see what the shouting was
about. Other boys joined in. Jodh Singh hurried on, his heart
bursting with fury and shame. Those who saw him read his
guilt in his looks. They watched him with hatred and sullen
anger. They did not do anything; no one had yet suggested
action against the warlock. Jodh Singh hurried on. Outside the
village and away from the noise and men, he still hurried, trying
to make his legs take him away from his heart. Hatred for
Dharma Nand surged up in his breast; he knew he was Uma
Nand's son and he hated Uma Nand because he could read in
his looks resentment at the injury done to him at Pokhra, because
he was a patwari, because he was grey and cynical. And now he
hated Dharma Nand too.

'I will be even with him,' he thought. 'I will be even with him.
One day I will show him that I am not called a panther for
nothing.' He hurried on towards Gadoli.

Hugh Upton had just come back to the valley for a further
attempt to settle the panther when he heard the rumour about
Jodh Singh, from another patwari, not Uma Nand. He told
Margaret that evening after dinner.

'I'm rather anxious about it,' he said. 'They all seem sure it's
Jodh Singh and it will be difficult to convince them it isn't. It
would be no use telling them men don't turn into panthers.
They'd think to themselves that that's just one of the things
Englishmen don't know, though of course they wouldn't say so.
And they'd think it is one of the things they do know, because
it's something they've been brought up on.'

'But what will they do?' she asked.

'Heaven knows. They're frightened and angry and people do very funny things when they're frightened. It's odd that people who make such gallant soldiers should be so frightened of wild beasts and ghosts.'

'Not odd they should be frightened of ghosts or anything they don't understand, is it?'

'Well, perhaps not. But they were very frightened and angry about the panther even before this idea got into their heads. Perhaps because it's the women who get killed. Ordinarily, they're the most law-abiding people on earth, but I should hate to predict what they might do now.'

'You mean, you think he's in danger?'

'I think he may be in very serious danger. Perhaps from a mob of villagers who've lost all reason in a sort of collective funk, or perhaps from one man who's had his wife killed.'

'Poor boy. It'll be terrible for him if he finds out what they think, even if they don't do anything to him. He's a sensitive creature. And so unsure of himself for all his cocksureness about politics. What a predicament for a young intellectual! Can't you do anything?'

'I don't know. I'm thinking what I can do. I must do something. There'd be a fuss if a leading political agitator was murdered by mob violence. Much more than if he was a supporter of government, I feel sure. As you say, it'll be a shock to him and he may be the one to make it most difficult to do anything. If he turns haughty and won't co-operate with me in disproving the idea, it'll only make them more certain.'

'A Coriolanus complex,' said Margaret. 'New to science. He hasn't shown much sign of that in the past. Well, do think hard. I go on liking that boy, and feel very sorry for him.'

Hugh tucked the problem neatly away in his mind and bent his thoughts for two hours to problems of the promotion of clerks, the transfer of patwaris, and the grant of gun-licences. Next morning he lighted a pipe and set himself seriously to consider it. He figured that he must give as many villagers as possible ocular proof that Jodh Singh was asleep in his bed on a night when the panther killed elsewhere. It would not be easy, for as Margaret had said, the boy would probably be in a complicated frame of mind and would not be likely to respond if he received a message summoning him to the camp. Hugh would have to go to Gadoli himself. Then there was the problem of getting the panther. The trouble was that it always had the initiative. There was a kill and Hugh moved to the place, saw the remains if he was in time and set his traps, or watched over the kill or over a live goat, in the hope that one day its habits would change and it would come back to the same place. But he was always one kill behind it. He had only fourteen days in the valley; he could not spare more at present. Would it be justifiable to spend some of these precious days in dealing with the Jodh Singh problem? He decided that he had a reasonable chance of proving that Jodh Singh was not the panther, while judging on past performance he had very little prospect of getting the panther by any means used so far. And since the panther always went somewhere new and it had never yet killed in Gadoli, right in the centre of its country, Gadoli might be as good a place to go as any other. He might for once catch up with it and be there when a kill occurred. Not that that would help Jodh Singh, who had just gone there.

There was one risk in the Jodh Singh affair. Suppose Hugh persuaded him to co-operate in a test, with men sleeping by him and others on watch by his side at night. And suppose by a freak of chance that the panther chose that moment to live for a fortnight on wild game or on dogs that no one missed. Things would be worse than ever for Jodh Singh if it stopped killing men just when he was under observation. But it had been almost as regular as clockwork so far. There was no reason to suppose it would change. The risk would have to be taken. He called the patwari and his orderly Dewan Singh and gave orders for th

camp to move to Gadoli, and for all the headmen in the neighbourhood of that village to be summoned to a talk with the
Deputy Commissioner in Gadoli the day after he arrived. He
wrote a letter to Jodh Singh asking him to tea in his camp on
the day of his arrival, sat and considered it for a moment, slowly
tore it up with his square blunt fingers, and wrote another asking
Jodh Singh if he and Margaret might call when they arrived and
drink tea with him. That, he thought, would do more to show
the villagers what he thought of this nonsense than anything
else he could possibly do.

'Horrid tea we shall get,' said Margaret when he told her. 'All
buffalo milk and sugar. Never mind, it's all in a good cause, and
we can have some more when we get back to camp.'

Jodh Singh was bitter when the letter reached him.

'The Deputy Commissioner is being kind to me,' he thought.
'He is doing me this honour to show the people he does not
believe this story. Well, I will be grateful and flattered.'

But all the same, though he would not admit it to himself, he
really was grateful and flattered. He began to make arrangements.
If it had not been for the hostility of the villagers, he would have
received his guests on the roughly paved terrace before his house
and everyone in the village would have crowded round to watch
the great man and his visitors drink their tea. But he dare not
risk that now and must ask them indoors. So a room was made
ready, with two undyed woollen rugs and the skins of a panther
and two chamoix on the floor. The skins had been dried, not
properly cured and the hair was beginning to come out. There
were three rather rickety chairs and a table that was both clumsy
and weak. Govind Singh had not aspired to European customs
and Jodh Singh had never given any thought to his home. Three
chairs, however, were enough; he was not going to let her see his
wife; she would pity him for marrying such a woman and her
husband would despise him. He would not show it, but in his heart
he would despise him. There was no china and the visitors would

167

have to drink from brass tumblers without handles, that would be too hot both for their fingers and their lips. The tea would be boiled, tea, milk and sugar together, in a round brass pot without a lid and would taste of wood-smoke. And what could he give them to eat? Unleavened barley bread in pancakes would not be suitable. Autaru was dispatched to intercept the camp on its way and beg some bread from Hugh's servants. White buffalo butter could be provided, and hard-boiled eggs. Englishmen always ate eggs. And bananas. Jodh Singh's mouth curled in scorn when he saw the best he could do and thought of the Uptons' neat camp arrangements. But they must take us as we are, he thought fiercely; we are a poor and oppressed and backward people and it is well they should see us as we are. Ignorant, backward hill-folk, and I am one of them.

Hugh and Margaret were familiar with this sort of reception. They wished people would give them what they liked themselves, and not try to imitate customs foreign to them, but it was seldom any use suggesting such a thing. They were also used to embarrassing apologies for the inadequacy of what was put before them, but not to the tone into which Jodh Singh slipped for a moment. He began conventionally. He came to meet them and said very politely:

'It is very good of you to honour my humble house. I am deeply grateful to you, Sir, and especially to Mrs. Upton. It is very poor and backward.'

Then he led them to the house and showed them into the room prepared, and when he spoke again, his voice was harsh with pride and pain.

'This is all I can offer you. We are poor and backward people. It is shameful, the way we live.'

Then he was the polite young man again. They talked of nothing while Autaru poured out the tea from the round pot. He did not spill much, and Margaret, although she was trained by now to accept anything, was pleased that he did not stir the tea in their brass tumblers with his fingers, nor insist on shelling the eggs and handing them the grubby result. After a little, Hugh said:

'Jodh Singh, I want to talk to you about this ridiculous story that's going round. You needn't worry about my wife; she knows all about it and wants to help you as much as I do.'

Jodh Singh sat forward on his chair and looked at the floor. He had known this would come. It was all very well for her husband to want to talk about it; he didn't; it would blow over. He could go to Bantok earlier than he had meant and people would forget. But he knew that peasants have so little to remember that they do not forget. He did not say anything.

Hugh went on:

'I think it may be serious for you unless we do something to show the villagers how silly it is. Don't you?'

'I shall go to Bantok,' said Jodh Singh gruffly to the floor.

'Well, that might be a good thing if all else failed. It would save you from immediate danger.'

'Danger?' said Jodh Singh, completely surprised.

'Yes. Hadn't it occurred to you that someone whose wife had been killed might want revenge, thinking as you know they do think? Or a whole village might take things into their own hands.'

'No, I had not thought of that. No, Sir, they would not do that.' But he remembered some of the stories he had heard and did not feel sure.

'Well, you see what I mean. By going to Bantok, you escape immediate danger — at least, probably you do, though someone might follow you. But what would it be like when you came back? You'd never live it down. The real answer is to disprove it.'

Jodh Singh was still sullen. He had forgotten most of his shyness in thinking of his own problem. He said:

'How can we — how can I disprove it?'

He paused, but before Hugh had time to speak, he went on:
'If I thought they wanted to kill me, I would go to them and talk to them.'

'I think it would only make things worse if you were to talk to them. I suggest the best thing would be if I were to talk to them and ask them to agree to a test. You would come and sleep in my camp and I would get men from several villages to watch you while you slept. That's all.'

Jodh Singh suddenly looked up at him like a child.

'You do not believe it, do you?' he asked quickly. But the mask was back in place at once; his eyes sought the floor. 'No, no, of course, you do not. No educated man believes these silly tales.'

Hugh leaned back in his chair. Poor little snipe, he thought; he half believes it himself. He said:

'I know very well that it is a perfectly ordinary panther, which one day I shall kill, or someone else perhaps may. But you and I know it's no use trying to explain that to the villagers. We have to prove that it isn't you. And that should be easy. Once it has killed, somewhere else, twenty miles away, when there are men standing round your bed watching you, no one will think it's you.'

Jodh Singh was silent. He hated the thought of being watched at night. He was going to be a great leader, one day. How could he give in to this and submit to such an indignity? But he would never be a leader if he didn't. But suppose — suppose — it was ridiculous even to suppose it — and it wasn't a thing he could say to this big man.

Margaret's clear voice broke in:

'Please do,' she said. 'It's the only way to clear you completely.'

He looked at her for a second only, for the first time since Hugh had spoken of this thing. How lovely she was. But for the moment she was only an irritation. He ignored her and spoke to Hugh:

170

'What shall you tell them they are to do if it is — if I do — if I do turn into a panther? What shall you tell them? We — I know it is not true, but they believe it, and they will want instructions.'

'I shall tell them to kill any panther they see.'

'And what if they kill me and show you my body — and say I turned back into a man when I was dead?'

'In that case, they would be arrested, and tried for murder. And in my opinion they would be hanged.' How much nicer if I could say I will hang them, thought Hugh.

Jodh Singh stood up.

'I think that is what they will do, but I will do what you say,' he said. 'Thank you very much, Mrs. Upton, for your interest. I — I know I am a very interesting case.' He suddenly turned his back on them both, for his eyes were full of tears.

'Good man,' said Hugh. 'Well done; I'm sure you're right. Come to my camp to-morrow before the meeting. Thank you for our tea.' He hurried Margaret away with his eyes. She said:

'I wish I could help you. I'm glad you've decided that way.'

They went out together, leaving him alone. There was a small group of villagers outside, all men, no women or children. They were quite silent and expressionless. Hugh and Margaret took the path to their camp, an orderly going ahead to show the way. There is no room to walk abreast in Garhwal and Hugh made his wife go first because he liked watching her. No one can talk intimately in single file, so they waited till they reached the tents and were drinking the promised brew of real tea. Then he said:

'He's quite right. There is a risk of the guards killing him. But it's got to be taken. What he's really afraid of is that the story's true.'

She said:

'I don't know when I felt sorrier for anyone. He seems so completely alone. Hasn't he got a wife?'

'He was married this winter, I heard, to a local girl. I don't suppose she's much of a companion.' He felt, as he said it, that little ache that the thought of Margaret always gave him, of wonder and joy because she was his, and of pain because she was not and she never could be his.

She said:

'How little we know of other people, and how less than nothing of these people.'

Next morning was the first for some time that they had not been either marching or setting traps or preparing to sit up for the panther. Margaret got out her paint box and slipped out after breakfast; she was glad to find the kind of subject she wanted close to the camp, in a place from which she could see the gathering of the headmen Hugh had summoned. She would try to paint the sunlight falling through the twisted limbs of an oak on to the ground by the end of a tiled cow-house; it was not going to be easy to deal with in one morning and the light would have changed completely by the afternoon. She worked as fast as she could all morning. But when she came back after lunch, there was no need for hurry and before she settled down to what little more she could do, she spent a few minutes idly contemplating all that was before her and letting her mind go where it would. Beyond her oak and cowshed were the steep hills on the north of the river, not so precipitous here as at Bantok and showing more signs of human life, but little enough even so; there were three little patches of terracing in the whole stupendous sweep of grass and cliff and forest. The hills went straight up from the river for four or five thousand feet. From Gadoli, which was only about two thousand feet above the river, nothing could be seen of the snows behind them. But eye and mind tire with immensity, she thought; what would I not give for the chalk downs, and a little winding lane! She tried to picture such a lane in late spring, the hedges starred with may, every branch crusted with the stiff blossom, the white petals on the wet soil at her feet; she tried to see the long bank below the hedge; bluebells and campion and fool's parsley, misty blue and pink and foamy white; she tried to see a little patch at closer range, fronds of bracken beginning to uncurl, palest green and rusty bronze, eyebright, flowering nettle, a constellation of primroses. She put down her face to the blooms and tried to inhale the faint earthy scent of the primroses. But it isn't the same, she cried. What was it Hugh had said? Memory's a poor thing. The headmen were beginning to arrive from the meeting. She started to paint again.

Hugh had given a few moment's thought to stage management. If he put Jodh Singh in a chair and sat in a chair himself, the two of them would be isolated in grandeur and separated from the headmen, who of course would have to sit on the ground. But he wanted Jodh Singh near him and after inviting himself to tea with the boy yesterday, he could hardly make him sit at his feet on the ground. They are so sensitive about such things, he thought. He spoke to Jodh Singh beforehand and asked him to sit on a rock, a little in advance of the chair where he would sit himself, and to face both him and the audience. He kept the boy in his tent till the patwari told him that the headmen were assembled. Then he came out, bringing Jodh Singh with him, and motioned him to sit on his rock. He himself sat in the chair, looking rather like a teacher conducting an infant class in the open air. He began to speak, slowly and clearly. He was not one of the very few Englishmen who have learnt the language with the care needed for a diplomatic appointment. He knew the simpler grammatical forms and had a small vocabulary; he was neither fluent nor idiomatic, but he was good at putting his thoughts into the form of simple sentences that were within his powers and for that reason what he said was perfectly clear. He spoke the Hindustani of the plains, but the headmen at least could understand that, if many villagers could not. He said:

'Headmen of villages, I have called you together because I have heard a strange story. I have heard that you think the panther who has been killing here is not a panther, but a man. I myself believe it is an ordinary panther and that one day I shall kill it, but in such a matter what is the use of words? No man will change what he believes in his heart for words. He will believe what his eyes see. Now I am told you believe that the man who becomes a panther is Jodh Singh here. It is a strange thing to me that you should believe this, for you know he has done much for you. The village folk have heard that he has worked for them with great eagerness of heart. But since some of you believe this thing which to me is foolishness, I want to give you proof that it is not so. Let us put the matter to proof and see with our eyes. Let each headman find me two men from his village, full-grown men, not children, and men who are shareholders in the village and fathers of families. No one whose relation has been killed by the panther. Let those men come to my camp here and come with me for a week, bringing their food. From them we will choose a guard every night of eight men who will watch Jodh Singh as he sleeps. There will always be four who are waking and watching. We will mount guard as they do in the battalions. Then we shall know in the morning that he has slept in his bed all night. And if we hear that the panther has killed in the body while Jodh Singh was sleeping here in his bed in the body, we shall know this thing is foolishness. What do you think of this test? Would it not then be proved?'

He waited, and let them talk among themselves; but not for long, because while he did not want to let them feel they were being rushed, he did not want the meeting to get out of his hand. There might be one obstinate old man who would sour them all if he were given the chance. When he judged the moment had come, he went on:

'There are two other things to explain. The guard will be armed with poles and axes or kukris —'

174

'No guns?' asked someone.

'No,' said Hugh, who had thought of this before, 'guns are well enough in the army where each man knows his duty and the punishment if he does wrong; but not here in civil life where everyone follows the wish of his heart. I do not want to be shot in my bed by a guard who becomes excited.'

'It will be very dangerous, lord,' said the man who had asked about guns.

'What, with eight guards, four awake and four ready to spring to their feet, all with axes ready to strike? Nonsense. And I shall be sleeping a few yards away with a rifle. Now, the second thing. If the guard see a panther, they are to kill it. But they are not to touch a hair of any man's head. If they attack a man they will be hanged. Is that understood? If they see a man behaving strangely, they are to wake me. Is that understood? Now, is there anyone here who does *not* agree to this test?'

He sent the patwari among them to see if there were any objections. Someone said:

'Lord, let Jodh Singh also be handcuffed to the bed.'

Hugh had thought of this, and felt it was a humiliation to be avoided. He said quietly:

'To what profit? If the hand becomes a paw, it will slip through a handcuff.' But he was not at all sure that it would. Probably a panther's wrist was thicker than a man's. Anyway, it did not seem to convince the audience, who muttered among themselves, until someone said:

'It would be safer, lord.'

Jodh Singh spoke for the first time. He had sat with bowed head, looking at the ground, never moving. Now he said:

'I have no objection. I am on trial. It is very suitable that I should be handcuffed.'

'Then it is settled,' said Hugh getting up. 'See that your men are here to-night. They are to report to the patwari, each man bringing his food and blanket, and a pole, and an axe or kukri.'

Hugh set the guard himself that night and explained what would happen if any harm came to Jodh Singh in his own body. The guards were submissive and frightened. Jodh Singh was silent, his face frozen and grey. He looked ill, his cheeks fallen in. He suffered himself to be handcuffed to the bed without a word, then turned on his side and pulled the blanket over his head.

For four nights the guard was set and nothing happened. It was a different group of men every night, but the others, those who had served their turn or were still to serve it, Hugh kept in the camp to spread the news when proof should be obtained. By day, Hugh travelled, with the help of a pony where possible, to every village in the neighbourhood where the panther had killed, to see the place, to talk to the people, to make sure that everyone understood the curfew order which was the only preventive action that could be taken. Every night he explained their orders to the new guard, who had their post only a few yards from his tent, so that he could be awakened if necessary. Every morning he went to see them and dismissed them. The fourth morning someone bolder than the rest, a man who had been a soldier and therefore was not afraid to talk to an Englishman, said:

'Of course nothing has happened, lord. What would he be likely to do when he is watched? He is too cunning. He has stopped killing now. Consider, how long it is since he killed.'

It was just what Hugh had feared. The panther had stopped killing at the wrong moment. When the test began, there had been no kill for a week, so that news of a fresh kill was now long overdue. It was worrying. Jodh Singh seemed in a kind of stupor. Hugh himself was becoming irritable; he had seldom stayed in one place so long as this since he came to the district and he was really doing nothing useful; he felt that time was slipping through his fingers and getting the better of him. But there was nothing he could do until the panther killed again. Sitting over a live bait in the hope that the panther might wander up to that particular spot, out of the sixty miles by ten that was his beat, would really be asking too much of chance.

But after breakfast on the fifth day there was sensational news. A man panted up the hill from a village ten miles away, which was on the main road running up the bank of the river. He had been sent to tell a story, but it took some time to piece it together by questioning and even then only the barest outline emerged. It was not till later, when Hugh saw the place, that he understood exactly what had happened. There was a shopkeeper, one Hukm Singh, who had a two-storied house, a shop below and living-rooms above, close to the road. He came from a village higher up the hill, but he was a younger brother and he had first been in the army and now he had started this shop. There had been some sickness in the house and as it was getting warm down there by the river, the shopkeeper had started to sleep out of doors on his veranda rather earlier than he usually did. Last night his stomach was not well and he had got up in the night, gone down by the staircase and walked a little way from the house and the road to an open field to relieve himself. He was nervous because of the panther and kept well away from any bushes or shadows in the bright moonlight. He came back with several anxious looks over his shoulder, but when he reached the top of the stairs he sighed with relief. Now he was safe. He put his hand on his bed to get in and at that moment heard the stairs creak behind him.

Hukm Singh turned and saw the panther come softly up the stairs. He would never have heard its step, but the stairs moved under its weight. He jumped back to the head of his bed, which was placed with one side close under the rail of the veranda, the other side facing the head of the stairs. The panther was at the top of the stairs facing the foot of the bed. Hukm Singh stood beyond the head of the bed against the veranda rail. He stood staring at the panther, which did not move. He was looking out of the corner of his eye for a weapon, but there was nothing within reach except a round stool of plaited cane near his hand. He picked that up as a shield. The panther did not attack him, but sprang lightly on to the bed, and continued to look at him. It was playing with him before the ecstasy of death, as a lover plays with his mistress before the ecstasy of love. Still on the bed, it took a step towards him. But he did not recoil. Instead he thrust the stool into its face with all his strength and at the top of his voice began to shout. The panther was surprised; no man had ever before anticipated its attack and taken the initiative himself. It half rose on its quarters and gripped the stool with mouth and paws together. That gave Hukm Singh the fraction of a second in which to fling all his weight on the stool, and it was in just that particular moment of time, less than the blink of an eye, that the panther's weight was wrongly disposed, because it was surprised. Its muscular strength was four times that of a man, but it was not balanced to use its strength; and with a hoarse scream of indignation it vanished over the veranda rail. Hukm Singh did not waste any time. He was inside the upper room with the door barred before the panther was back on the veranda. He heard it pace up and down. Once it flung its weight against the door; he could hear its breath, as it stood motionless, panting after the effort; he could smell the reek of it. Then it made off. It was too cunning to stay there long.

When Hugh heard this, he said to Margaret, who had been listening to the story as it was gradually squeezed out of the messenger:

'This is the best chance yet. It hasn't killed and must be hungry and wanting revenge. It may be hanging round that same place again to-night; and I shall be waiting for it. And incidentally it lets Jodh Singh out.'

He gave his orders. All the guards on Jodh Singh, both those who had served their turn and those still to come, were to be collected at once, and he would talk to them. Immediately after

178

that he would start with a rifle and his orderly Dewan Singh for Hukm Singh's house. Camp would move to somewhere more convenient, but not too close. He chose a village less than three miles this side of Hukm Singh's shop, feeling that to move the camp any closer might disturb the panther.

The guards agreed gravely when he spoke to them. They had to admit that Jodh Singh had been sleeping quietly in his bed when Hukm Singh was wrestling vigorously with the panther.

'He did not even talk in his sleep,' one of them volunteered.

'Then he cannot be the panther,' Hugh argued relentlessly, and they agreed rather doubtfully that this must be so. But they were not utterly convinced, the weak spot in the defence being that if your powers of wizardry are strong enough to turn yourself into a panther, it should not be beyond your art to be in two places at once. Thus there were no congratulations to Jodh Singh on the fortunate end of his ordeal; the guards drifted away, undertaking to tell the villagers that Jodh Singh had been asleep when Hukm Singh's adventure took place, but both Hugh and Jodh Singh knew that something would stick:

'At first people were saying Jodh Singh was a warlock and turned himself into the panther; later on they were saying he wasn't. God alone can say what the truth of it all may be.' That was what they would be saying in the villages for many years.

Jodh Singh came to thank the Uptons before they left. He made Hugh uncomfortable by saying:

'Sir, you have been very kind to me. You have been like my father to me. I wish to thank you. I thought bad thoughts of you before, but now I know you have always been kind. I do not want any foreign rulers, but I thank God that He has sent us such a ruler as you.'

He did not seem to expect a reply, but turned to Margaret and said to her:

'Please try to think well of me whatever you may hear.

Thank you very much, Mrs. Upton, because you have been kind. You are my only friend.'

'Of course, I'll think well of you,' she said. 'I do already and you know I do. And in any case, I expect we'll be seeing you soon. You seem to get about nearly as much as we do.'

Hugh was impatient to be after the panther and they left at once. Jodh Singh never saw either of them again. A month later, Hugh was unexpectedly transferred to a city of the plains, where he resumed the life of continual crisis and overwork he had come to regard as normal. He went without question, without expressing a personal preference, just as he tried to carry out unquestioningly the policy set him from above. The district had to learn the ways of a new master who also had not a little to learn. Since it was before the days when Englishwomen decided that they could after all work in the plains in summer, Margaret had the choice of a lonely hill station or England. She spent the summer in London. There she reopened that wound she had hoped was scarred over.

Jodh Singh was left without a friend. He stuck to his plan of going to Bantok. He needed the healing airs of that lonely place more even than he had after the affair at Pokhra. Politics must wait till the memory of his ordeal had died.

PART THREE

THE UPROOTED, 1938

I

WHEN the runner arrived, the men were just beginning the business of pitching camp. The mules came jingling in, hung about with bells and red tassels, with big blue and white beads round their necks. The drivers lifted off their loads and their curious saddles, like a thin tube of matting doubled back on itself so as to give a line of padding on either side of the backbone. As each mule was freed, it rolled its gaunt sweaty back on the turf, turning over from one side to the other with the uncouth effort which all the horse tribe seem to need for this simple act. The drivers, the idlest and most feckless of mankind, lighted cigarettes and sauntered off to make themselves comfortable. There were porters as well as mules, for the camp sometimes split when Christopher Tregard, Deputy Commissioner in 1938, wanted to go to a village where the paths were too difficult for mules. The porters were mostly Nepalese, for since the forced labour ended there were not many local villagers who were willing to carry loads for other people. Each porter went his own pace; they were less gregarious than the mules, who came in groups of two and three with a common driver. The loaded men came one by one; each one as he reached the camp sat down with a deep grunt, let the weight of his burden on to the ground, and then eased the ropes and webbing that held it to his shoulders and head. Then he lifted off the pad of sacking that protected his back, a simpler affair than the type the mules used, moved off for a drink and a few minutes' rest, and then came back to help the orderlies with the tents.

The camp was at the foot of a bank of forest that ran steeply up in an unbroken sweep for four or five thousand feet, till the trees thinned out and gave way to bare fells. Where the steepness of the slope broke below the forest, there was a shelf of green turf before the cultivated terraces began. At one point in this shelf a small stream ran out, making a break in the forest; if you stood facing the camp, you looked at a gently rising stretch of turf on either side of the stream, with tall trees closing in behind. Facing the other way, you looked through miles of space straight across the valley to the majesty of Dunagiri's twenty thousand feet, her snowfields and cliffs of ice. The vastness of the valley and its ice-fed streams was something the mind could not comprehend; and to that was added the mountain, revealed in her entirety from crown to roots. There she was; you just looked at her and were filled with wonder. Christopher and Susan stood gazing for a few moments without speech. Then they turned towards the camp.

Christopher smiled:

'I like that site,' he said. 'It might be in the New Forest. Chestnuts, do you see? And turf — have you ever thought of the thousands of miles of this planet where there's no turf? Oh, and there's the first yew. Red berries and all. D'you remember: "Colour threads the darkness as yewberries the yew"?'

Susan did remember, and was just saying so when the runner arrived. The bag had been passed on from man to man, but they were eleven stages from headquarters and it had taken four days to reach them. An orderly hurried up to break the seals and cut the string. He took out two big bundles of files, which were put aside till there should be a tent to work in, a table, and a stenographer; he gave Christopher a bundle of newspapers and some letters. Christopher sorted out Susan's letters and sat down on a rock to read his own.

Christopher and Susan had started out that morning of September 1938 from Vishnumath, on the first day of a new world. The rains were over, the sky was washed and bright, the air was crisp. They had left the tiny bungalow at eight o'clock, feeling exhilarated by the prospect of brisk walking. But it had happened as it always did. Immediately outside the gate a man appeared, hurrying towards them. He said:

'Lord, come and look at my wall!'

'Where is your wall?'

'Just down there, lord. Only ten steps. Close to your road. Please look at it, Presence. There is great tyranny. I am a very poor man.'

They reached the wall. There was a house on the upper side of the mule-track and on the lower side an orchard. In front of the house, the track, which was usually of the natural gravel, rock or clay from which it had been cut, was cobbled with rough stones, so that the surface was much more durable than elsewhere; on the valley side of the stretch of cobbling, for its exact length, ran a low wall, two feet high; built of roughly shaped stones, mortared, with carefully-cut flat stones on the top. A pleasant wall to sit on; obviously part of one plan, the house, the cobbled stretch of track, the wall, the work of a man who wished to make himself a settled home and did not want half the width of the track washed down into his orchard by heavy rain.

'Well,' said Christopher, 'I see your wall. What is your trouble?'

The owner of the wall stretched out his hands over it in a protective, almost caressing gesture. His hands said that the wall was his wife and little children, that he loved it dearly, that it was in danger. But his mouth made only an inarticulate sound, and then said:

'Lord — my wall — . . . .'

'Can anyone explain what the trouble is?' Christopher asked.

'Yes, Presence, I can,' said the patwari, who had arrived as if attracted by some telepathic knowledge. 'The Public Works Department say that this is their track. They have to mend it and it all belongs to government. And they say this wall is not shown on their records, and therefore this man built it without permission, and it is an encroachment, and must be removed. And when this man wouldn't move it, they reported it to the court, and the court has ordered him to move it at once or be fined.'

Christopher gave a deep sigh.

'Well, now, how old would you say this wall was?' he asked.

The patwari put his head on one side.

'I cannot say, Presence.'

'But does it look to you new?'

'No, it does not look new.'

'And who built this wall and this house? It is all one work — look at the carving on the stone at the corner of the house and the corner of the wall; it is the same pattern.'

'It was my grandfather,' said the owner, who was a man of more than fifty. .

'Yes, it was his grandfather,' agreed all the bystanders.

'Is that true?' Christopher asked the patwari.

'Lord, I have only been here three years. It was here when I came.'

'Well,' said Christopher, 'I do not go only by what I am told, but here what I am told agrees with what I see. There's no doubt this is old. Look at this carving! Do you carve stone doorways like this if you build a house now? And what sort of roof would you put on your house if you built one now? Corrugated iron — but this is all tiled. No one who built a house this size would put tiles on it now. No, I think this house and this wall were here before the Public Works Department had any records — and that's not very long in any case. All right, old man; don't be afraid; no one shall touch your wall. I will see to it. Have you written me a petition? No. Then write it quickly and give it to the patwari here, and he will bring it to me this evening. Do you understand?' he added to the patwari. 'I want his petition brought to me at the next camp and you are responsible for bringing it. Bring it this evening when all the petitions come.'

Susan and Christopher started again.

'But *why*,' asked Susan, 'why should anyone want to destroy

186

his wall? It looked a very useful wall, and it was holding the track together. I should have thought there ought to be a wall like that all the way along.'

'Well,' said Christopher, 'the Public Works people say that walls on the lower sides of these tracks turn them into torrents, and the water runs along them instead of across them and tears up the surface. But in this case it was just red tape, blind obedience by some junior chap to general orders from Naini Tal or Lucknow. Most unintelligent.'

They walked on, along a winding path that followed the contour of the hill, but rising slightly. It was pleasantly varied. There were patches of terraced cultivation, with men ploughing the little shelves of fields for the winter crop at the same time as others were cutting the maize and the autumn crop, so that there was green and brown and gold and the deep crimson of the red millet, smiling in the sun. But the cultivation soon gave way again to forest and they were in the deep shade where the smell of rotting leaves and moisture pricked their nostrils. Every leaf in the brown carpet at their feet was rimed with frost on the underside. There would come the sound of running water and they would cross a stream, clear water chattering happily over brown pebbles, or white water at the foot of a fall scooping hungrily at the stone in whose hollow it churned; the chill of the fresh water would strike them, and then they would be past it and out in the sun again, gazing across that immense valley to the snowfields. But they never got very far without interruption. Up would bob a blanket-clad figure, his legs in thick shapeless trousers of handwoven wool, almost like felt, his body swathed in a plaid of the same stuff, fastened by a pair of strong iron pins, chained together so that one of them could not be lost without the other.

'Lord, look at my field.'

'Where is your field?'

'Over there, lord. There – there – there –' the reddish-brown face between the locks of long hair would screw up into still more intricate convolutions of wrinkles with the effort of pointing out the place.

'All right, I see it. What about it?'

'Lord, it is a very dangerous place. Look at the forest all round. It is full of animals. Pigs — deer — bears — ' a pause between each, and a long-drawn hiss of intaken breath to show how big and many and dangerous the animals were — 'panthers — monkeys — porcupines — tigers. . . .'

'You want a gun-licence, I suppose. But which is your village? Aren't there any guns there?'

'There is my village, there — there. *Very* far from my fields, and there is a gun there, but he uses it to guard his own fields. He won't come to mine.'

'And where is your house? Out by the fields? I see. All right, I've seen where it is. Come to the camp this evening and we'll see what the other people in your village have to say and whether you've got a good character.'

They went on, and came to a village. It was tiny, twenty or thirty houses round an old stone temple, and a stone tank into which the clear water shot in a bright sunlit curve from two spouts roughly carved to the shape of a cow's head. There was a school, and the two went gravely round it while ragged little tots sang a shrill song of praise.

Outside the village, again there was the cry:

Lord, look at my field.'

'Where is it?'

Just down there, lord, only ten steps.'

'Ten steps? All right — one, two, three — ten. Am I there?'

'No, lord, not that sort of ten steps. Farther than that.'

'Below that village?'

'Yes, lord, a very little way below that village.'

'About three miles, and two thousand feet down, in fact. And why do you want me to look at your field?'

'Lord, there is a dispute!'

'What is the dispute about?'

'About my field, lord. Just look at it, lord, and then I shall get justice. Only if you come can I get justice.'

'But tell me, now,' said Christopher, 'what good would it do if I saw the field? Would the field speak to me? Would the crops lift up their voice and tell me the truth?'

'No, lord, but you would see what a good field it is.'

'But I should have to go and see the other man's field too. I should have no time for anyone's business to-day but your business. And just by seeing I cannot give you justice. I must have your opponents there. Have you made a suit before the courts?'

'No, lord, but the other man has.'

'Well, if you can bring the other man to my camp this evening, I will try to give you justice and make an agreement between you.'

'I will bring him; but there will be no justice if you do not look at my field, lord!'

All morning they heard the cry: 'Look at my field, lord,' and several times if it really seemed that it would do some good Christopher scrambled down or up the hillside. But usually the cry was born simply of a pathetic belief in personal rule. Each man wanted a direct order. No abstract business of law in a court miles away, but an order on the spot, after inspection.

But at last the camp was reached, and the runner panted up with the letters.

'Anything interesting?' Susan asked when Christopher had skimmed through the more urgent and personal.

'Nothing very startling,' he said, 'but there's one thing that is rather interesting to me at any rate: you remember that man Jodh Singh I was telling you about?'

Susan wrinkled her brows.

'Jodh Singh? Which Jodh Singh was that? There aren't

189

enough names to go round here; there seem to be only about a dozen and there are so many people.'

'Yes, but this one's rather special. Don't you remember the story Margaret Upton told me about how everyone thought he turned into a panther? I was telling you when we came through his village.'

'Oh, yes, of course I remember that. A lovely story. Has he turned into anything else?'

'No, but I have a feeling he may be going to, or at any rate, that I may be going to hear quite a lot of him. I've been interested in him ever since Margaret told me the story; she obviously thought there was a lot in him, and felt desperately sorry for him, and I felt, in the way one does, you know, a special sort of interest in him because she was so interested. . . .'

'If I'd known Margaret was going to be there, I shouldn't have let you go to Naini Tal by yourself,' said Susan.

Christopher put out his tongue at her.

'I regard her as an elder sister,' he said. 'A very nice and decorative one. The kind that's an asset. But as I was saying when you so rudely interrupted, Margaret talked about him and I was interested, but I wanted to hear Hugh's side, so I got hold of him in the bar one night and asked him. Now Hugh wouldn't strike you as a chap with much imagination. . . .'

'None whatever, I should have thought. But I don't know him as well as you do, of course,' said Susan thoughtfully.

'More than you might suppose, as a matter of fact. At least, I think so, even from a woman's point of view. I sometimes wonder whether even Margaret quite realizes how sensitive he is. He pretends not to be. Anyhow, he had imagination as a district officer. More than anyone who's been here since — '

'Until you came, darling?'

'Until I came, as you so rightly say. Well, Hugh told me that he strongly suspected, though he never had any proof or shadow of it, that the panther story was started by a patwari who'd been accused of bribery by Jodh Singh. And that patwari's son, one Dharma Nand, has just come to be tahsildar of the Northern Circle, which is Jodh Singh's home country.'

'Dramma,' said Susan appreciatively.

'Well, setting for dramma, or so I thought when I heard it. And so I expect did Dharma Nand. Poor devil! It's not much of a plum anyhow, the Northern Circle, seven days' march from a road, no decent schools, and everything double the price it is in the plains; and anyone would be a bit nervous of coming to Jodh Singh's part of the world. . . .'

'Why?' Susan was interested in everything about the district. It was Christopher's work.

'Well, now,' said Christopher thoughtfully, 'how can I explain fairly? He obviously impressed Margaret as fundamentally a nice and honest person, and an idealist. Hugh thought the same, though he put it differently. Hugh said his ideas were half-baked and unpractical and he was a bit of a visionary, but full of enthusiasm, and full of guts. But terribly emotional and quick-tempered. Now every other district officer since has described him as a pest, because he will start complaints about officials which have usually nothing in them. I reckon, from what they've written about him, and what I've heard and seen myself, that he's completely honest in the sense that he's not interested in money or just making himself important; but he's intolerant, can't see any point of view but his own and flares up if people disagree with him, and highly emotional. Someone comes and pitches him a yarn about some patwari taking a bribe and he gets in a passion and rushes off to start a war at once, without attempting to hear the other side of the case. Well, if you throw mud long enough, some of it sticks, and there's hardly an official in the district who doesn't bear him a grudge for some accusation that has never been proved, perhaps, but has been worrying and harmful.'

'Doesn't sound as if he'd be very popular,' said Susan.

'Not with the patwaris. And there's hardly a member of the District Board he hasn't fought. But the villagers — well, they're a little frightened of him, because they don't understand him. I shouldn't wonder if the panther story sticks, you know. Peasants have long memories. And he does have these unaccountable rages. But although they're frightened, they do look on him as a champion when they're in trouble. They don't forget what he did for them over the forced labour. And he has great charm. He so obviously feels and believes what he says. I can't help liking him whenever I meet him. He's trying in a way to do the same kind of thing as I am; his blood boils at the same things as mine — only I wait to make sure they're true before I let it boil.'

'Oh, yes, I remember you telling me about the forced labour. But tell me more about the panther part. Do they really still believe in were-wolves or were-panthers, or what would you call them?'

'It's very difficult to know what they do believe. I think that most of them in the villages do believe it's a thing that does happen. And if you believe it may happen and meet someone to whom it is supposed to have happened, and who is obviously not quite like other people — well, it just adds a little extra something the others haven't got. I should think that now it probably rather adds to his prestige than otherwise. The reformed warlock. You could never be quite sure, you see, that the panther that was eventually killed was the one that was doing the killing. The killing stopped, but that might be just because the warlock turned over a new leaf.'

'Y-e-e-s, I wonder — do you think, Christopher, that the panther story might have had an effect on him? Mentally, I mean. Still?'

'Bound to have some effect. Both Hugh and Margaret said that the most pathetic thing was that he seemed half to believe that it might be true. You mean that he might go on half believing, or perhaps about one-eighth believing, that it had been true?'

'Yes — I hadn't put it to myself as definitely as that — but that was the kind of idea at the back of my mind.'

'I dare say. In fact, I should say you're probably right. It would encourage him to think he was different from other people and in a way flatter his vanity. He certainly is different; a sort of scourge of God, the self-appointed champion of the oppressed. So you see why a tahsildar in these parts is not on a bed of roses. And this poor devil has the added complication of a family feud with the scourge.'

'Most worrying for him. Well, anyhow, what's happened?'

'Well, trouble between them has started at once, though in a minor way. Jodh Singh goes into a sort of retreat every summer to a lonely village on the north side of the river, a most inaccessible place, where he communes with nature, certainly with nothing else. And the moment he comes out of his retreat — in fact, I didn't know he was out till to-day — he sends in a complaint about Dharma Nand taking bribes. He says Dharma Nand went to a village where there was a dispute and they feasted him on goats and wine — he means spirits, of course; no wine here, worse luck — and made their women dance naked before him and supply all his needs. He adds a little note here that Dharma Nand is a young man and notoriously gluttonous of women. And then they gave him five hundred rupees. And then he made an order in their favour.'

'But if Jodh Singh's honest, as you say he is, why does he send in a complaint like that? It isn't true, is it?'

'Well, you can't be sure, of course. I shall have to make inquiries. But I must say, it doesn't sound true to me. Dharma Nand's a young chap with a good reputation and this is his first independent post. And he's only officiating. He's bound to be on his best behaviour. I expect it's the story the other side told Jodh Singh. I've had this kind of thing from him before and I've talked to him about it. My impression is that people come

to him with a yarn and he gets so worked up and full of indignation that he really believes every word of it. Then he gets
committed to it and simply won't accept any arguments on the
other side. He really is incapable of understanding them, once
he's excited about a case; he hasn't the mental detachment. He
has a sort of reservoir of moral indignation which is always
ready to come to the boil. And being a creature of emotions, the
fact that he doesn't like Dharma Nand to start with will only
make him more ready to believe anything against him. And
incidentally, the complainants are the Marchas, who are great
pets of his.'

'Oh, the Marchas. Yaks and things. Why does he like them?
Is he fond of beetle porridge?' Susan had once wandered up to
the skin tents of a Marcha camp and looked into the cooking-pot.

'Well, it's rather typical of him, as I picture him. You see,
they're wanderers, not really settled folk. Their villages are
under the snow most of the year. And they're nobody's baby.
All the settled villages hate them because they eat up all the
grazing and waste firewood. They're always getting into
trouble over that. And it's like Jodh Singh to take them up;
there's no political advantage in it, in fact, the opposite. He's
done a lot for them. Look, the tents are up. I must go and do
petitions. But I think we shall hear more of Jodh Singh and
Dharma Nand before long.'

Christopher called one of the orderlies and Susan went to the
tent to get her box of medicines. Christopher sat on a tree-stump
and the orderly shouted at the top of his voice that justice was
available for anyone in the neighbourhood who wanted it.

They came, a dozen or twenty wild figures, with long hair
and blanket plaids made from the coarse black wool of their
little horned sheep. Among them were most of those he had
seen in the morning and all had troubles of much the same kind.
Gun-licences, fields, wood from the forest to build houses and
cowsheds, leave to break new ground, those were the kind of

things they wanted. And that individual want had always to be balanced against something else, the right of the village, who did not want all the grazing land cut up for cultivation; or the good of the forest, which must be protected for the sake of future generations and because it is the forest that holds together the hills and stores the water. At last they were finished, orders given and peace made where possible. Christopher stood up:

'The court is closed,' he said. 'Now, medicines?'

Most of the petitioners wanted medicine. And a number of other people were already getting doses and powders from Susan. The petitioners moved over to join the group of patients and Christopher came too in case he could help. Susan listened gravely to their troubles, with some assistance from an orderly when the dialect became too obscure.

'Castor oil,' she would say. And an orderly would pour out castor oil from an enormous bottle in incredibly large doses. But there was no shirking. The patient drank it slowly, as though he enjoyed it, and ran his finger round the inside of the brass cup and licked it to make sure that not a drop was wasted.

'Quinine and aspirin, for you, my friend —'

'Tannofax on that burn — but you must take it to hospital if it doesn't begin to heal in two days — can you make him go, Christopher?'

'Cough lozenges for you, but really, you know, I can't cure asthma —'

'And as for you, what you've got is either an appendix or duodenal ulcer —' She glanced quickly at a first aid book, 'Yes, I'm sure that's it. Don't you think so, Christopher? We can't cure you, brother. You must go to the hospital at Vishnumath. The doctor will cure you. The sahib will give you a letter to him.'

The patient looked sad. He turned to Christopher.

'Please cure me, lord,' he said. 'Your medicine is better than the doctor's. You *can* cure me.'

'I'm very sorry,' said Christopher, 'but honestly, I can't do it.'
The patient sighed.

'Well, lord,' he began, 'I've got another illness too. A dreadful
sore throat. Can you give me some medicine for that?' The last
man swallowed his dose, the last little party went away with
precious bundles of pills or stoups of castor oil or bottles of
disinfectant for distant friends and relations. The light began to
fade. The bulk of Dunagiri grew vaster, her snowfields flushed
with rose, as the colour died from trees and grass. A little icy
wind crept across the valley.

'Tea,' said Christopher. 'Hot, strong and sweet like a kiss.
That's a Russian proverb.'

'It's no use your pretending you learnt that from a Russian
girl friend because I know about your past and you never had
one,' said Susan.

'Well, I know someone who did and I got it from him. And
anyhow, you only know as much of my past as I've told you.'

'You'd have told me that,' said Susan.

Susan was slim and young. Christopher Tregard had met her
in Delhi, where he was bidden to decorous dinner parties given
by kind mammas and aunts, from which eligible young men and
nice young things would troop away to dance together. She
laughed at the same things as he did, and she spoke to him of
England, the downs and meadows, bluebells in the clear green
light of the beech woods, the damp bracken, birdsong in spring,
and cowslips in the banks of the soft south-west. They danced
together, they rode together; at each party he looked first to
see if she was there.

There is a magic moment in Delhi between the seasons, when
the winter is past, before the heat begins. It comes overnight, it
goes without warning. Suddenly the green stems in the gardens
are crowned with flowers and the evenings are heavy with
their scent. Their life is short; soon the hot winds will wither
them and the earth will be dusty beneath the searing sun. But

for those few days, the hollyhocks nod their pink and white sun-bonnets; the tender blue of larkspur melts against the dancing cornflower; the snapdragons are gallant yellow and glowing orange; the rose scatters her petals; pansies hold up their faces like happy children on the floor at a party; and the poppies are cups of liquid light, floating in purest colour, scarlet, white and gold.

On such a day, Christopher turned away for a moment from a group of people chattering in the sunshine before lunch. He saw Susan leave the house and come towards him through the flowers, fresh and cool and dark. His heart turned over within him; he knew that she was his and he must never let her go.

They were married six weeks later and in the autumn Christopher was posted to Garhwal. Susan and he held hands and danced when they heard the news; they could have hoped for nothing better. That was two years ago and they were still sure there would never be anywhere in India where they would sooner be. They went everywhere together; when they first came to the district, the villagers in some particularly inaccessible spot would ask incredulously:

'But will the lady be coming too?'

And the orderly sent on ahead would reply:

'Why not? Where the needle goes, does the thread not follow?'

This evening Christopher finished his tea and settled down for a couple of hours to the files and letters which the runner had brought. After dinner, Susan curled up on a camp chair in a dark blue jersey and slacks. She said:

'You know, really this is the life for us. Why do we ever want anything else?'

'Well, yes, if it could go on for ever. It has been fun, hasn't it? Do you remember our first march, when they brought you a sheep, and you came to me with tears in your eyes and said: "But it's alive! The poor thing looks so trusting!" Now you come stamping with fury and say: "Look at this skinny creature they've brought to-day! Nothing on it at all! Feel these ribs!" '

'Yes, and do you remember all the times we've come into camp late, in the dark, cold or wet or both? The time when we had to cross the river on stepping-stones by the light of one lantern; and the smooth water gleaming and slipping away like a mill-race? And that night on Dudhatoli when the tents got lost because you would go by a new way no one had ever been before, and it poured with rain all night, and we had to keep warm as well as we could by a bonfire?'

'Weren't the men nice about that? Never the sign of a grumble or an I-told-you-so. That's one of the nicest things about being here; everyone is so cheerful.'

'And us being gipsies,' said Susan. 'And in being able to hear about all you're doing. I don't think I could ever go back to being folk in housen.'

'We'll have to sometime. This can't last for ever. At the end of three years they'd move me to some Dustypore in the plains. And then it will be time to go.'

'Was it so very dreadful in the plains? I don't mean Delhi, because that's different; I mean in a district.'

'Oh, no, I don't regret a minute of it. I feel about all those years rather as I did about going to school. One hated the thought of going back at the end of the holidays; I hated it so much that I used to be sick; and yet if anyone had suggested never going back again, I should have been appalled. The hot weather wasn't very nice, of course, but even about the hot weather there is something attractive, at least in retrospect. You count the days till it's over, but there's something tough and astringent about it; everything is stripped bare, no curtains on the windows, no mattresses on the beds, no women. You have a feeling that you really are earning your keep and are in the front line, which is good for one's self-conceit. But I've done it. I don't want any more. It can't be good for one to go on being abroad when one wants so much to be in England. And from the point of view of duty — no one seems to want us to stay.'

'But, Christopher, how can you say that? You know I want to be home more even than you do, but these people, the villagers, they do want you.'

'Yes, I know. What I feel may be self-deception; I suppose my reason is not to be trusted because I want so much to see the English country and to be among English people again; but it seems to me wrong for us, the English, as a people, to take refuge behind the peasant and say we must stay because he wants us. Every people must express itself through its vocal classes; we shouldn't dream of saying that American opinion was exclusively what the farmer thinks in the Middle West; and the vocal classes in India want us to go. It's true they're out of touch with the peasant, but that is just because we're here. It's a thing which can't right itself so long as we are. It was different for people like Hugh. They'd had the best part of their life under the old tradition and when changes came it was their plain duty to carry on, and they did. But for our generation, the good we can do has to be balanced against the harm to our own lives. And for me, the point is approaching when the balance tips over against staying. Once I'm out of this district, my value goes down sharply. Frustration is the key-note in the ordinary district now. You have to acquiesce in much you hate and can't achieve anything you want. No, we must go where we belong and settle down and make a home for the children, and drive our roots deep into the soil. We shall have to be folk in housen some day.'

'Well, of course, I know that; and I don't mind so long as it's folk in nice housen, not little horrors in rows. A nice rambling farmhouse with lots of bedrooms where people can come and stay, and lofts with apples in them, and places for playing trains. And I see what you mean about the vocal classes, but it's hard to believe they want us to go. It's so easy to forget the rest of the world when one sees only these nice people who come to you for everything and live almost exactly the same life as they did in Mr. Bennett's time.' She stopped, then said:

'But tell me about camp in the plains. I mean the nice part, not the frustration. What did it feel like and smell like? You see, I wasn't with you and I want to know what it was like when I wasn't there. I can't picture it a bit because I only know Delhi.'

Christopher tried to tell her. He talked of one of his camps down by the river, where he went every year in the spring because the stream changed its course in the floods, washing away the fertile fields and replacing them with sand, so that a fresh record had to be made every year. He tried to recall a day, seeing as he relived it the pictures he had seen then. Called by lamplight; a cup of tea and some bread and jam before you start — but Susan was used to that — and then you were out in the cool morning, on Sweet Janet or Corvette, cantering easily along a sandy road to the first village. The light was sweet and fresh, there was a sense of infinite space, sand and water and sky, with milky clouds in clear smooth bars on the horizon, and here and there the aromatic fragrance of crops. It was light soil and peas were a favourite sowing; their white blossom, sparkling with dew, repeated the tones of sky and sand. At dawn, it was a country for the Dutch and English water-colourists, space, emptiness, cool colours; but later, when the sun was high, it was beyond the power of painter. You found a sandy bank with a tamarisk bush above, and sat in that tiny patch of shade to eat a large late breakfast. It was not really hot, for there was always a breeze by the river, but sand and water flashed and glittered, it was bright sky and blinding sun, light trembling and glittering and incandescent, the flashing flight of the white river tern, and the cry of the water-fowl. Back to the tents in the early afternoon, and then, in the cool of the evening, the villagers would collect and for two or three hours you would try to settle their troubles on the spot, by word of mouth.

Then there was the winter camping, when the morning ride was sharp with cold, the level green fields wet with dew or touched with hoar frost; the smell of sugar-cane juice, rich and warm, as they boiled it into brown toffee-like molasses on the edge of the field where it had grown; the return to camp in the evening when the smoke lay in level blue lines above the villages and the peafowl were settling for the night with noisy flappings in the treetops, the air chilling the arms that had been bare in the sunshine; and the smell of the camp, smoke and straw and bullocks.

'But it's no use,' said Christopher, 'I can't recapture it to myself, let alone make you see it. Try to remember for yourself a day on the downs or in the Alps. You try, but memory can only call up a shadowy sort of ghost, one of the strengthless heads of the dead which have no reality till they drink some blood. Go to the place again, and it all comes back with the first breath of wind that carries the scent of thyme, or of pine woods in the sun.'

Susan sighed. She said:

'Oh dear, I'm afraid you're right. Shan't we be able to remember all the loveliness we've seen here?'

'We can help each other. But not much. You can't really call things back.'

'You can call them back a little way,' said Susan, 'but your memory's inadequate. What was that thing in Francis Thompson we liked, about the wild sweet witch? Read it to me, will you, Christopher?'

Christopher found it and read:

In the most iron crag his foot can tread
A dream may strew her bed
And suddenly his limbs entwine
And draw him down through rock as sea-nymphs
might through brine.

201

But unlike those feigned temptress-ladies who
In guerdon of a night the lover slew,
When the embrace has failed, the rapture fled,
Not he, not he, the wild sweet witch is dead!
And though he cherisheth
The babe most strangely born from out her death —
Some tender trick of her it hath, maybe —
It is not she!

Christopher looked up when he had read it. He said:
'He's talking about the poet, of course. Every poet there's ever been. I suppose everyone who tries to paint or write must have that feeling. He has an idea, but when he puts into paint or words, the result is pitifully inadequate compared with what he dreamed it might be.'

'What I meant,' said Susan, 'was that the memory of anything lovely is inadequate in the same kind of way. If you were a perfect artist, you could make your past days, and your dreams, both live. But I suppose lots of people have had the same thought before.'

It was Mr. Bennett's thought of sixty years earlier, but he had lacked Francis Thompson's words to express it.

'Yes,' said Christopher. I don't think memory and what the artist makes are really the same, but they are inadequate in the same kind of way. It's odd you should have thought of those lines. Because I'd been thinking about them too, after we read them the other night. Only my thought was a little different; I thought that for many people, who don't paint or write or express themselves in that way, the same is true of their lives. What you make of your life — well, it's usually very different from the dream that strewed her bed for you as a young man. If you had dreams at all, of course. That must be true of my friend Jodh Singh, whom we were talking about this afternoon, if I'm at all right in my picture of him.'

'Yes, poor man,' said Susan. 'What sort of trouble do you expect about him?'

'Oh, I don't know. I just feel it's an electric sort of atmosphere in which anything might touch off a disturbance. Something that was nothing to do with either him or Dharma Nand might happen, some dispute, and those two get sucked in on opposite sides, and gradually get absorbed in it, till the whole district was excited about it. But I dare say I'm talking rot. Let's go to bed.'

It was cold outside the tents and the stars had a frosty twinkle. The moon was just rising over the eastern shoulder of Dunagiri, lighting a long slope of snow with milky radiance. Vastness and cold and silence, the stars, and the icy bulk of the mountain; a wind breathed in the trees and they swayed against the clear sky.

'Let's try very hard not to forget,' said Susan.

IN the fifteen years since the episode of the panther, Jodh Singh had kept only one of the resolutions he had made when he was younger. He never missed going to Bantok for some part at any rate of the summer. It seemed to him that only when he was there could he really be himself, as he wished to be. During the rest of the year, as he wandered about the district from his head-quarters at Gadoli, with no companion but his servant Autaru, he was continually being forced by the world and the pressure of events into words or actions which he did not feel were really his. He had never realized himself again as he had done in those first days of the agitation about the corvee. When he spoke to the villagers now, there was always somewhere a tiny corner of his mind that remembered the jeering faces at Pokhra, when he had walked past the court-room with the Dom in a procession of two, the handcuffs and the guard set over him in the night at Gadoli.

In the villages they looked on him with respect and even fear. He was not like other people. You never knew how he would take things. Someone would suggest what was obviously the wisest course, a judicious attempt to delay throwing oneself completely into the fray until it was clear which way it would go, and he would flare up in a rage that was terrible to see. There was hardly a member of the District Board who had not winced under his tongue at some time or another. Hot-tempered, some-times raging like a wounded panther, unaccountable to the worldly mind, moody and solitary; but all the same, he was a champion to be sent for by the weak when they were in trouble. Every villager knew that if Jodh Singh took up his cause, or the cause of his village, there would be no lack of courage or of energy in the way it was fought.

But when he was at Bantok, or better still, in the high pastures with the sheep, and could sit gazing south over the blue foothills, or north towards the icy peaks, he felt like a god, remote from passion. He could see then how year by year his emotions had led him, and how again and again they had led him wrong, and he would resolve that when he went back to the world of men he would let them dominate him no more. Nor would he again lose himself in drink when he was miserable, inflaming the passions from which he was trying to escape. And then one day there would come that opportunity for which he still waited, the chance that he would seize as he had once seized it in the days of the corvee, a chance that would let him show what was really in him. For he still knew that he was capable of more than he had yet shown the world. His moment would come, and it would make him truly a leader. They had recognized already that he was different from other people; everyone in the district knew that he was set aside for something special. It had been that which they had recognized in an obscure way when they thought he was the panther; and indeed in a sense it was true, for he was a panther, a whip, a purge, to cleanse the land of evil. And one day his hour would come and his full stature be revealed.

These were his thoughts when he was alone; and then he would forget thought and live in the body, enjoying flowers and sunlight and the clean air, or he would play with his son as if he were himself a boy again. But when he went back to the world of men, there it was, ready to pounce on him; it would spring before he was poised to receive it, and his passions would mount and push him into swift action. He would be back in the current again, hurled from wave to wave with no time to recover his breath between one crest and the next.

This was just what had happened when he came back from Bantok for the last winter of his life. The world had sprung on him at once. There was waiting for him one of the Marchas from the upper valleys, with a tale of tyranny and oppression. It was two years now since Jodh Singh had extended the favour of his special patronage and protection to the Marchas, the half-Tibetan people who live in the valleys leading to the passes to Tibet. They are a folk who lead a strange life. Half the year their villages are buried twenty or thirty feet deep in snow. They move down in autumn when the first snow falls, men, women and children, with herds of strange creatures, half yak and half cow, and flocks of sheep and goats, pitching their black skin tents at the camping-places prescribed by long usage. Their beasts carry their tents and cooking gear and food, the women carry their babies on their backs, queer little mummified bundles slung between Tibetan tubes for mixing tea and butter, and a host of oddities; and the goats and sheep carry panniers of the salt and wool and borax and the rare skins they have brought from Tibet. They move down towards the plains, trading as they go, selling sheep and goats and the goods in their panniers, buying grain and sugar in the plains to carry back to Tibet. They depend for food and fodder on the forests and the grazing grounds of the villages where they camp. After mid-winter, they start to move back and they reach their own villages just as the snow begins to melt. Even then, they do not live long in houses. They plough the fields and sow the barley, and a small buckwheat with a pink flower like London Pride, which will not grow below eight thousand feet. Then in July, when the snow melts in the passes, the men move on to Tibet, where they sell their grain and sugar and refill their panniers for next winter. They are a hardy folk and a Marcha woman will drop her child one evening and move on with the flocks next day, carrying her bundle, like a ewe from her own flocks.

This way of life had been all very well in the old days, when there was plenty of grass and fuel for everyone, but as people grew more and forests less, there were more and more villages who resented watching the Marcha flocks and herds eating their jealously preserved grass and the Marcha women recklessly burning wood from their forests. It was for help in one of the quarrels arising from this resentment that the Marchas first turned to Jodh Singh. He had never been one to wait and consider and weigh the arguments, for and against; and as he grew older he grew more impatient. The story the Marchas told appealed to him, because they were wanderers like himself and opposed to vested interests. He took up their cause without waiting to hear what the villagers had to say on the other side. When he did hear the villagers, he regarded their arguments as selfish. He came very quickly to look on the Marchas as his people, especially committed to his care, because they had no other friends.

While he was fighting their case, they told him of their need for a trade agent and general store at Vishnumath, the last village of any size before the climb to the passes begins; and he had spoken of this to a cousin of his at Gadoli, another Govind Singh, who was becoming increasingly restive at the control of his father, Jodh Singh's money-lending uncle. Govind Singh and Jodh Singh in alliance had decided to start a shop at Vishnumath, to be run by Govind Singh. They had carried the day against the uncle, as in the last resort Jodh Singh always could, and had set up the shop, thus strengthening Jodh Singh's bond with the Marchas.

That had been two years ago. Now, when Jodh Singh came back to Gadoli from Bantok for the last time, he was met by one of the Marchas who had come on in advance of their main camps to tell him of fresh trouble. Last year, there had been a quarrel with one of the villages where they pitched their tents, but there was no doubt that by old custom the Marchas had a right to camp there and the Tahsildar had decided the case in their favour. But there had been unpleasantness and threats of violence. The Marchas were peaceful folk, nomad traders, not soldiers; they did not want trouble. They were afraid the villagers would not respect the Tahsildar's decision and so this year they had camped near by in another village, where they thought the villagers would be more amenable. They said that this was a place where they had always camped, but this was not true; and Dharma Nand, the new Tahsildar, soon got to the truth and turned them out. Now they came running to Jodh Singh, with a sad tale of corruption and intrigue.

As soon as he had heard the name of Dharma Nand, Jodh Singh had felt that suffocating uncontrollable anger that constricted the throat and filled the head with blood, a drunkenness of anger like the drunkenness of the high pastures that he knew so well. He remembered the boy who years ago had run after him and called him a panther; and now that same boy had come to lord it over him here, in his own country, among his own people, a creature from the lower hills who looked down on the people of the upper hills as backward, a lickspittle, a toady who had taken the safe course of government service instead of helping his country by opposing foreign rule. And the Marchas' tale showed him corrupt and unfair, as bad as the rest of them. Jodh Singh did not stop to consider. He would show the swine that he was not called a panther for nothing. He sent the Marcha to wait outside and sat down at once to write his complaint to the Deputy Commissioner.

But he regarded that complaint as no more than the opening shot of his cannonade. He went about looking for material for further attacks on a man whom he was firmly persuaded was extortionate and tyrannous. He found material of a kind and sent in one petition after another. The atmosphere in the Northern circle became indeed, as Christopher had said, electric and charged with tension. A trivial incident would be enough to release that tension in storm.

It was not long before it occurred. The murder of Raghubar Dat, the high priest's cook, was a sordid and petty affair in itself, but one of which the consequences spread wide.

It happened in Vishnumath, when the first snow had fallen. The high priest and his retinue had come down from Badrinath, the great temple, some six weeks earlier. The temple was deep in snow all the winter, and twice a year the acolytes and thurifers and choristers moved between Badrinath and Vishnumath, and with them the shopkeepers and the keepers of hostels and lodgings and all who lived on the pilgrim traffic. Down they came in autumn to Vishnumath, moving up again in the spring when the snow began to melt. But they were dull in winter, with no pilgrims; they felt the need for a relaxation which it was hard to find in Vishnumath, a hill village where the snow lay for two months, though not so deeply nor for so long as at the temple. This particular night, Raghubar Dat wanted a drink. He was a hill Brahman, a Dimri, and it was the custom of his caste to drink spirits, one reason for the contempt in which a Brahman of the plains would hold him. There was no liquor in his own quarters and in any case he wanted company as much as drink. He was bored, he wanted to be cheerful and excited. He had cooked the high priest's evening meal and there was nothing more he had to do that night. He went out to look for amusement.

Outside in the snow, he paused. There was really only one place where he could be certain of finding drink and that was in the Marchas' cabin. It was true the Marchas were almost as repulsive a caste as the aboriginal Doms; it was said, though they denied it, that in Tibet they would eat yak's meat and a yak is practically a cow. But they always had liquor, because they had a special dispensation from the Government to follow their age-long practice of distilling their own drink from barley. They were not supposed to sell it or give it to anyone else, but no one worried much about that. There was one family of Marchas who did not go down to the plains with the rest, but stayed behind in Vishnumath, and there was always drink to be had there. And one of the women was an attractive piece. That was the place. Raghubar Dat's pause lasted only a moment and then he moved off to the Marchas' cabin.

The Marchas were not particularly glad to see him. He had been there before, and their private opinion was that he was not sufficiently free with his money to make up for his bad manners. In fact, Keshar Singh, the leader of the community, had told them that next time Raghubar Dat came, they should refuse to let him in. To-night, however, Keshar Singh was out and not one of the others felt sufficiently sure of himself to be rude to a Brahman. And Raghubar Dat gave them no chance to deny him entrance. He banged on the door of the smoky little hut and when they opened to see who was there, he stooped at once and came straight in, crouching as one had to, for the door was not four feet high.

It was snowing again outside and there was a sharp wind, which whistled in the cracks of the cabin and in the cedar overhead, a noisy blustering night, when one would be glad to be indoors. The Marchas, two women and three men, clustered round the fire of yak's dung and wood. They squatted on the floor; it was their lifelong habit, but in any case it was the only way to be comfortable because the ceiling was too low to stand upright and the smoke was much thicker in the upper part of the room. If you kept near the floor, you avoided the worst of it. They were smoking tobacco, handing round the pipe-bowl, men and women taking their turn alike.

Raghubar Dat slipped quickly into the place of the man who had opened the door. The others surlily made more room. Raghubar Dat knew them, and greeted the men by name. Then he looked sideways at Tara Devi, the woman sitting next to him. She was the elder of the two, the wife of Keshar Singh, but she was young. She was the one who took his fancy. He asked her for a drink.

She replied shortly and sulkily.

'There is no drink,' she said. 'We finished it yesterday. We are making some more to-morrow.'

'Ah, come now,' said Raghubar Dat. 'It's no use telling me

that. You people are never without a drink. I know you're not
supposed to sell it, but between friends now, on a night like
this — '

'There isn't any,' she said, still more sulkily.

Raghubar Dat put down a rupee, a whole rupee.

'Come now,' he said, 'give me a little. Just a little.'

'Give him some,' said one of the men. He thought it would
save trouble to give in to one so importunate. Tara Devi looked
at him. The firelight shone on her wide-boned face, the clear
whites of her slanting eyes. Her cheeks beneath the grime of
smoke and cooking were as firm and red as the flesh of a ripe
apple. Her look said that the man who spoke was a fool and had
let her down, but she said nothing. She rose crouching and
turned to get the bottle. She wore a full red petticoat over
trousers and felt boots. As she squatted again with the bottle in
her hand, Raghubar Dat looked with pleasure and desire at her
squareness, the swell of her breasts beneath the close-fitting
bodice, the silver ornaments round her neck and the smooth skin
beneath them. A woman of the villages would have been
swathed in shapeless blanket. He took his drink; and they all
drank.

Raghubar Dat asked for more. He produced another rupee.
The party began to mellow and to talk. Keshar Singh, the
leader, the husband of Tara Devi, came in. He looked at Raghubar Dat with a scowl, but said nothing. They made room for
him in the circle and he too drank, but he would not talk. He
saw with anger the looks Raghubar Dat cast on his wife. The
drink inflamed his sullen anger, but there was nothing he could
say; he sat and glowered.

Raghubar Dat grew bolder and his tongue bawdier. His jokes
grew more and more shameless; it could not be said that he was
making direct advances to Tara Devi, but all were conscious of
the thought behind the words. The other Marchas laughed at
his sallies, but shamefacedly, their eyes on Keshar Singh. Tara

Devi grew more angry and more silent. She passed the bottle as she was asked, with no further protest. It was for her men to say when the visitor had had enough.

Then Raghubar Dat's hour came. With his fourth drink he grew bolder still. He leaned forward and turned towards Tara Devi, sitting on his left.

'You are beautiful, beloved,' he said. And his right hand passed across his body and caressed her left breast, and then strove to enter her bodice.

Keshar Singh was sitting on his right. He put back his hand to a wooden butter tube that stood against the wall behind him. He pulled out the plunger. It was eighteen inches long and as thick as a rolling-pin, of maple-wood polished by years of use till it was hard and smooth. Keshar Singh half rose from his squatting position and with one violent movement swung the plunger over the head of the man beyond him and brought it with all the strength of his arm on to the back of Raghubar Dat's head, below his cap as he bent towards Tara Devi. Raghubar Dat toppled forward. He fell with his head on Tara Devi's lap, and a thin trickle of blood ran from his nose on to her red skirt. His cap fell off towards the fire and someone automatically picked it up to save it from burning.

They lifted him and laid him on his back.

'He is badly hurt,' said one.

'He is dead,' said another.

Keshar Singh looked at his head. He put a hand on his heart and listened for his breathing.

'He is not dead,' he said, 'but the bone of his skull is broken. He will die. But he might talk first. We must take care he does not talk.'

The others nodded.

'Give me a blanket,' said Keshar Singh. He put the folded blanket over Raghubar Dat's mouth and nose and pressed. When he moved the blanket, he listened again. Then he said:

'Now he is dead.'

'We must hide him,' said one of the other men.

Keshar Singh thought for a little.

'We must take him out and push him over a cliff,' he said. 'Then they will think it was an accident.'

'It would be better if they did not find him at once,' said Tara Devi. 'They will take him to the doctor at Chamoli and he will cut him up and find liquor in his stomach and then they will guess he had been here. It would be better if the vultures found him first before the doctor.'

Keshar Singh thought again. He said:

'They will look for him to-morrow when he does not come back. Let us hide him now, then throw him over a cliff to-morrow night when the search is over. Then they will not find him till the vultures have been at him.' He paused and thought. 'We will take out his stomach anyhow, and it will look as though the vultures had done it.'

'Where shall we hide him?' asked one of the younger brothers. 'There is no room here and people come here all day, all kinds of people.'

Keshar Singh considered again. Then he said:

'There is Jodh Singh Ji's shop. There is the place underneath it where we put the liquor. We might try that.'

They continued the discussion for some time before they opened the low door and lifted out the body, rolled in a blanket. It had stopped snowing, and the wind had dropped, but the stars were hidden.

'Do not put it down,' whispered Keshar Singh. 'Keep it off the snow.'

The three men moved away over the fresh snow, carrying the body between them.

ON the second morning after the death of Raghubar Dat, that is, some thirty-six hours after Keshar Singh had struck his blow, a young man was driving out the family flock of sheep and goats into the snow from his home about two miles from Vishnumath. It was no use taking out the cows in the snow, but until it grew deeper, it was worth sending the smaller and hardier beasts. They would find leaves on the bushes and would scrape away the snow from patches of grass and find a certain amount of nourishment, not enough to keep them, but enough to reduce the demands on the stored hay that had been cut from the forests by the women during the summer and laboriously carried down to the village on their backs. And there was a small sheltered grazing-ground, where the drifts would not lie deep, to which no other flocks had access and which Pancham Singh had been reserving for just this purpose. It was a shelf in the face of a cliff and could not be reached from the Vishnumath side. There were precipices above and below and the only path to it was a narrow track along the face of the hill from the lonely homestead where Pancham Singh lived with his brothers. He had come there every day since the first snow fell, and, with the wind as it had been, not much had lain there. It would be worth going for some time yet.

Pancham Singh tramped along cheerfully, his feet warm in fragments of old blanket bound with a network of grass rope. Coming and going was all right, but it was not much fun waiting while the animals grazed. He would collect sticks, of course, to take home, and also to make himself a fire. It was women's work really, but they were very short of women. They were a stock who bred males and the last two generations had had to expend all their hoard of rupees on wives; this generation would have to save before they could marry. He reached the grazing-ground and at once collected sticks to make a fire on the ashes of yesterday's. The wood was soaking wet, of course, but he had some dry grass and chips with him. He squatted down and pulled out a brass cartridge case with a wooden plug, full of tinder made from lichen collected on the high pastures. He struck his steel, shaped like a tiny knuckleduster, on a flint, and soon had his tinder glowing. When the smoke of his fire was rising in the still air, he strolled round the little shelf to see how his flock was getting on.

He went up first towards the upper cliff, and there he stopped. Half among the bushes, half on the open snow, lay something dark. For a fraction of a second he thought it was a bear, but it was quite still and it was too small for a bear. A black sheep had fallen over the cliff perhaps; that might mean a meal of meat. He went closer. It was a man. He was quite dead.

Pancham Singh did not wait to look at him closely. He saw that this was not a peasant like himself, for he was wearing a suit of shaped clothes, not a blanket plaid. He covered him with branches to keep the vultures from seeing him and decided he could leave the flock to itself for the half hour or so that would be needed to get to the homestead and back. There was obviously neither a panther nor a bear lying up on the shelf, or the flock would have winded him by now and would be huddled together in a frightened circle. He had with him a black long-haired dog with a wide brass collar studded with spikes. He left the dog to guard the flock and went as quickly as he could to tell his brothers.

Amar Singh, the patwari, reached the grazing-ground by midday. He was a short man, almost completely square, with a hooked nose and a reddish-brown face. He was a good patwari, intelligent and conscientious, who did his best to be honest within reason. He recognized the body at once as Raghubar Dat's, for he knew the man well by sight. He had of course suspected that it would be he, for he had heard yesterday that the high priest's cook had not come home and that the retinue had been out looking for him. He had not worried very much, supposing that he had fallen over a cliff when drunk. Raghubar Dat's reputation was not a good one.

When he heard of the corpse, however, he began to suspect something more serious. He asked questions as he walked up the narrow path towards the grazing-ground. Pancham Singh was positive there had been no corpse there yesterday. Now it was credible, though not very likely, that Raghubar Dat might have fallen over the cliff in his cups the night he disappeared. Not very likely, because it was difficult to see why he should have gone to the top of that particular cliff, a mile from Vishnumath, on a snowy night. It had not been the sort of time or place one would be likely to choose for either a drinking-bout or a love affair; and drink and women had been his interests. Still, he might have agreed to meet someone outside the village and lost his way. It was just possible.

But to suppose that he should have disappeared, near his home, and remained alive for twenty-four hours, and then fallen over a cliff by accident — that was surely stretching probability too far. It looked at once as though he had been killed the night he disappeared, his body concealed, and only now pushed over the cliff to make the death appear an accident.

This was Amar Singh's simple reasoning as soon as he heard Pancham Singh say the body had not been there the day before. And when he saw it, his reasoning was at once confirmed, because while the rest of the body was untorn, the stomach had been taken out. If the vultures had done this, they would have torn at least the face and eyes as well, but they had not; and again, Pancham Singh had been positive that there had been no vultures when he found the corpse. It looked as though someone, for some reason of his own, wished to make sure the stomach was not examined.

The patwari hunted in the bushes, but he could find nothing

else connected with the body. No hat. Hardly anyone in India goes about with his head uncovered. In the hills, everyone wears a round cap; the villager has a shapeless woollen affair, woven from the yarn he has spun himself; those who have employment away from the village usually wear a black pill-box. It is worn indoors and out. There was no cap with this body.

Amar Singh had the body dispatched to Chamoli for post-mortem with a brief report. He could not form any opinion on how long it was since death, nor on how the wound on the back of the head had been caused. He himself went back to Vishnu-math and began to ask questions from the high priest's house-hold. But he got nothing there. No one had seen Raghubar Dat go out, nor heard him say where he was going. But they could make a guess why he had gone out. There were bottles in his quarters which had contained spirits, but they were empty.

He must have gone out for a drink, and that meant the Marchas' cabin. There the patwari went. He was met with stony denial. They had not seen Raghubar Dat that evening. Well, yes, he had been to them in the past. Not for a drink, no. They could not imagine why he had come. They had not wanted him to come again and had not been friendly with him. They had seen nothing of him that evening; nothing at all.

Amar Singh felt sure they were lying. Most of the answers came from Keshar Singh or Tara Devi, the other three keeping silent. Amar Singh sat back and looked at them, their high Mongolian cheek-bones and slanting eyes, their long hair. Their glances were downcast, there was a positive sulkiness and resent-ment about them all, and fear, he was sure. But were they frightened only because this might bring to light their activities in the matter of liquor, or had they something more serious to hide? He had of course long known that they peddled small quantities of liquor and had a shrewd suspicion that they had rather larger dealings in which Govind Singh, Jodh Singh's partner in the shop, was involved. But was there something more?

He began again to question Keshar Singh and Tara Devi. He asked them the same questions all over again, quickly, any question that came into his head. He did not pay much attention to their answers. The corner of his eye was all the time ready to dart a glance at the others, the silent three, of whom he asked nothing, but he was careful not to release that glance. He waited, talking and bullying. Then he said:

'I shall have to search this room.'

And then at last he let his eye flick to the youngest of the three men, quick as the dart of a lizard. And he caught the look he had hoped for, a half turn of the head toward a corner where there was a pile of gear, clothes, a butter-mixer, cooking pots.

He felt he was safe in making a search. These people were not the kind to hire lawyers and make a fuss, they were too simple. And in any case there was no doubt they were on the wrong side of the law over liquor. He went straight to the corner where the youngest man's eye had turned.

He looked at the butter-mixer with curiosity and pulled out the plunger, but pushed it back again. He had hoped for a weapon, but there was nothing of that kind. There was a folded blanket. He looked at it carefully. There were dark stains of something that had gone hard. It looked like blood. He asked about it.

'That's the blanket we carried the goat in,' said Tara Devi. Amar Singh wrote down her reply. It did not sound very convincing. Why should anyone carry a goat in a good blanket? But they might have a gun they had no licence for, and they might have shot a chamois and smuggled it home in a blanket.

Then he found a cap, a round black cap. Keshar Singh said it was his. He wore it when he went to Chamoli. It was not the sort of cap he usually wore, but it was difficult to say he had never worn it and Amar Singh saw at once that it would be impossible to prove it was Raghubar Dat's. It was, for instance, indistinguishable to the ordinary eye from the cap he wore himself. If Raghubar Dat had had a wife living with him in his quarters she might have been able to identify it, though even that was doubtful, but she was in his village three days' march away, looking after the farm.

But even without the cap, Amar Singh felt he had the rudiments of a case. He took the Marchas out into the snowy track. He looked at their clothes. There might be some blood there. Sure enough there was, on the front of Tara Devi's red skirt. She said it was from the goat, the same goat that had been in the blanket. But the doctors would be able to say whether it was goat's blood, and Amar Singh said he must take possession of her skirt, a demand which caused a good deal of delay, because Tara Devi maintained she had no other skirt. At last someone lent her one. Amar Singh then arrested Keshar Singh and Tara Devi; as he had only two pairs of handcuffs and nowhere but his own quarters to lock them up, he felt that two were as many as he could manage.

The body of Raghubar Dat had been sent with a team of eight porters, who had orders to waste no time on the way and they covered the thirty odd miles to Chamoli within the twenty-four hours. As soon as they arrived, the Tahsildar, Dharma Nand, read the report that they brought; he decided that a possible case of murder in which the corpse belonged to the high priest's household was too important to be left to a patwari and he sent his assistant to take over the investigation. The Assistant Tahsildar also wasted no time. He arrived on the fourth day after the murder.

He set to work to get a confession.

ABOUT a fortnight after the murder of Raghubar Dat, Susan and Christopher were sitting out of doors in the clear starlight, muffled to the ears in all the clothes they possessed. They were camped on a bluff in the middle of a wide shallow valley and they could see the hillside on either side of the stream, up and down, for ten miles each way. There were perhaps thirty villages in their view. It was the feast of lights, and as they gazed at the dark bulk of the forest-clad hills, below the clean line where the ridge cut the stars, one by one, from every village, there crept a winding golden caterpillar, which crawled down the hillside and then broke into fiery clusters. From the nearest village a caterpillar came directly towards them. Every male in the village was carrying a torch, a blazing bundle of resinous splinters tied together with a grass rope, of which an end several yards long was left free. As the long winding line reached the open fields below Christopher's camp, each man flung his torch from him to the full length of the rope and then, as it checked, tightened the strain, and leaning backwards swung the tangled flames in planetary circles round his head. Each man had to dodge his neighbour's torch and keep his own swinging; twenty circles of flame and sparks crossed and curved and intersected amongst a wild confusion of leaping figures, with here and there a face lighted for a momentary glimpse as a torch passed close. When he tired of making others jump over his catherine wheel, each man broke off into a pas seul in which the rope was shortened and the flaming brand made to spin in a smaller circle over which the performer skipped himself, while next, in even smaller circles, it would flash under one leg, over an arm, back in an inverted curve, under the other leg, behind the back.

The torches burnt themselves out, the men stood panting and happy, waiting for congratulations on their skill and vigour.

Then a bonfire was made, and the drums began their stammering syncopated rhythm; the men danced a story of the Pandavas, heroes of old Hindu legend, and the wars they had fought in the hills. They moved round the fire in contorted attitudes, their arms and hands accenting the rhythm in angular motion; then the drums quicken, the knees bend more sharply, the angles of elbow and shoulder become more acute, like the knotted limbs of the hill oak; the dancers are ecstatic; the rhythm sinks again, the dancers shuffle less violently.

In such a lull, a figure pushed forward from the darkness towards the two camp chairs where Susan and Christopher were sitting. This was not a blanket-clad peasant, but a man wearing a shaped suit, a shopkeeper or a minor official. He stooped and laid his hands on Christopher's feet.

'Lord, forgive me,' he said.

Christopher removed his feet out of reach under his chair and cautiously asked what there was to forgive.

'Lord, it is Jodh Singh Ji.'

'What has happened to him?'

'Lord, he has been arrested and locked up.'

'Why?'

'Because the Tahsildar is his enemy.'

'But why does the Tahsildar say he has locked him up?'

'They say he hid the body of Raghubar Dat. But it is false, lord. Why should he? It is all for enmity.'

'I see. Well, I can do nothing about it to-night. In any case, I expect he has been released on bail. I have had no reports on this yet and must wait till I have. If there is reason to suspect him, I cannot interfere with justice.'

'But, lord, it is Jodh Singh Ji. You know him. You know his temperament. I am afraid. I do not know what he will do.'

'Whoever he is,' said Christopher, 'it cannot make any difference to the law if he has done this.'

'But he has not done it. He is innocent.'

'Well, we shall see. I promise to look into it and see what I think. Come again to-morrow morning. I may have had a report by then. Who are you, in any case?'

'Lord, I am his cousin, Govind Singh. We have a shop at Vishnumath.'

'Oh, yes, I see. Well, come again in the morning.'

Christopher suggested to Susan that they should leave the dancing now. He gave the headman of the village the price of a goat for the dancers and they went into the tents. There he undid the bags of mail, which had arrived late that evening, and looked through them for a letter from the Northern Circle. It was there sure enough, and also a letter from Jodh Singh and he read them both without delay

'Now,' said Susan when he had finished, 'tell me all about it. Or do you want to do something important?'

'No, I can't do anything to-night. It would be a help to talk about it. You be Watson.'

Susan was wearing a dark blue sweater, slacks the colour of the sails in a Breton fishing-smack, a long camel-hair coat. She curled herself up in a big camp chair and pulled up to her chin a honey-coloured blanket that left nothing to be seen but a tangle of dark curls and a small round face that by nature looked always amused but was now serious.

'Now,' said Christopher, 'I told you about this rather sordid affair, the murder of the high priest's cook — the title of the crime's the best part of it. Well, since I last heard, the Assistant Tahsildar has got a confession from the younger of the Marcha women, who has turned King's evidence. Better not ask how he got it. Jodh Singh says they did extremely intimate things to her with red pepper and also made her lie in the snow with nothing on till she talked, but he is inclined to believe rather exaggerated stories. I shall have to look into that separately.'

'I suppose they must have done something, or she wouldn't have confessed,' said Susan.

'Yes. And for that reason I don't expect her confession will help much in court — even if she sticks to it, which she probably won't. But it may all the same be true. She says that Raghubar Dat came to them for a drink and got fresh with the other woman, her sister. Apparently he had rather a reputation for that kind of thing. And under provocation her husband hit him on the head. They thought there would be a search next day and so they hid the body till after the search and then pushed it over a cliff, hoping it would look like an accident.'

'Wait a minute,' said Susan. 'Was that really any good? Because if the searchers didn't look in the place where the body was going to be tipped, there would have been nothing gained by hiding it; but if the searchers did look in that place and it was empty, and then next day the body suddenly appeared there, it would be worse for the murderers? Or wouldn't it?'

'You're being much too clever for Watson. And also for the Marchas. You must remember they've never read any detective stories. They haven't had that thorough grounding in crime that every young Anglo-Saxon has the right to expect. Anyhow, that's what she says they thought. And she says they went with the body to Jodh Singh's shop, and he was staying there, and they asked if he would help, and he agreed, and they put the body under the shop in a sort of secret cellar that they knew about and had used for smuggling liquor.'

'I see,' said Susan. 'But — oh well, you tell me what you think about it.'

'Well first the murder, apart from the Jodh Singh part. Raghubar Dat went out somewhere, on a snowy night; the only place anyone can suggest he could have gone to is the Marchas, because he was a drinker and he often did go there for drink. His body is found two mornings later. There's a wound on his head which might have been caused by a blow or by a rock. The doctor says he had been dead about thirty-six hours when found; and a shepherd whom no one sees any reason to disbelieve says

223

the corpse was not in the place where it was found the morning after death took place. Also the stomach had been removed with a knife.'

'Disgusting,' said Susan. 'And I can't see why.'

'Well, the only reason I can think of is that they thought a post-mortem would show his stomach was full of drink, which would point to them. But it wasn't very clever really. Anyhow, all that makes it pretty clear the body was concealed somewhere. Therefore, the presumption is murder, though there may have been an accident which they were afraid might be taken for murder.'

'Yes. How silly people are when they try to hide things. It always seems to land them in trouble.'

'I don't know what I should do myself if I suddenly found a corpse on my hands in suspicious circumstances. I've never tried. It might take a lot of courage to come clean. However, that's beside the point. Now — it looks very much like murder. The next question of course is, who did it? And it looks very like the Marchas, even if you disregard the confession. They were the only people he was likely to visit that anyone can suggest. No one else seems to have seen him. There was a blanket in their hut with blood on it, and blood on the elder woman's skirt. They say it was goat's blood, but the doctors say it's human. There is an extra cap in the cabin, of the kind Raghubar Dat wore, but it can't be positively identified. It seems to me ten to one that he did go to their hut and died there; no, more, a hundred to one; and the real doubt in my mind is whether they meant to kill him, or whether he was killed by accident and they decided to hush it up. They might even have been justified in killing him if he really assaulted the woman and that was the only way they could protect her — but that's most unlikely. No, as far as the murder goes, I'd say it was a clear case. Really, from my point of view, the problem is whether Jodh Singh was concerned in hiding the body. The first evidence for that is the confession. It may be that the rest of the confession is true, and that the bit about waking Jodh Singh and asking him to help was dictated, just to implicate Jodh Singh. The patwaris don't love him a little bit.'

'Do you think that — what's his name? The Tahsildar — would really go as far as that?'

'I must say all my instinct is against believing he would. But his Assistant, or the patwari, might have done what they thought he'd like them to do. You know, Thomas à Beckett — who will rid me of this turbulent priest — that kind of feeling.'

'It doesn't sound very convincing to me, but I don't begin to understand the official mind.'

'And long may you not,' said Christopher. 'As a matter of fact, Dharma Nand has written here that he finds this very embarrassing because of his known enmity with Jodh Singh, and he asks me to have the formal magistrate's inquiry done somewhere else. He also says he's going up to Vishnumath himself to hear what the witnesses say and to make sure they're not under pressure. That sounds all right, and I want to believe him; but of course the defence would say he was going to make sure the witnesses don't recant. But to return to the story. Of course, it's possible they hid the body in the smuggler's cellar without telling Jodh Singh. In fact, I shouldn't have expected Jodh Singh even to know that the cellar existed; it was used only as a smuggling depot, and the only entry was from outside the house at the back: it was a concealed entrance. And it's most unlikely to my mind that Jodh Singh knew about the smuggling. It wasn't his kind of racket at all. I should have expected that Govind Singh was doing the smuggling, without Jodh Singh's knowledge. I've always heard Jodh Singh never concerned himself at all with the way his cousins did business. He just wasn't interested. And it's a mean niggling sort of way of breaking the law; most unlike him. But it would be quite in character for him to make up his mind that the Marchas weren't morally guilty and decide to help them. I don't think he has much abstract respect for the law, and his arrogance — in one kind of way — is terrific.'

'Perhaps it was really Govind Singh who helped them and they changed it to Jodh Singh because the patwari told them to.'

'The only thing against that,' said Christopher, 'is that a shop-keeper, who's always thinking of profit and loss, isn't really very likely to run the immense risk involved in hiding a body on the premises for someone else's benefit. Jodh Singh of course never counts the cost of anything. Only you'd think he might have seen your point, that it was silly to hide the corpse anyhow.'

'Well,' said Susan, 'if there's nothing against Jodh Singh but the confession, and you don't think that's any good — have they really got anything on him?'

'What I think about the confession is that it'll be retracted. When she gets into court, she will say she didn't really mean it and it was all extorted from her under pressure. But there is something else, as well as the confession. There's a man who lives on one of those little solitary farms you find in the upper part of the district, about a day's march from Vishnumath. He says he came in to do business with a man who has a shop in Vishnumath, as he does once a year, and stayed the night. Well, that's quite plausible. The shopkeeper confirms that he spent the night there. Jodh Singh says rather vaguely that they're both enemies of his, and I happen to know it's true of the shopkeeper. He's a member of the District Board, and Jodh Singh accused him about a year ago of having got himself a contract to build a school and of having made a very good thing of it. I think Jodh Singh was right. Anyhow, they had a flaming row, and I remem-ber hearing about it. Well, the other man, Dharam Singh his name is, was staying in this shop, and he had a pain in the night, one of those convenient calls of nature, as they say, that witnesses always do have when there's something interesting going on. He went outside and while he was there he heard some men come and knock on the door of Govind Singh's shop. And he says Jodh Singh came and spoke to them. He recognized his voice and saw his face by the light of a lantern he was carrying. He couldn't see the men because it was too dark.'

'Fishy,' said Susan.

'I agree; very fishy. It's too good to be true. But I must say I should be hard put to it to give really convincing reasons for disbelieving it. Well, there it is; undoubtedly, there is a case of a kind made out against Jodh Singh. I'm inclined to suspect it, but I don't see that I can do much beyond making sure he's given bail and having the magistrate's inquiry held in another circle. I shall warn the magistrate to sift it all very thoroughly, though I must take care not to influence him. But every official is prejudiced against Jodh Singh; and in any case, even if he's discharged from the magistrate's court, he'll have been put to a lot of trouble and will have lost a great deal of prestige. I'm afraid it'll drive him into a furious, irresponsible kind of mood; and he still has immense influence. It may cause a lot of trouble. I told you something would happen. This is just the kind of thing I imagined. Let's go to bed.'

Next morning, Christopher told Govind Singh his conclusions. He could not interfere but he would make sure that bail was allowed and would have the inquiry held in another circle. Govind Singh seemed dazed. He could only say:

'Lord, it is Jodh Singh Ji. I do not know what he will do. He will be very angry. And it is false. It is all enmity. Why should any man be so mad as to keep a corpse in his house for someone else? He will be very angry.'

V

JODH SINGH was sitting on a bluff above the village of Vishnumath. It was a steep rocky promontory, uncultivated, where nothing grew but sparse grass and a few pines. He could see from here a long way up and down the river, and across it to a peak that was visible from his home at Bantok.

His heart was full of anger and despair. Anger at the meanness of his enemies, despair at the wreckage of his life. And there was shame because his name was fallen low. He had been released on bail in the end, but for two nights he had been handcuffed and locked up in a back room of the patwari's quarters, eating his heart out, consumed with fury and impatience. Anger flamed up in a quick bright blaze when he thought of the way he had been treated, he, Jodh Singh, the leader of the district, the champion of the oppressed. Arrested and handcuffed, not for any political offence, but for concealing evidence of a most sordid murder. And whatever doubts the Deputy Commissioner might feel, Jodh Singh himself had none as to who was responsible. He knew it was all a plot. Dharma Nand and all his enemies had banded together against him. Dharma Nand had told them what to say. It was he who had planned this. Dharma Nand had schooled his assistant and the patwari, and those two had taught the Marcha woman what to say. The drunkenness of anger filled his heart and constricted his throat; his head felt as though it would burst.

And then he plunged into an abyss of misery when he thought of the plans he had made for his life. Year by year he had fallen below what he had hoped, but until now his feet had been turned the right way, even though he struggled aimlessly with the cactus and the boulders at the foot of the snow-clad peak that some day he would climb. The child born of his dream had up till now some tender trick of its mother, though the wild sweet witch herself was dead. But now he would never rear it; the child too lay dead at his feet. He could no more hope to lead the district after this. He saw before him nothing but a long dreary prospect of charge and counter-charge, inquiry in this court, trial in that court, the hired lawyer and the perjured witness, all the meanness his soul hated. For now his enemies would never be content. If he escaped from this, they would dig another pit about his feet. They would compass him about for fear lest he should strike back at them first. He would be locked up again, to rage baffled at the bars and pine for freedom, as he had in the patwari's quarters. He could not bear captivity.

Then there was money. Things had not gone well with the money-lending uncle, and now that Jodh Singh was down his creditors would make for him like vultures on a corpse. Debt would be their portion, and all its degradation.

He looked across the river towards Bantok and thought of his happiness there, the home he loved and his son. He looked at the track winding away from Vishnumath towards the bridge that led there. That was the way to his home, but it was not for him to tread it. He would never go there again. To-morrow he must go south to face his judges.

His mind turned to the witnesses against him. Lachchman Parshad, the shopkeeper whose corrupt contract he had exposed, mean, money-grubbing, a foreigner from the next district, a sneaking sophisticated Kumaoni, an intriguer like every one of his race. And Dharam Singh, who had no cause to hate him except that he had taken the part of the Marchas. Dharam Singh had not even the personal excuse for a grievance that the shopkeeper had. But Dharma Nand was the worst. From the day he had shouted in the village street that Jodh Singh was a panther and a man-eater, Dharma Nand had hated him and plotted against him, like his father before him. And this was his latest plot. Well, they should feel his fury. They should know what it was to anger a panther.

He had a kukri with him. He drew it and looked at the sharp heavy blade. He felt its edge. Years ago someone had given it to him, someone he had helped. He remembered the serious wrinkled face of the old man who had come to him when the case was won and given him the kukri, laying his hand on his arm and begging him to keep it and to take it with him wherever he went, because his enemies were many and he travelled in lonely places. He had kept it ever since, with his few belongings, in the basket covered with goatskin which Autaru carried for him on his travels. He had never used it for anything, but he liked to have it, partly because he had not often been given a present in return for what he had done, and partly because he felt a pleasure in the thought that he had to go armed because of his enemies. Its presence made life more exciting, and Jodh Singh more important. It had been there in his basket when they came to arrest him, but as soon as they led him away, Autaru had hidden it, with an obscure feeling that if they found it they might regard it as incriminating. They had not found it when they searched and now that he was released he had it again. He did not usually carry it on his person, but this morning he had slipped it under his coat and brought it with him, he could not tell why.

He thought of his enemies again. He knew where they were. They were to start to-morrow for the south, like himself, for the inquiry before a magistrate. Dharma Nand had gone up to Seragad Tok to question the main witness against him, Dharam Singh. Jodh Singh knew the place, for he had been there in the Marchas' quarrel about the camping-place. The Tahsildar would be in a tent near Dharam Singh's house. The shopkeeper, Lachchman Parshad, was in his shop in Vishnumath.

Again the drunkenness of anger swelled and mounted in his veins, suffocating, intolerable. There was a roaring in his ears, lights danced before his eyes. Something seemed to happen in his brain like the shift of pattern in a kaleidoscope, and suddenly he was lighter, clearer, cooler. He could see the world very small and very clear and far away, as though through the wrong end of a telescope. His body seemed to dance and sing; he could hardly feel it. He knew now what he would do. He would go and see them. He would show them what his anger meant. He would make them see how wrong they had been. They should understand everything, all he ought to have been. And he would take his kukri in case he needed it. He stood up and moved towards the path for Seragad Tok.

That evening, Dharam Singh and his son Man Singh, a boy of about twelve, were sitting quietly talking after their evening meal. Dharam Singh was going away next day, to give evidence in the south, and he was telling Man Singh what to do in his absence. Most of the work would be done by Makar Singh, Dharam Singh's younger brother, who lived in the other dwelling house, which with a huddle of cowsheds made up the buildings of the homestead; but there would be plenty for the boy to remember too. Dharam Singh was recently a widower and the two of them slept alone, but his brother's woman cooked for him. Father and son chatted quietly. There was no light except the fire, but it was a good fire, and they were warm and happy talking together.

There came a tap at the door and a low voice.

'Who is there?' said Dharam Singh. He could not hear the answer and went to the door to listen. The boy rose to his feet.

'Let me in, Dharam Singh,' said a quiet voice outside. Dharam Singh thought it was a message from the Tahsildar camped near by. He opened the door.

The boy Man Singh could never properly remember what happened after that. He heard the stranger speak, and something in his voice must have frightened him, for he stepped back out of the light of the fire and stood in the shadow of a corn-bin, and then there were more words, not loud but angry, and suddenly a blow and his father uttered a choking cry. Man Singh sank to the ground in his dark corner. He covered his eyes with his hands. He heard a dreadful chopping noise, and a harsh panting, and then he heard the door close. He crouched trembling, not daring to move.

He did not move for a very long time. Then the door opened again and he crouched closer and stiller. A voice said:

'Oh Dharmu!'

Someone came in and said:

'Where are you both? Are you asleep?'

Man Singh knew the voice but his brain was too frozen to tell him who it was and he kept quiet. He heard a step go to the fire and the sounds of wood being thrown on and the ashes being raked together. The voice spoke again, slow and wondering:

'My feet are wet and sticky!'

And then the voice cried in horror:

'What has happened! He's been killed!'

He heard a quick rush of steps and then the door slammed. He crouched still.

Makar Singh, Dharam Singh's brother, had been at the Tahsildar's camp talking to the orderly about the arrangements for the move next day. He had come back to tell Dharam Singh what had been decided. When he found his feet wet with blood, and the fire blazed up to show his brother lying with his head almost severed from the body, he ran out into the courtyard and stood still for a moment panting with fear and horror. There was no one in his own home but the women and children. He ran to the door and called:

'Are you awake? It is Makru.'

They answered sleepily and he told them to bar the doors quickly and open to no one but himself. Then he ran to the Tahsildar's camp. He found the orderly whom he had just left. The orderly was already in bed, but when he heard what had happened he said at once that the Tahsildar, Dharma Nand, must be told. The moon was at the end of its first quarter and had just risen. By its light they could see the Tahsildar's tent glimmering fifty yards away. There was no snow here yet.

They stopped outside the tent and asked permission to enter.

There was silence and they called louder. There was still no answer, and at last they went in. They found Dharma Nand fallen forward across a table at which he had been writing. He must have half risen to speak to his visitor, and dropped without a sound when the first savage blow fell on his skull and split the bone. Blows had been rained on his head. There was blood everywhere.

Early in the small hours of that morning, Lachchman Parshad, the shopkeeper at Vishnumath with whom Dharam Singh was supposed to have stayed, was roused by a voice calling his name. He slept on the upper floor of his house, above the shop, and he could hear someone on the veranda, which was reached by an outside staircase. There was a small window by the door, a tiny opening not a foot across with a wooden shutter, and before he unfastened the door he looked out to see who was there.

The moon by this time was high in the clear sky, and its light was reflected from the snow. He recognized Jodh Singh with a kukri in his hand.

'Let me in,' said Jodh Singh. 'I want to talk to you.'

Lachchman Parshad was frightened by his voice, his look, the weapon in his hand. He thanked the gods his door was barred and told Jodh Singh to come in the morning if he had anything to say. He crept into bed again, but did not dare to sleep, and as he lay trembling he too, like that other shopkeeper fifteen years ago, heard feet like an angry beast's pad back and forth on the veranda seeking entrance. Once the door was seized and rattled, and he heard it shake with the weight of a heavy body; blows were showered on the lock; it held, and he heard the breath of his enemy come in gasps as he stood motionless, panting after the effort. Then he heard steps going quickly and softly away.

In the morning, he found that the door of the shed where his goats were kept had been broken. Jodh Singh had burst his way in, and slain them all. Twelve goats lay decapitated. He had not taken their flesh for meat. The headless bodies lay there as witness of his rage.

VI

CHRISTOPHER was moving south and was several days' march away when he heard the news that Jodh Singh had disappeared and that two of his enemies had been killed in a night. There was nothing for it but to cancel the rest of his tour and turn north again. He arrived to find that terror had come to that part of the valley round Vishnumath, and that as in the days of the panther men slept with barred doors and did not go out after dark. Jodh Singh had taken the Tahsildar's gun from his tent and some cartridges known to be loaded for large game. He had fired once at the patwari, but had missed him and had escaped into the forest. The patwari was sure that food was being taken to him by villagers he had helped in the past, but it was impossible to find who was sending it or how it was sent. The patwari had taken Autaru and Govind Singh into custody as obvious links between the outlaw and the means of life, but this had not stopped the supply and he could not hold them long when there was no charge against them. Christopher ordered their release, although he had not the men to have them kept under continuous watch.

The difficulty was the same for the hunters of the man as it had been for the hunters of the panther. Until he revealed his whereabouts by some open act, a kill or a murder, the hunt was always far behind. The initiative lay with the hunted. There were hundreds of miles of forest where a man could lie hid; there were caves and shelters without number, and unlimited fuel with which a man might keep himself warm. Jodh Singh had influence all over the district; there were a score of villages in the Northern Circle alone who remembered him with gratitude. He could descend on any one of these and demand food and be ten miles away by morning. To the villagers' gratitude to their old champion and their natural sympathy with any breaker of the law was added the powerful cement of fear, plain bodily fear and a superstitious horror that Jodh Singh was something more than a man. He seemed to place everyone who met him under a spell of terror.

Christopher sent for a force of armed police. He moved in patwaris from elsewhere and left quieter circles in the hands of probationers. He kept a small mobile force with himself and stationed men in any village which he thought likely to be helping the fugitive, hoping that somewhere someone would catch an echo of his flying footsteps and make it possible to pick up the trail. But it was no use. For nearly a month he heard nothing. He made up his mind he would have to go away to the south and leave it to the new tahsildar to avenge the murder of his predecessor.

But just as he had reached this decision, something happened. He was staying in a bungalow on the edge of the forest, at the head of a shallow valley, just below the snow. After dinner he did some work he had neglected all day; then he stepped out of the bungalow to look at the stars before going to bed. The moon was at the end of its first quarter and had just risen. The forest lay still in the windless cold; from far away a wind sighed and crept nearer over the tree-tops as though the night was turning in its sleep. There was the sound of a stream close by, but behind the running water he could hear the silence of frost and snow and the stars and millions of leaves. There came the sharp bark of a fox; he shuddered in the cold and turned to go; and as he turned there came a voice crying in the night from beyond the stream.

'Lord!' it cried, 'lord! Can you hear me?'

Christopher was silent. He listened intently.

'Lord! Can you hear?'

'I hear you,' Christopher called and moved behind a tree.

'Listen, lord. It is I, Jodh Singh. Come and see what has

happened here by the shop on the track beyond the stream. Come and see what has happened.'

It was the first time Christopher had known Jodh Singh address him in Hindustani.

'I wonder if it's a corpse or an ambush,' he thought to himself, and called for the patwari and the six armed police whom he kept with him as a mobile squad, to be put on the trail if anyone should pick it up.

Ten minutes later they were stumbling down the hill together. The track and the shop were beyond the stream and there was no path leading that way directly, the usual route being round the head of the valley. They went straight down through the forest, pines, scrub oak, scarlet rhododendrons and thorn bushes. It would have been difficult ground in daylight; by the light of a half moon it was frightful; they tripped over bushes and rocks, tangled themselves in briars, fell into holes. Christopher felt that if it was an ambush they were making all the noise Jodh Singh could want. He must know just where they were. But if he was lying up to shoot them, he must be near the shop on the track. He had not got a rifle, but a shotgun, and in the moonlight he was unlikely to fire at anything more than twenty yards away. The only thing to do was to move as though going straight to the shop, and then when fifty yards away make a detour and reach the track well below it. There would then still be an anxious moment as one approached the shop but at least it could be done comparatively quietly, and at the same time distracting noises could be made by flanking parties.

They crossed the stream and struggled breathless up the farther slope. Christopher swung the whole party sharp to his left, down the valley; then a last burst straight up and they were on the track about a hundred yards below the shop, without misadventure.

Christopher thought his feelings must be exactly those of an experienced tiger approaching last night's kill, wondering when a tree would spurt death. He decided to take a lesson from the tiger. Circle round before approaching; stop and wait and listen — those were the tiger's maxims. But it's no use trying to listen for Jodh Singh when I've got this gang of heavy-footed policemen with me, he thought.

After some consideration, he decided to send the patwari and one policeman in a detour above the shop, to strike the track fifty yards beyond it. They would whistle when they reached the track. Two policemen would take up a position thirty yards below the shop, two more thirty yards above. Each of these parties would also whistle, so that each knew where the other was. After the whistles there would be ten minutes complete silence, in which everyone would be trying to hear Jodh Singh move if he was there.

At the end of ten minutes, on a whistle from Christopher, everyone would start making a noise, beating bushes, throwing stones. In the middle of this, Christopher would walk up the track to the shop, with a constable ten yards behind him ready to fire at the flash if there should be one.

The parties moved off, crashing and stumbling as before. It was remarkable how quickly the noise died. What had seemed deafening when one was in the middle of it dropped to no more than the snap of an occasional stick as the distance increased. The three parties whistled to show they had taken their stations. Then came the silence.

There was a spring near the shop and water overflowed on to the track so that the black leaf mould of its surface was always wet. It was trampled by the feet of men and animals into a bog of tiny patches of water, interspersed with black points and hummocks, both glittering in the light of the moon, which shone directly down the track. Christopher gazed at that broken path of glistening black and silver up which he would soon have to walk. He strained to hear a sound that might be an excuse for doing something else, but he knew the sound would not come and there would be no way out. He had often waited in silence before, to take the life of a beast; he knew the pounding heart that comes at every sound that may be the tread of a tiger. But for the moment, he was the hunted; it was his life that might be taken this time. This time there was no false alarm, only the sickening certainty that he must walk up that path.

He looked at his watch. Only five minutes. I wish it would be over and I could start. I wish it would be over. Six minutes. Seven. Eight. I wish it would be over. Nine. Ten.

Christopher swallowed twice and blew his whistle. Crashings began in the forest above, below, beyond the shop. He waited a last wait of thirty seconds, his eyes on his watch. Then he walked slowly up the track towards the shop. He felt better at once. Now it was settled. It was to be or it was not to be his death; there was no more to worry about.

Nothing happened. He reached the shop without sound from man or beast. He banged on the door.

'Who is there?' he called. 'Oh, shopkeeper! Let me in.'

There was silence inside. The constable who had been following Christopher came up, and the others came crashing through the bushes. The patwari called:

'Open the door, you fool. It is the Deputy Commissioner.'

Still there was silence.

'They've been murdered,' said one of the constables. 'All of them.'

No one else spoke. No one had thought of bringing an axe; the head constable doubtfully drew his bayonet, but the patwari had a kukri which was obviously more suitable, and he set to work to chop a hole in the door by the latch.

'Wait,' said Christopher. 'The door is locked from the inside. He must be inside with them. Come back with me.'

He led them away from the shop to a point where his talk could not be heard by anyone inside and gave his orders. When the door was opened, everyone must be on one side or the other, to give a clear line of fire through the door; and in the doorway against the moonlight there must be something that looked like a man, to draw Jodh Singh's fire. The constables set about making a dummy. But it was a double-barrelled gun and no one would fire twice at a dummy, Christopher reflected; he would lose one man with the second barrel, and it would be himself. He did not fancy the thought of a shotgun fired at short range into his stomach. He explored the back of the shop. But there was no entrance big enough for a man's body.

The dummy was made, something that would pass for a man in the moonlight if it moved quickly before the eyes. Operations on the door began again. Snap. The last fragment was chopped through. Nothing remained but to thrust in a hand, draw the latch, and open the door. Christopher looked round to make sure that the man with the dummy was ready.

'Now!' he said.

The door was flung open. The dummy swung out for a second across the open doorway and darted back.

Nothing happened.

'Again!' said Christopher.

Again, nothing. The dummy had failed. The next step seemed a concerted rush. If Jodh Singh was inside it would almost certainly mean the loss of two men; surely it would be better to wait till morning? And then to consider whether to fire the hut. Christopher decided that it would. Four pairs of men, at the four corners of the hut; one man of each pair to sleep. One man to go now and get blankets. He moved round to post the sentries.

As he came to the upper side of the shop, he noticed a cattle-track leading up the hill at an acute angle with the main track. He would have seen it before if all his thoughts had not been concentrated on the hut. The patwari's encircling party must have crossed this. But had they? They would have thought it was the main track and had probably come straight down it to the shop, and if that was so, no one had explored the main track. The patwari confirmed his surmise, and Christopher, expecting nothing in particular, moved up the main track in case something had been missed.

Twenty yards up was a forked stick, on which there was a paper and a sealed letter, addressed to himself, and at the foot of the stick was a packet. He struck a light and set it to a lantern. Then he read the papers. They were written with a blunt indelible pencil.

The open paper said:

I, Jodh Singh, son of Govind Singh, son of Kalyan Singh, Rawat, of Bantok, the deliverer of Garhwal from the forced labour, formerly a member of the Legislative Assembly at Lucknow and a member of the District Board, killed my enemies Dharma Nand and Dharam Singh because they were liars and had borne false witness against me. Now I have decided to kill no more of my enemies and I will surrender to the Deputy Commissioner and to no one else on the fourth day from to-day at midday, at the shop on the track near the bungalow, where this paper was found. Let the Deputy Commissioner be present to accept my surrender.

The letter said:

Dear Mr. Tregard,

At the foot of this stick is a packet of personal belongings which I wish to be sent to my son at Bantok. I do not wish that they should be handled by the police and dragged into court. They are personal papers and a ring. There is nothing that has to do with this case, and I shall plead guilty, so it does not matter. I beg you to send them to my son at Bantok as you believe in Almighty God. I trust no one but you. There was an English lady who was my friend and believed in me and so I trust you.

I trust no one else. I have not meant to do any harm, but to lead a good life. I do not understand what has happened to me. Please believe me, that I meant no harm.

Yours sincerely,

Jodh Singh Rawat.

Christopher opened the packet. There was a ring and a bundle of letters, certificates of good conduct from school and college, letters of thanks from villagers, two letters from Hugh Upton written in the days of the forced labour, all the carefully treasured evidence of Jodh Singh's successes against the world that laughed at him. Christopher put them in his pocket and said:

'I think there is no one in the hut. Let us see.'

They went together to the hut. Christopher opened the door and walked in. There was a bed inside and a man lying on the bed. His head was covered with the blanket. Christopher pulled back the blanket gently, moved the hands that covered the face. To his surprise, they were warm. The man said:

'I know nothing. I saw nothing. I heard nothing.'

That was all they could get out of him. So powerful had been the spell that Jodh Singh had put upon him that he had lain quite still, frozen with terror, throughout their operations on the door and their planning outside.

They went back to the forked stick and looked for tracks. But many men had been that way during the past day and they had no tracker who could have puzzled out such a trail. It was two hours since Jodh Singh had called across the valley. There was nothing for it but to take him at his word and wait for his surrender on the fourth day.

At noon on that fourth day, Christopher was at the shop with the patwari and six armed policemen. The stage was set; it was a familiar scene. The surface of the track, black with leaf mould, stretched before them. It was puddled with water. There was a leaden sky that looked like snow. On the hill above them, and again across the stream, the forest swept up to that lowering sky. Only the wet black track and the tiny clearing round the hut were free from trees. Christopher's heart was beating fast; he could not have said why he was so stirred. He lighted a cigarette to show that he was calm and waited till he had smoked it before he acted. Nothing had happened. He called, loudly, slow and clear:

'Jodh Singh! Are you there?'

There was silence. He called again.

This time there was an answer:

'Yes, lord. I am here.'

Christopher waited a moment. An order might frighten him away. He called:

'I am here to meet you.'

There was silence again. Christopher called:

'Are you coming down to surrender?'

There was a long silence. Then the voice cried, suddenly and very loud:

'No! No! Never!'

There were two shots from above and a few slugs whistled over their heads and spattered on the trees beyond. They heard a crashing above and a shout:

'Jai Badri Bisal!'

The muskets of the police were loaded. Christopher said:

'Get ready to fire!'

The crashing of bushes and branches came straight down the hill towards them. Jodh Singh burst out of the trees into the clearing by the hut, his kukri in his hand, running as hard as he could. He made straight for the line of police. Christopher said:

'Fire!'

The body of Jodh Singh rolled to his feet.

VII

THERE was a new Kalyanu at Bantok, a great-grandson of that first Kalyanu who had fought the bear. He was the leader of the little community at the homestead and it was he who planned the sowing and harvesting and the paying of land revenue. He had gone across the bridge to Gadoli to talk business with his kinsmen and he was there when the news came of Jodh Singh's death. A special messenger had come from the Deputy Commissioner with a packet of papers for Jodh Singh's son. The messenger put them into Kalyanu's hand.

Kalyanu went back sadly, for at Bantok they had loved and reverenced Jodh Singh. He crossed the bridge, and made the three days' journey, cliff and torrent, corrie and grass slope, rock and pine. There were fresh crossings to the streams, where the spates had washed the old stepping-stones away, but except for this, the way was unchanged since his great-grandfather had travelled it in the opposite direction in his hammock, leaving Bantok. The young Kalyanu reached Bantok on the third day and decided he must go at once to the upper farm and tell the news to the household. Snow was lying up there, but it had not yet reached the lower homestead.

As he climbed, he thought of the things to be done on the farm. Among the narrow shelves of ploughed land near the homestead, he thought of the weeding and hoeing that was needed, and the spring harvesting and ploughing. He wondered how soon snow would fall, it was badly wanted, for these lower fields were dry; but it did not look like snow to-day. The sky was clear. Then he was above the little snaky fields, out on the long hillside of grass, where the feet of his ancestors and their goats and sheep had worn a path like a thread through the golden grass. He moved slowly across the vast hill, a tiny dark point. He wondered if the stocks of hay cut in the summer would last them through the winter. He thought they would.

The way led below the rock face and turned to zigzag directly up the hill. Here he came into the snow, but there was a beaten track, and it was easy going to feet wrapped in blanket tied with grass rope. Through the tiny terraced fields of the upper farm, through the narrow place where the first Kalyanu had killed the bear, to the rocky spur where Jodh Singh had built his house.

. He gave the news. The widow wept, though she had lost nothing of Jodh Singh, for he had never been hers. The son took his papers and went away to read them, dry-eyed. They kept Kalyanu late and it was dark when he went back. The moon was in its third quarter and had not risen. He ate his evening meal and went to bed. The dark lay close as a blanket over the homestead and the hills and there was silence behind the distant roar of the torrent. It was very still and the trees too were silent.

But towards morning, when the moon had risen, there came a little wind. The moon silvered the grass on the steep side below the bluff, as the wind sighed over it in a long ripple, like a caress on the skin of a panther. The wind sighed again and the blue pines breathed deep in reply. The roar of the torrent rose faintly and the wind sighed in the pines, but behind all sound was the silence of the mountains, silence and the silver of the moonlight.

Charmouth, Dorset
May–July 1946

MORE ABOUT PENGUINS

For further information about books available from Penguins in India write to Penguin Books (India) Ltd, B4/246, Safdarjung Enclave, New Delhi 110 029.

In the UK: For a complete list of books available from Penguins in the United Kingdom write to Dept. EP, Penguin Books Ltd, Harmondsworth, Middlesex UB7 0DA.

In the U.S.A.: For a complete list of books available from Penguins in the United States write to Dept. DG, Penguin Books, 299 Murray Hill Parkway, East Rutherford, New Jersey 07073.

In Canada: For a complete list of books available from Penguins in Canada write to Penguin Books Canada Ltd, 2801 John Street, Markham, Ontario L3R 1B4.

In Australia: For a complete list of books available from Penguins in Australia write to the Marketing Department, Penguin Books Australia Ltd, P.O. Box 257, Ringwood, Victoria 3134.

In New Zealand: For a complete list of books available from Penguins in New Zealand write to the Marketing Department, Penguin Books (N.Z.) Ltd, Private Bag, Takapuna, Auckland 9.

NUDE BEFORE GOD
Shiv K. Kumar

Just as Ramkrishna, a painter, is convinced there is far more to life than portraits of fat industrialists and buxom nudes, he is murdered. But his problems don't end there. Under a special dispensation granted by Yama, the Lord of Death, he is able to spy on those he left behind—his unfaithful wife, her murderous lover, his unhappy dog, his jealous collegues.... Just when their actions are beginning to really get to him the plot takes a wholly unexpected twist.

'A most amusing book on a daring subject'—*Graham Greene*

ARJUN
Sunil Gangopadhyay

Arjun thinks he is in love with a beautiful college girl, but he falls prey to the fear that he is wooing someone far above his station. For Arjun is a poor, if brilliant and re-sourceful, refugee from East Bengal living in a squatter's settlement on the outskirts of Calcutta, whereas the girl he is keen on is the daughter of a wealthy doctor. But his love-life is the least of his problems, he soon discovers, as a crooked landlord and a disreputable factory owner join forces in an attempt to evict the people of Arjun's community from their hard-won land. Arjun now has to choose between fighting alongside the people he has grown up with, against the forces that threaten to engulf them all, or escaping to the safe haven his wealthy Bengali friends are willing to provide. He chooses to fight in a stunning climax to a powerful and sensitively written novel.

THE DEVIL'S WIND: NANA SAHEB'S STORY
Manohar Malgonkar

Nana Saheb was arguably India's greatest hero in the country's early battles against the British. This novel, by one of India's finest writers, brings alive the sequence of events that led the adopted son of the Maratha Peshwa Bajirao II to take on the British in the Great Revolt of 1857.

'A fascinating novel'—*The Sunday Times*

'A tragic and tremendous story'—*Pearl S. Buck*

'(Malgonkar writes) compellingly'—*Paul Scott*